P9-BYB-232

REAPER

THREAT ZERO

ALSO BY NICHOLAS IRVING

Reaper: Ghost Target
The Reaper
Way of the Reaper
Dark Winter

ALSO BY A. J. TATA

THE CAPTAIN JAKE MAHEGAN SERIES
Foreign and Domestic
Three Minutes to Midnight
Besieged
Direct Fire

THE THREAT SERIES
Sudden Threat
Rogue Threat
Hidden Threat
Mortal Threat

REAPER
THREAT ZERO

A SNIPER NOVEL

NICHOLAS IRVING

WITH A. J. TATA

ST. MARTIN'S PRESS ⚜ NEW YORK

REAPER: THREAT ZERO. Copyright © 2019 by Nicholas Irving. All rights reserved. Printed in the United States of America. For information, address St. Martin's Press, 175 Fifth Avenue, New York, N.Y. 10010.

www.stmartins.com

Designed by Omar Chapa

The Library of Congress Cataloging-in-Publication Data is available upon request.

ISBN 978-1-250-12736-5 (hardcover)
ISBN 978-1-250-12737-2 (ebook)

Our books may be purchased in bulk for promotional, educational, or business use. Please contact your local bookseller or the Macmillan Corporate and Premium Sales Department at 1-800-221-7945, extension 5442, or by email at MacmillanSpecial Markets@macmillan.com.

First Edition: May 2019

10 9 8 7 6 5 4 3 2 1

For Laura and Snowy, my two best muses

—*A. J. Tata*

For Kayden Irving

—*Nicholas Irving*

ACKNOWLEDGMENTS

Thank you to my tremendous writing partner, Nick Irving, the character upon which Vick Harwood is "loosely" based. Nick's creativity is inspiring and his positive vibes and focus are refreshing. I look forward to continuing this journey with Nick.

Scott Miller and the team at Trident Media Group are the best in the business, and I'm thankful that Scott thought of teaming Nick and me together for the Reaper fiction series.

Thank you to our editor, Marc Resnick, and assistant editor, Hannah O'Grady, and the entire St. Martin's/Macmillan team for their professionalism and support in making *Threat Zero* the best story it can be.

And most important, thank you to our readers, who make all of this possible.

—*A. J. Tata*

This work would have not been possible without the team support of the St. Martin's Press and Trident group family. I am greatly indebted to General A. J. Tata, Marc Resnick, and the editors who have been supportive throughout the work of this series.

I am forever grateful to the readers and listeners of the Reaper series, for without you, none of this would be possible. And to my family and military brothers and sisters in arms, I thank you eternally.

—*Nicholas Irving*

REAPER

THREAT ZERO

CHAPTER 1

As it turned sharply uphill toward Camp David, the convoy of black Suburban sport utility vehicles filled with family members of President Bob Smart's cabinet snaked through the shooter's scope.

A single black Dodge Charger led four hulking black armored vehicles ferrying excited men, women, and children to the well-known presidential retreat in western Maryland on a warm May morning. Windows were rolled down. Children's arms hung outside catching the wind and sun. Parents smiled in anticipation of the fun weekend.

As the automobiles made the U-turn, shiny metallic paint winked through the misty air as the sun burned away the dew. The convoy turned off the main road into the Catoctin Mountain Park, leaving behind the grassy fields before ascending into the thick forests. Little publicized, but accessible to the leader of the deadly Threat Zero Team, as the ambush squad called themselves, the itinerary for the annual family day was right on schedule.

As the first vehicle slowed at the hairpin turn, Zero One—the leader—pressed a garage door opener sending unit, which transmitted a signal to a receiving unit antenna sticking up from a faux curbstone. The blown Styrofoam curbstone contained twelve improvised explosive devices called explosively formed penetrators, or six-inch copper plates, that became molten fists when fired from the PVC pipes.

The EFPs fired in a flurry of black smoke and flame. The black rectangular hood of the first Suburban popped off, flew into the air, and bounced off its own windshield. The precisely placed EFPs punched through each of the armored SUVs like rocks through a flimsy porch screen. All four SUVs were hit, two were on fire. Doors opened. Women and children stumbled out. Then two men rolled out of the fourth vehicle, both on fire.

Zero One leveled his scope on the first of the two men, fired. Switched to the second man, fired. Saw the woman in her jeans and five-hundred-dollar shirt, shot her through the head. Two children on the ground, injured. He took them, as well. The other members of his team fired on their targets. Each was assigned a vehicle to avoid squirters that might escape. Zero One eyed the trail vehicle, which he had assigned himself. The fire burned rapidly, flames licking the sky. Anyone inside was incinerated by now.

He moved his scope to monitor vehicle three, which he had assigned to the newest member of the team. Two women were lying on the ground, blood seeping from their heads. Good shots. While that Suburban was not burning, smoke was boiling under the hood. Someone stumbled from the vehicle, gasping. Zero Three nailed the adolescent through the head, spinning the child around. He fell into the open door and slid down, arms and legs splayed open, as if he were making snow angels.

After no further activity on vehicle three, Zero One scanned up to the lead vehicles. Two men from the lead chase car were aiming rifles, scanning for the threat, for them. Zero One fired once, killing the man who was using the open Dodge Charger door as cover. Another team member killed the other man, eliminating the threat. Police sirens screamed in the distance. Time to pack up and move.

"Rally," he said into his microphone. The team executed their well-rehearsed clean-and-collect plan. They then collapsed to an apartment where they had one final task before they would escape and evade in much the same manner that they had entered the ambush location.

The entire attack had taken three minutes.

CHAPTER 2

The charcoal barrel of an SR-25 sniper rifle pressed into the flesh beneath Sammie Samuelson's chin, aiming upward into his skull.

Vick Harwood had been watching one of the cable news shows on his smartphone—some former senator from Virginia named Sloane Brookes was discussing her presidential aspirations—when he got the Facebook Live notice. Brookes had been commenting on the president's latest tweet that referred to her as "Slippery Sloane" and alleged she was conducting shadow diplomacy with Iran in the wake of the cancellation of the nuclear deal. Brookes had quickly pivoted away and reminded the host of her support for free tuition for all college students, paid for by trimming the defense budget.

All that melted away, though, as he stared at his smartphone, watching the Facebook Live feed from Samuelson's Facebook account. He recognized Samuelson's slightly deformed skull. The unmistakable scar from a mortar attack was a bright red four-inch hash mark just below a tuft of hair not much larger than a

Mohawk. Samuelson's face was pocked with wounds from rock and shrapnel sustained during the attack in Helmand Province, Afghanistan. His eyes were in their signature half-lidded stare, nearly catatonic. Eyebrows pinched together, making his normal unibrow look even more authentic. This was a pose that Samuelson could conjure whether he was joking or dead serious.

Harwood hoped this was some kind of sick joke.

Thumbs-up, crying face, open-mouthed shock, angry face, and heart emoticons floated across the screen in a steady stream.

"Don't do it, man," Harwood muttered. He quickly fired up his MacBook, clicked onto Samuelson's page, and enlarged the feed to full screen. He pressed off the feed on his smartphone and dialed Samuelson's number.

A few seconds later a phone began playing George Thorogood's "Bad to the Bone," a specialized ring tone that Samuelson had marked just for the Reaper's phone calls. There was no doubt this was Samuelson with the barrel under his chin. His eyes narrowed slightly at the sound of the phone, but he didn't move. His pupils unflinchingly stared into the Facebook Live feed, presumably done so from a smartphone.

"Pick up, Sammie. Been through too much, man," Harwood muttered. The phone clicked through to voice mail with Samuelson's deep voice saying, "Send it," in true spotter parlance.

"Sammie, come on, man, talk to me," Harwood said. The voice mail did not play through Samuelson's smartphone speakers. The computer screen showed Samuelson's apartment in the background. It was an untidy studio overlooking a windswept valley of green grass and rising, forested hills. A breeze carried debris and traces of smoke. Over Samuelson's right shoulder was a desk with an assortment of newspapers, magazines, and loose-leaf papers. Beneath them there appeared to be a MacBook of some variety, a silver monochrome edge peeking out from beneath the mess.

"I'm sorry, Vick," Samuelson said.

"What are you sorry about?"

Harwood practically shouted at the computer screen. He studied Samuelson's face. The lips moving in slow motion. The high-definition display on the monitor highlighted every scar, every imperfect line, a cut on the lip, the bristles from missing last week's Ranger haircut.

"It's all right in front of you," Samuelson said. Samuelson's chin pressed deeper into the muzzle of the weapon.

"Whatcha watching," Monisha said, opening the door to Harwood's spare bedroom turned makeshift office.

"Get out, now, Monisha!"

Harwood turned his head. Saw the young teenager he had adopted. His promise to her was to mentor her into college and medical school. She was basically a fourteen-year-old orphan when he had saved her from two men who had connected with her on a prostitution web page.

"Don't yell at me, Reaper. I ain't done nothing wrong," Monisha shot back.

Harwood looked at Monisha, her honey-brown skin covered by a gray army running shirt and blue jeans. She wore black canvas PRO-Keds that were fashionably unlaced. Her eyes grew wide as she gazed over his shoulder at the monitor. Brow furrowed, teeth clenched, Monisha shouted, "No!"

She knew Samuelson as well as anyone in her life. He and Harwood were her role models. Big brothers. All she had.

Standing to block her view, he turned to look at the screen.

The shot rang loud in the small bedroom, echoing from the MacBook speakers. Harwood was caught in between Monisha's horrified stare and the explosion of blood spraying onto Samuelson's screen.

Through the pink haze of the Facebook Live feed, Samuelson's head—what was left of it—hung loosely to the side, blood draining over the ragged edges of his destroyed skull like red wine over a jagged goblet.

As soon as he could refocus, Harwood heard a noise at the back door. It was the slightest tick of a lockpick set. He removed his Beretta pistol from its holster—he always kept the handgun within five feet of him—and whispered to Monisha, "Get in the closet, now. You know where to go."

"I heard it, too," Monisha said. She had excellent instincts and had proven to be an able assistant and spotter on the range. He had taken Monisha to shoot pistols and rifles so that she would be comfortable with his lifestyle as an expert sniper. Still on active duty, Harwood was required to have a "Family Care Plan" for Monisha in the event he was deployed. He had chosen the parents of Command Sergeant Major Murdoch to care for her, and they had gladly accepted the duty, doting on Monisha from the outset.

Glass shattered in the hallway as Harwood locked the closet door behind Monisha. She would take the hidden stairway into the basement as they had rehearsed.

Harwood moved toward the noise, leading with his Beretta. A shadow crossed the floor to his front. Pushing his back against the wall, he heard the intruder snap off two shots. If Harwood had not insulated the house with sheets of metal between the wooden studs and plasterboard, he would be dead or seriously wounded right now. But he had designed their home in Columbus, Georgia, primarily to protect Monisha against the hazards of his life as a renowned army sniper with many enemies.

Swiping his thumb up on his smartphone, he pressed the Kitchen button on his security system. The camera showed a compact man looking directly at the fiber optic camera. Two more shots and the picture went blank on Harwood's phone. He was dealing with a professional marksman if not assassin. Harwood's specialty was as a sniper, earning him the nickname Reaper, for his thirty-three kills in ninety days. A record for the U.S. Army Rangers.

Still, he was more than competent with the basic handgun of the U.S. Army, the Beretta nine-millimeter pistol. He needed to move though, because he could sense the intruder coming toward him.

Harwood did a running baseball slide across the kitchen doorway, firing upward from his back as he slid across the opening. The attacker had closed the distance so that they were less than ten feet apart. Using the kitchen island as cover, the man ducked as Harwood laid down suppressive fire. His intent was to give Monisha time to evacuate and draw the attacker away from her.

Ultimately, he intended to kill the son of a bitch, which would buy them both all the time in the world. Easy fix. No time for that, though. He pushed the images of Samuelson to a compartment in his mind where he stored all the painful memories of his young life. In full combat action mode, Harwood pushed up to one knee, raced through the dining room, dodged the dinner table, and raced headlong into the kitchen.

The attacker's back was facing Harwood. He waited until the man heard him, looked in his direction.

Then the Reaper snapped off three rounds in the center mass of the man's face. Checking to make sure he was accurate, Harwood's concern shifted to the potential for backup intruders and ultimately the mess he was going to have to clean up from this guy's exploded head. He inspected the body for forms of identification or any intelligence. Black pants, black shirt, and black outer tactical vest were all devoid of any helpful information save a small radio connected to a fiber optic earbud stuck in the man's left ear canal.

Harwood removed the earbud, wiped off the blood and wax,

and stuck it in his ear, listening. For a few seconds static carried through the small device.

Then: "Zero Five, confirm kill."

Zero Five? The term meant nothing to Harwood. He was an active duty Army Ranger sniper. Call signs and nicknames were a staple of his regiment, but he'd only heard "05" as a suffix to a call sign previously—such as "Eagle 05," which usually indicated the second-in-command. "06" was typically the commander. He removed the small radio from the outer tactical vest and stuffed it into his pocket, immediately focusing outward, away from the growing pool of blood on the kitchen floor.

"Need code word for cleaners," the voice said into his ear.

Deep baritone. Command voice. Like a drill sergeant or captain, someone who was used to barking out orders, making stuff happen. Inflected with the slightest hint of impatience.

Harwood's mind raced with options. None awesome. His favorite thought was to somehow lure the cleaners into the house and kill them. Monisha had enough time to get into the safe room, lock the door, and survive. It was like a nuclear bomb shelter in the backyard. There was no way in or out other than a combination lock and heavy gauge metal blast-proof door. Harwood knew that he had enemies, both foreign and domestic, and as Monisha's surrogate big brother, he had taken the greatest precaution possible. Perhaps extreme, but Harwood had two speeds: on and off. And "on" was 100 mph, always considering the worst thing that could happen.

Harwood moved to the rear door that had been breached. He had triple locks and had been careless this morning when he had looked outside in the backyard. He should have locked all three when he had returned from his security checks before prepping to take Monisha to school. Scanning the backyard, Harwood saw no visible threats. The yard was a well-manicured one-hundred-foot-by-one-hundred-foot square of St. Augustine grass, thick blades providing a level and smooth carpet all the way to the eight-foot-high fence.

Perfect fields of fire for him. The only imperfection in the backyard was the imperceptible three-foot-by-three-foot square of sheet metal that led into the safe room. It was covered with the same grass and only Harwood could discern it, primarily because he knew it was there. Detecting no threats in the backyard, he moved to the living room, kept low, and took position between the front door and the bay window.

The street featured the usual traffic of parents driving to work or carpooling to school. A yellow school bus stopped at an intersection a half a block away. Monisha's bus. The driver looked over his shoulder at Harwood's house, waited a beat, perhaps expecting Monisha to come sprinting from the door as she had done so many times. After about fifteen seconds, he gave up, and pulled away with one less student than the normal pickup of five.

As the bus pulled away, Harwood saw a gray sedan, maybe a Ford Taurus, parked on the street. Two men sat in the front seat. The car was aimed away from Harwood's modest brick rambler built in the Georgia countryside outside of Columbus and Fort Benning.

Harwood low crawled to the sofa, pulled his SR-25 from beneath the davenport, slid back to the bay window, and used a hand to slowly push open the windowpane, tilting it ninety degrees. He eased the muzzle of the weapon out of the window and lined up behind the scope. Boxwood shrubs were just beneath the window and the barrel of the weapon, masking Harwood's movement. He flicked on the digital recording device in his scope and laid a steady aim on the two men. They were white, broad-shouldered men, not unlike his dead assailant in the kitchen. Likely accomplices. He had never seen this car or these people on his street.

"Send it," Harwood said, pressing the push-to-talk button on the radio.

From the front seat of the car, two heads turned toward the house. That was enough confirmation for Harwood.

His best shot was on the passenger. The driver's head was mostly blocked by the divider between the front and back doors. He leveled the crosshairs. Exhaled slowly. Pulled the trigger.

The man's head erupted, kicked backward. As Harwood was moving the rifle to attempt a shot on the driver, the car sped away.

He was okay with that. Two down, one to go. While he doubted there were more than the three, he couldn't be sure. He inspected the rest of his house. The garage. The side yards. Nothing.

He called Command Sergeant Major Murdoch, his mentor.

"Blue on blue," Harwood said when Murdoch answered.

"Roger that," Murdoch replied.

He pressed End and found the closet, gained access to the stairway, and climbed into the tunnel leading to the safe room. He stooped as he walked twenty meters past concrete blocks on either side and two-by-eight flooring above. He spun the dial on the heavy metal door, opened it, and found Monisha inside working on the computer.

"I watched it all, Reaper," she said.

Harwood had outfitted the entire perimeter with cameras, which Monisha had been monitoring from the basement. "Damn, you good."

"Work on the grammar, will you, Monisha. I'm not raising a hood rat."

Monisha cackled.

"Yes, sir, Reaper. I'm going to be a doctor, for sure. But like you say, you've got to remember where you've been to know where you're going."

Harwood nodded. "That's right. And where you're going is to stay with Minnie and Pops for a few days until we figure this out."

Monisha leapt out of her chair and did a slight moonwalk, spun around, and high-fived the air.

"Yes!"

Harwood nodded.

"Not that I don't love you, Reaper, but they're the best."

Harwood was concerned about the child's apparent unconcern about the events that had just occurred. She compartmentalized too well and needed to be more afraid, or at least more aware of concepts such as danger and risk. When he found her a few months ago, she had been tied to a bed naked by two white supremacists who fully intended to rape and murder her. They ended up dead by his hands and even then, she had responded coolly, as if she was just turning another trick.

"You know we have a dead man in our kitchen, right? And that I just shot a man in the street. These men were trying to kill us."

Monisha's eyes grew wide. She stuttered, then stopped and looked down.

"Yes, I know, Reaper. I'm scared, and I cover that fear with the good stuff."

"As long as you can feel that you're scared, Monisha. Like we talked about. You need to feel that. You need to know it's real." He touched his chest with his hand. "We lost Sammie."

"I know it's real. I watched it too, Reaper."

He had never been married and had no previous children. Adopting Monisha to keep her out of the court system and from being pimped out again was his solution to saving her. The FBI had allowed him to keep half the money that his previous adversary, the Chechen, had deposited into his account in an attempt to frame him for the murders of high-profile generals and politicians. The $250,000 was in a secure investment trust and could only be used for secondary education and associated expenses. Harwood paid for everything else out of his own pocket and meager sergeant's salary. He wrestled with balancing his time between parenting Monisha and doing his soldierly duties. Mostly, though, he struggled with raising a fifteen-year-old girl, a chore for anyone, he presumed.

"How we going to clean up the dead guy?" she asked.

"I'll call the right people," Harwood said.

"The cleaners? I watch TV, movies and stuff," she said.

"No. I'm calling the police. Keep this aboveboard."

"All right. What about school? Is it dangerous for me?"

"We'll probably keep you at Minnie and Pops's place for a few days. Minnie was a teacher, so she can work on things with you."

"Roger that, Reaper man." Monisha smiled. She was a smart child but aged beyond her years from a childhood that no child should have to endure.

The combination lock to the outer door clicked and spun until Command Sergeant Major Murdoch opened the door. A former collegiate heavyweight wrestler, Murdoch had to lean well forward to navigate the low tunnel to the safe room. He popped up and looked every bit the impressive Ranger that he was. White sidewall buzzed haircut. Bulked chest and arms. Square chin and chiseled face.

"Status?" Murdoch asked. "Other than the guest you've got in your kitchen. Looks like he's making himself comfortable."

"Damn, you funny, Sergeant Major," Monisha said.

"Who gave you that mouth, young lady?" Murdoch snapped.

Monisha stepped back, shut her mouth, which was the typical reaction most people had when Murdoch spoke.

"Pretty sure I killed one guy in a four-door Ford Taurus sedan. Got the license plate on my scope video. Samuelson committed suicide."

"Samuelson's *dead*. We know that much. Let's not jump to conclusions about anything else," Murdoch said.

"You saw it?" Harwood asked.

"Son, half the world's seen that by now. It's all over the news. Most of the Rangers in the barracks watched it. It's everywhere. The questions are, why would he do that? And, if he didn't do it, why would someone want him and you dead?"

Harwood flashed back to the Chechen and his need to confirm that kill, but there was no confirmation. Some blood in a life raft was the only indicator that the Chechen had been wounded. Was he still alive?

"Hundred bucks says it's not the Chechen. This feels different," Murdoch said.

"It's got to be something Sammie found."

"In Maryland?"

"He'd gotten a job as a tech guy at a subcontracting company working on defense programs near Frederick, Maryland. Western part of the state. He sent me a bunch of texts."

"Let me see," Murdoch said.

Harwood pulled up the message function of his MacBook and clicked on "Spotter."

DUDE, CHECK THIS OUT
SEND IT
CUT/PASTE FROM DEEP WEB: FAMILY DAY
AT CD IS BEST LOCATION. EASY. BLACK
SUBURBANS W DODGE CHARGER CHASE
CAR. HAIRPIN TURN.

"What's CD?" Monisha asked, looking over their shoulders.

"Camp David. He lived in a town just outside of Camp David."

"Look at this," Murdoch said. He pointed at the television monitor tuned to a news program. A news helicopter showed a road with four black Suburbans destroyed and smoking, the Dodge Charger chase car relatively intact. Bodies littered the field on either side of the narrow road.

"Women and children," Harwood said.

"Some look my age," Monisha seconded. Her voice was quiet, subdued.

Harwood pulled up the Facebook video of Samuelson's apparent suicide. The live feed automatically converted to a video on the individual's Facebook page. He fast-forwarded until he could see the window behind Samuelson.

There was a field and a road with a hairpin turn.

"Looks like a good spot to attack the convoy. Right there from his window," Harwood said, pointing at the paused frame of the video. He saw things he hadn't noticed before. The window was half open. A chair sat facing the window. The bottom sill of the window had light scratching. Saw the silver edge of what looked like a MacBook. Harwood could almost smell the acrid aroma of burning gunpowder.

"You don't think Sammie did that, do you?" Monisha asked. Not much was lost on her. She studied the images with Murdoch and Harwood.

Murdoch's phone buzzed.

He answered and muttered a few, "Yes, sirs," before hanging up.

"I've got to send you packing," Murdoch said. He turned from Harwood to Monisha and nodded. "First, I'll take Monisha to my parents. I've already got someone coming to clean up your house. Meet you at the headquarters where I will sign your papers. I'll get next-of-kin notification rolling on Samuelson once we have confirmation. He was out but he's still a Ranger. Always will be."

Harwood nodded. The thought of a mission sent a charge through his body. All he ever wanted to be was an Army Ranger. He was excited, but Murdoch was giving him that stare to keep his mouth shut, a look Harwood knew well.

"Who were next of kin?" he asked anyway. He had spent less than a month in combat with Samuelson as his spotter. They had shared some time convalescing after the Chechen incident in Savannah, but still, they didn't talk about much other than the superficial niceties that prevented them from sinking into the analytical depths of their dangerous profession. He couldn't recall Samuelson mentioning any of his family. Maybe a sister? Or maybe that was a girlfriend.

"His parents are living. And a sibling out there somewhere that they're checking on. They're in his paperwork. I've got it. Meet me in an hour. Pack your shit." Then to Monisha, "Let's go, Monisha."

Monisha hugged Harwood and said, "Don't get killed or nothing, Reaper. Need my brothers. Sucks about Sammie."

Harwood hugged Monisha and watched her exit with Murdoch. He gathered his SR-25 and other tools of war before heading to Fort Benning.

CHAPTER 3

Harwood landed at Dulles International Airport's Signature Private Jet facility late in the same evening of the ambush at Camp David. He had received credentials from his command sergeant major that he hoped would clear a path for him instead of having to fight his way into the crime scene.

Being a Ranger was everything to him and to Samuelson. His sadness about his former spotter was balanced by his appreciation of being able to investigate Samuelson's death. One last "send it" with his buddy, if nothing else.

He carried his duffel bag off the airplane and found the 2019 BMW 5 Series vehicle that was waiting on him. He located the keys on the rear wheel and clicked the button, half expecting it to blow up. Images of combat were hard to erase. They stuck with him like childhood memories, indelible markers of his life. But instead of an explosion, the lights winked and the doors unlocked with a click. Tossing his bag in the back seat, he unzipped the outer pouch and retrieved his Beretta, checked his magazine—full—and then slipped into the front seat. He punched up Samuelson's address and prepped for the one-hour drive. He'd be arriving around midnight, which was perfect, he thought.

He found Highway 15 and began following the Google Map route on his phone, which he had placed in the cup holder. As the female voice soothingly told him to "turn left" and "turn right," he thought of Samuelson and the unthinkable. Was he involved in the slaughter of ten Secret Service agents and twelve family members of the president's cabinet? No one had survived. The EFPs had killed half of them at the outset and then the snipers had mowed down the remainders. The youngest was a seven-year-old girl in second grade. The oldest was the wife of the secretary of the Interior, who had been an Army Green Beret and twelve-combat-tour veteran.

Harwood had studied the names and dossiers of each individual on the flight into Dulles. Was there a point to the attack? Of course. There always was. Was it to inflict terror? Perhaps. Was one single person targeted with the others as collateral damage to hide the truth? Maybe. Did Samuelson kill himself or was someone on the other side of that phone camera? Anything was possible.

Discovering the truth would involve being allowed inside the ropes of the crime scene, which Murdoch had assured him would not be a problem.

His phone buzzed. Monisha.

"Hey," Harwood said, pressing the button. The BMW's Bluetooth had picked up the audio.

"Hey, Reaper," Monisha said. Her voice was sullen.

"What's wrong? Minnie and Pops okay?"

"Yeah, they okay. Just wondering if you are?"

Harwood smiled. "Yeah, I'm good. Just trying to figure this thing out. I talked to your principal today on the way to the airport. He said it was cool for you to miss a few days as long as Minnie gave you the lessons. One of your classes is flipped anyway, right?" One of Harwood's new roles as Monisha's guardian was learning about the K–12 education system. A flipped classroom was one where the teacher made videos of the class, uploaded them to a website, and the students watched them at home after school. The next day, all of the students received a quiz on the material, allowing the teacher to divide the class into those that had mastered the material, had a few questions, or didn't understand it at all.

"Yeah. It's easy. We watch it on YouTube. Teacher gets all crazy, but she's good. Makes me laugh."

"Easy thing to do."

"Just because you lack a sense of humor, Reaper, doesn't mean I have to."

"I'm working on it," he joked.

"Yeah, keep working on it. Long way to go."

Their faux criticisms were a symbol of each of them testing the boundaries of their developing parent-child relationship.

Silence filled the airwaves for a moment, unusual for any conversation with Monisha.

"I heard what the sergeant major said. Send you packing can mean lots of things."

"It can," Harwood said.

"Nothing to do with me, I hope?"

Typical child response. Blame herself. He could hear the question in her voice.

"Nothing to do with you. Come on, Monisha. We've talked about this. We take care of each other," Harwood said.

"True that. You'd be lost without me."

"Heard that."

"I ain't stupid, you know," Monisha muttered.

"Never said you were, Monisha. Now you should get some rest."

"I know you on some kind of dangerous mission."

"I'm always on a mission, young lady. Now go to sleep," Harwood said.

In the distance he saw spinning blue lights and telescoping spotlights surrounding the crime scene.

"Night, Reaper. Don't get killed."

"Night, Monisha. I'll do my best."

"You always say that," she said. Her voice was drifting.

"And I always do," he said. "Now, get some sleep."

"K."

They hung up as Harwood approached the crime scene. He loved Monisha as any adoptive big brother/parent could love a child. His heart ached for what she had endured during her first fourteen years and if he could change the course of her life for the better then he would be accomplishing something productive.

He approached the cluster of vehicles parked randomly all around the apartment building sitting off the main highway about a quarter mile. He passed a couple of gas stations and convenience stores before turning onto the feeder road to the residential area. A Maryland State Trooper flagged him down immediately. Smokey Bear hat, crisp uniform, Glock perched on the wide leather belt, and flashlight shined into Harwood's face.

"Off limits," the trooper barked.

Harwood grabbed the leather credentials from his coat pocket.

The trooper's pistol was in his face quickly. Flashlight in his eyes, pistol aimed at his temple.

"Disarm," the trooper said.

"I'm showing you my credentials, Officer."

Harwood had been pulled over many times for "Driving While Black," and understood the latent sentiment that the officer perhaps felt. Still, it sucked. He was an Army Ranger on a mission to help his buddy.

"What credentials?"

"I was sent here to link up with the investigation team and to identify the remains of former Army Ranger Sammie Samuelson."

The pistol lowered. The flashlight canted to the coat pocket.

"Slowly."

Harwood retrieved his orders assigning him to the President's Task Force on Counterterrorism.

The trooper studied them with the flashlight and nodded.

"Sorry, Ranger. Tough day up here."

"No worries, Officer."

"I was Airborne. Thanks for what you do."

"Likewise."

"You're the second to arrive. The task force is meeting in the apartment manager's office. They've cleared out. You can go there and they'll show you up to the shooter's room."

The shooter.

Samuelson?

No way.

Harwood parked, retrieved his rucksack and slung it over his shoulder as he walked into the manager's office. Three desks were evenly spaced apart in the room with a large-screen television showing the news in the background. Reporters were flocked about a half mile away with the ambush location in the background. The office had become an operations center, with FBI agents and assistants looking at MacBooks, leaning over shoulders, and talking to one another.

Deke Bronson, the head of the domestic terrorism task force, looked up and said, "Oh my God. Who let you onto the premises?"

Harwood half expected Bronson, whom he had previously interacted with on a different case, to smile and shake his hand.

But neither the smile nor the shake was forthcoming. Bronson was serious.

"Samuelson was your spotter, Harwood. You can't be in here. You're not objective."

Harwood nodded and said, "Good to see you, Special Agent. Seems someone else has a different concept of the operation here."

Harwood handed Bronson his papers. The agent read the first page then flipped the second page over, showing a powerful forearm beneath the trademark rolled-up sleeves of his button-down shirt with English spread collar. Bronson had been a marine infantry officer in Iraq then transitioned to the FBI upon separation. When the spate of killings that ignited the Black Lives Matter movement began a couple of years ago, the FBI appointed Bronson, an African American, the head of the task force investigating the shootings and other incidents.

"This is bullshit," Bronson said.

"But official bullshit," Harwood replied. The two men squared off as the room grew quiet. Bronson's assistant Faye Wilde tugged at his shoulder. During the debriefs from the Poppy Slave Scandal as the media had named it, Harwood had befriended the redheaded beauty. They had even been out for drinks a couple of times.

"Let's go outside," Bronson suggested.

Wilde joined them as they huddled in the dark recesses of a stairwell leading to the apartments above. The spinning blue lights bounced off the walls.

"Faye still checking your Match dot com?" Harwood poked.

"Vick, stop," Wilde said.

"Vick?" Bronson said. He looked at Wilde and then at Harwood. "No. Fucking. Way."

"Not fucking. Just friends." Wilde tossed her hair and smirked at Harwood. The emerald eye contact was just enough to cause

Harwood to refocus on the task at hand before he let other thoughts pollute his mind. "Besides, he's on Bumble now."

"I need to see Samuelson's place," Harwood said. "Now."

Bronson looked back at the papers then laid wide eyes on Harwood.

"I'm sending Special Agent Valerie Hinojosa," Bronson said. "Definitely not Agent Wilde."

"Agent? Promotion. Congrats," Harwood said.

Bronson lifted a handheld radio to his mouth and said, "Agent Hinojosa, please come outside." Then to Wilde, "We're good here."

"Roger that, boss," she said and departed.

In the moments between Wilde's departure and Hinojosa's arrival, Bronson said, "Stay away from Faye, Reaper."

"You're not my daddy, nor hers, Bronson. But judging by my orders, which I need back, by the way, I'm not going to have the time to be the bird dog you seem to be," Harwood replied.

Bronson stiffened and huffed until Agent Hinojosa approached.

"Secret agent meeting under the stairwell or just a lovers' spat?" Hinojosa quipped.

"What? Is everybody a comedian? We've got twenty-two killed—twelve family members, ten Secret Service. We think it was domestic terrorism, and you guys are auditioning for improv?" Bronson said.

"Gallows humor, Marine," Harwood said. "Only way to survive."

Hinojosa didn't look anything like he expected she might. Reddish-brunette hair pulled into a severe ponytail, fair complexion, a few freckles across the bridge of her slender nose, high cheekbones, and wide copper eyes. Her ancestors probably traveled on the *Mayflower*. She was well put together in her navy wool suit with white silk blazer. Low pumps instead of high heels. Slight bulge under the blazer. What kind of pistol did she carry?

"So, what's up?" Hinojosa asked.

"This is Vick Harwood. Army Ranger. They call him The Reaper. He's on special assignment. I need you to watch him as he goes through Samuelson's room."

"Watch him? You need a babysitter, check your Tinder dates."

Bronson had a reputation of dating women in their twenties, ten years his junior. The dig produced a smirk from Bronson.

"None of them have clearances," Bronson shot back. "Nor do they work for me."

"Neither do I," she replied.

"Au contraire. You are on special assignment to my task force until further notice. You know this."

Hinojosa sighed. "I haven't been through Samuelson's room. Why does he get to go?" she protested.

"Not my call."

Hinojosa raised her eyebrows. "Higher than you, boss? Director?"

Bronson said nothing. Returned her level gaze. Fireworks.

"Oh my God. Higher?" Harwood didn't know if she was mocking him or truly shocked.

"Just take him up there," Bronson directed and stormed off.

In the wake of Bronson's departure, Harwood said, "How long you been part of his team?"

"I'm not," she replied. "They flew me in today from Texas. I've got skills they need."

"Such as?"

"Right now, you don't need to know that. My task is to babysit your ass. So, let's go," she said.

Harwood followed her. He understood the tensions and quick retorts. Most likely, the last thing Hinojosa wanted to do right now was to escort some interloper to Samuelson's room. They climbed stairs and walked through an open hallway, a pitched roof covering the walkway with clear views behind the apartment complex and to the front, toward the ambush location. Hinojosa lifted the yellow crime scene tape and opened the door. They walked through a standard apartment building hallway, apartment doors on either side.

"The other residents?" Harwood asked.

"Being interviewed as we speak. Using the gym facility as a holding area. Interviews in the conference room off the manager's office."

She removed a key from her blazer pocket and lifted more yellow crime scene tape as she stepped into what he immediately recognized as Samuelson's room. The window was still half open. The chair remained in front of the window. Twenty-two spent casings lay on the floor, scattered haphazardly, presumably ejected from the rifle as someone—Samuelson?—fired into the convoy of family members. An SR-25 sniper rifle lay on its side to their right, near the desk where Samuelson's smartphone remained. There was blood splatter on the ceiling, along with some chunks of brain matter. A single hole punctuated the artistic spray, the blood streaking outward in thin, jagged lines. To his left was the kitchen, which looked relatively intact. To his right, beyond the two chairs, one for shooting and one for suicide, was a tattered sofa. Beyond that was a door to the bedroom, a mattress on the floor visible. The sheets were rumpled and clothes were on the floor. Typical bachelor's apartment.

"Damn," Hinojosa said.

Harwood said nothing. Used his sniper skills to collect information. Scanning, logging, assessing. Something was missing. He looked back at the chair facing the window, the supposed shooter's platform. To the right was a small table and poorly upholstered chair. A couple of shirts lay wadded in the chair. Newspapers and magazines were on the end table.

Beneath the stack of magazines, he remembered seeing the MacBook. Now there was no MacBook. He would go back and check it, but he was certain he had seen it earlier.

"Did anyone remove anything?" Harwood asked.

Hinojosa looked at him.

"No. Why?"

"Just a logical question. So, we are looking at the apartment as it was, save Samuelson's body?"

"That's my information. Initial first responders on the scene were Maryland State Troopers, then Secret Service, and then us. The Secret Service turned it over to us. They collapsed on the president and the cabinet members who were awaiting the family members at Camp David. There's a Secret Service liaison in the manager's office. He may know more. I do know that forensics has gone through this place with a fine-tooth comb. Place was pretty clean. One set of footprints. Samuelson's fingerprints on the casings and rifle. GPR on the sleeves."

Gunpowder residue findings on Samuelson would not be unusual if he pulled the trigger once, but Harwood remained curious and would pursue the specific pattern of the residue, which he considered important. They spent ten more minutes walking through the apartment. The refrigerator was empty save a couple of half-full Gatorade bottles and some Clif Bars. The bedroom did not improve upon its first impression. It was a tangled mess of clothes that Samuelson had dumped where he was standing at the time. Running shoes, shorts, and shirt here; jeans, T-shirt, and boots there. Going back to the small living and dining room, he studied the spray pattern of spent casings. Each was marked with a plastic evidence marker that stood up like a small triangle with numbers one through twenty-two. Sitting in the chair, he leaned forward, closed his eyes, and then opened them, as if he were the shooter.

A quarter mile beyond him he had a perfect shot at each of the vehicles that had made the hairpin turn. He used a shooter's pose to silently work the rifle from the lead vehicle, the Charger, to the rear vehicle, a Suburban. He repeated the process, this time thinking about timing. Repeated again, thinking about casing expenditure. With each phantom shot on each vehicle, he looked over his shoulder and checked the brass and related evidence markers. Made a note that something was off about where the brass had landed. He couldn't quite place it, but it wasn't natural. If he had worked left to right or right to left, the spray should include some logical dispersion. But what the evidence markers indicated was a more tightly grouped array of casings. Not all bunched together, but neither were they logically dispersed as they should have been. Plus, the bedroom was a mess. The kitchen was nasty. But this living area floor was clean. The pile carpet showed vacuum streaks that looked like a backgammon board.

Noted.

Samuelson's dead. Let's not jump to any conclusions.

"Where's Sammie's body? I have instructions to identify him."

Hinojosa paused, looked away, and then came back to him with soulful eyes.

"Part of him is up there," she said, pointing at the ceiling. "And the rest is in the morgue in Hagerstown. Closest place with one. State troopers escorted the body there. We have a forensics team there."

Harwood nodded, considered her flip response, judged it to be out of character with the sorrowful countenance, and decided to change directions.

"Feeling left out?" Harwood asked.

She lowered her chin, perhaps the closest thing she would offer to a nod.

"I dropped everything I was doing in Texas to come up here. We all want to be useful, Reaper."

Reaper.

Harwood nodded, but continued staring at the table near the window. "Totally understand that," he said, absently.

"What's missing?"

Harwood walked to the end table, squatted and used the back of his fingernail to lift the magazines.

"There was a MacBook or some kind of computer underneath these magazines. Study the video of the FB Live event," Harwood said.

"That's something," she said. "As far as I know, nothing's been taken by law enforcement except for Samuelson's body."

They spent another ten minutes looking through the apartment. On the refrigerator were two pictures of Harwood and Samuelson in desert camouflage, holding their rifles, checkered kaffiyehs across their faces, leaden stares looking at the camera. They looked dangerous, almost psychotic. When Hinojosa turned to open the door, he removed the two pictures and pocketed them.

Harwood stepped into the hallway and watched her lock the door and secure the yellow crime scene tape back in place. His mind was buzzing. Why was the living room completely vacuumed and cleaned? Could Samuelson have technically pulled off the ambush alone? As far as Harwood knew, he wasn't an expert on construction of EFP improvised explosive devices. To place them in fake Styrofoam curbstone and make it look real took talent . . . and experience. Samuelson didn't have that.

"Any trace of explosives in the apartment?"

"No. But there was a key to a storage unit in a nearby facility. One of those places you rent monthly. The unit is in Samuelson's name. Paid in full with cash for three months."

"Prints?"

"Samuelson's and a few of the people who run the joint. That's what we've got so far."

"Makes no sense," Harwood said.

"No, it doesn't. But everything points to Samuelson."

"He either didn't care who knew what he was doing and actually did this, or was set up," Harwood said.

"This way," she said.

He followed her to the next apartment. More crime scene tape plastered a giant "X" across the door. She removed it on one side and opened the door with another key.

Inside was a perfectly normal-looking apartment with plaid sofa and love seat, cherry end tables and coffee table, and big-screen television. The apartment looked uninhabited, a furnished corporate kind of deal.

"What's this?" Harwood asked.

"We got a kid's cell phone video that showed this window was open also. Samuelson could have been going back and forth."

Harwood shook his head. "Wouldn't make sense."

"Unless you didn't want a rocket up your ass. Secret Service carries those."

They spent ten minutes walking through the pristine unit. Everything in place.

"Who rents it?"

"A holding company."

The walls showed a couple of nicks, minor chips in the paint. He stood at the window, which was closed. Then knelt, putting himself at a shooter's level. The view on the ambush scene was just as good, maybe better. Blue lights spinning. Floodlights glaring. Harwood took aim, pulled an imaginary trigger, turned to watch where the casings would eject. Saw the floor and sofa. Nothing visible. On all fours, he crawled to the green-and-burgundy plaid sofa and lifted a flap. Using his cell phone flashlight, he scanned beneath. Something winked at him.

"Either someone shot from in here or a kid found this and put it down there," Harwood said.

"What?"

"A brass 7.62 shell casing just like the ones in Samuelson's place. We need the techs to do a hundred percent sweep of this apartment."

She was on her knees, looking from the opposite direction. Her eyes poked beneath the dust cover of the sofa, looking like a feral animal searching for food.

"Oh my God."

"Roger that."

Harwood snapped a picture of the casing before using a latex glove to secure the shell, which he placed in his pocket. He stood and took pictures of the nicks in the wall. Some of the casings expended from the SR-25 would have been wildly bouncing off the walls in the rapid-fire succession mow down that had occurred. This room had been used for the ambush. Maybe Samuelson's had, too. But this one, for sure.

"This is something," Hinojosa said, standing.

"Roger. No video cameras?"

"Only in the parking lot. There are some along the exterior of the building and the stairwells but as you might imagine they were disabled an hour before and after the attack."

"Why would Samuelson do that? He couldn't do that, at least not that I'm aware of."

Hinojosa paused and lifted her eyes toward him. There was something familiar about her face, but he couldn't place it. She was beautiful with creamy skin. He chalked it up to her likely resemblance to a movie star or actress that he had seen. The eyebrows and forehead, so perfect, and so unique at the same time.

"Hinojosa? Married name?"

"Divorced name. In the process of changing it back."

Harwood nodded. "Fair enough."

Standing at the door of the apartment, a clock ticked somewhere. Like a second hand or a countdown. The crazy descending numbers of a basketball scoreboard clock showing the one hundredths of seconds. The frightening countdown of an IED bomb timer. How long had they been in the apartment? Five minutes, max?

"Quick," Harwood said. He grasped Hinojosa by the arm and opened the door, pulling her into the hallway. She seemed to understand and strode with a long-legged gait behind him. They reached the stairwell, spun down the stairs, and ran into the courtyard near the pool, ducking behind a storage shed. He pulled her close as he heard the click of the detonator followed by the explosion.

Samuelson's room erupted as a bomb cratered half the building. Heat licked at his face as he turned Hinojosa away from the blast. Debris blew past them, the shed pinging with shrapnel impacts.

CHAPTER 4

The fire trucks on hand circled quickly to spray down the blaze in the middle of the apartment building.

Harwood had pulled Hinojosa out of the blast radius at the last moment. Shards of glass and wood littered the area. The building had collapsed inward, with Samuelson's apartment and the ones on either side completely destroyed.

In the gym Harwood removed the SR-25 casing he had secured in the second room. Walked over to a man who had both arms covered in tat sleeves. His thumbs were working a smartphone he cradled in both hands.

"The playboy says you're the man who can find fingerprints," Harwood said.

"Max Corent. That's me. Found *you*, didn't I, Harwood?"

"You're the guy that connected my rifle to all the Chechen bullshit?"

"The one and only," Corent said. He lifted his glasses and stared at Harwood. "That was some wicked shit that went down."

A few months before, Harwood had faced off with his combat nemesis, Khasan Basayev—aka the Chechen—only to have the conflict unresolved. Was the Chechen dead or alive? Corent must have seen the contemplative look on Harwood's face.

"He's dead. Every shred of evidence we recovered showed he lost too much blood to stay alive in the Atlantic Ocean. Sharks, hypothermia, nobody to help him. He's dead."

"Hope you're right, Corent. Can you check this for prints?"

"Just a sec. Reading this tweet."

"Tweet?"

"Twitter. It's only been the new thing for the last few years. Get with the program, Reaper," Corent said.

"That's social media, man. C'mon. This is a crime scene. I need intel," Harwood said.

"Actually, journalism is dead. All those talking heads on television are opinion assholes. Left, right, it doesn't matter. You want the real scoop, it's right here."

He held up his phone and flashed his Twitter app at Harwood.

"What's the real scoop, then?" Harwood asked.

"I hear your sarcasm, Reaper, but listen to this from Maximus Anon. 'Camp David Ambush inside job. Explosion at sniper hide site destroyed evidence. Carly Masters was target. MTF.'"

"More to follow. Talk to me about Carly Masters?"

"The Secretary of Defense's daughter. General Masters. She worked for the Senate Intelligence Committee staff."

"Already there's someone with that level of detail? Who's Maximus Anon?"

"I'm telling you. Because you can have anonymous accounts we don't know who these people are. Could be someone in this room. But Maximus Anon is probably the most informative and well informed of all the researchers out there on Twitter. Spygate. Crossfire Hurricane. North Korea. Singapore. Iran. The mid-term bomber. He broke all that stuff before it happened." Corent waved his hand around the buzzing gym. "Most of them are clueless."

"Sounds like a bunch of bullshit. But I've got something real for you. That bomb didn't destroy all the evidence," Harwood said. He held out the shell casing wrapped securely inside the latex glove. Corent nodded and took the glove. The spent cartridge looked like a severed finger in the translucent material. He dumped it on a sheet of wax paper and used a pipe cleaner to lift it to the light. Squinting, he said, "Yeah. Def, bro. There's prints here."

"Good. How long?"

"Give me an hour if they're in the system. If not, forever."

Harwood nodded and walked the length of the gym where he saw about twenty residents standing and sitting along the far, mirrored wall. He caught a glimpse of Hinojosa walking briskly out the opposite door chasing after a stocky blond-haired man in tactical clothing. The man crossed the room and exited into an anteroom that was all hardwood flooring and mirrors. Harwood followed Hinojosa into the room. Several blue mats were rolled and tied in the corner. Yoga room. It smelled of sweat and antiseptic. The mirrors made the room seem larger than it was and reflected the man's back. On his belt was a hip holster with an HK pistol, a Blackhawk knife, and a tactical flashlight.

"Not everyone is a suspect," Hinojosa said, jabbing her finger at the man.

"Lady, I don't work for you."

Both heads turned toward Harwood as he entered.

"Fuck you want?" the man spat.

"Prob just take you down a notch," Harwood said.

The compact man came up to Harwood, inches away, looking up into his face. A lizard grin spread on his face, thick lips pulled back against uneven teeth.

"Holy fuck. If it isn't the Reaper himself." Taking a step back the man reached out his hand and said, "Stone. Erik Stone."

A little too rehearsed and a little too James Bondish, the salutation smacked of condescension.

Regardless, Harwood shook the man's hand and said, "Hinojosa is doing her job. Leave her alone."

Stone held up his hands in mock surrender. "Just controlling the environment until I know who's a good guy and who's a bad guy."

"What's your job? You work for Bronson?"

Stone laughed. "He might work for me. I don't work for anyone but the man."

"The man?"

"The president. And you're on my team, Reaper."

Harwood felt the folded papers in his back pocket. Remembered Murdoch's orders to him. That he was part of a special task force being set up by the president.

"I think it's the other way around, Stone. This is my team," Harwood said. He pushed back just to establish boundaries. Stone was an alpha predator. He'd seen the type many times before. If you didn't set the markers down immediately they assumed they owned every bit of space you didn't claim.

"Actually, you're both wrong," Hinojosa said. "You both work for me." She flashed her phone at them. A text from "Unknown."

Unknown: ANY WORD?

Hinojosa: PROCESSING EVIDENCE.

Unknown: FASTER

"You've got a call," Harwood said, nodding at the phone. It was Bronson. She placed the phone on speaker.

"You're on speaker," she said.

"We've got something. Link up with Max and me now," Bronson directed.

"Seems like everyone is working for everyone else," Stone said.

"Does it matter?" Harwood replied.

They retraced their route through the gym and into the conference room where Corent had a large fingerprint displayed on a big-screen television monitor.

Bronson and Corent were discussing something while Faye Wilde turned and looked at them with a grim façade. Harwood locked eyes with her, but she simply shook her head.

"Find a hit?" Harwood asked.

"Immediately," Corent said.

"We've already briefed the president and the director," Bronson said.

"That was fast."

"We're shutting down the airports, train stations, the works. We've already got a bead on him. We think he's at Dulles right now."

On cue, a man's passport photo displayed on the screen.

"Malik Sultan from Crimea. He helped Russia invade. Was a key informant. Known mostly for his explosives capabilities, he's graduated into money laundering and arms dealing. Kind of a high-end guy to do a hit like this, but he easily could have built the IEDs used in the attack and the secondary attack on the apartment building. Comms records show I ran connections."

A live-circuit television showed FBI and other law enforcement closing in on the unsuspecting Sultan as he stood in line to board the airplane to Amsterdam.

"They've got him," Harwood said. Three agents angled in from the left. Another three from the right. An air marshal came barreling out of the boarding gate door with his pistol drawn, aimed directly at Sultan as he scanned his ticket by the gate. Travelers scattered quickly. The FBI agents closed on Sultan before he could react. Classic takedown. Textbook.

Bronson nodded, said, "Good job."

"Okay, that gives us something to work with," Harwood said. He envisioned an interrogation followed by a mission to capture the potential other cell members. Seemed logical.

Bronson and Hinojosa exchanged looks.

"This way," Hinojosa said.

They entered an office off the conference room. She closed the door. The place was cramped with Stone, Harwood, and Hinojosa standing in the small space. A large desk was littered with applications and other paperwork. Two chairs faced the desk. An empty coatrack stood in the corner like a skeletal winter tree.

Hinojosa retrieved an iPad from the top of the desk, tapped a few buttons and they all watched Google Earth spin and zoom in on the Crimean Peninsula.

Ultimately the image became that of a large compound.

"Sultan's compound. His family lives here."

Stone and Harwood nodded, waiting.

"Our mission is to kill his family."

"Kill his family?" Harwood asked.

"Damn straight," Stone said, as if this was the best news ever.

"Yes. Presidential orders under the current authorization of the use of military force. You are Team Valid. These are valid targets."

"Families are noncombatants, technically," Harwood said. Schooled in the art of rules of engagement, Harwood understood the fine line between legit and revenge. Sometimes the two overlapped.

Hinojosa pulled up three images on the iPad. Side by side they looked like criminals from a Southie Boston lineup. The man on the left looked mid-forties with thick dark hair combed straight up and to the side, punk rocker style. A day of dark stubble dotted his jawline and chin. Flat black eyes stared back. A white T-shirt covered a muscular, but thin frame.

"This is Murat Sultan, brother of the man we just captured, Malik Sultan. They live in a compound in the highlands above Yalta on the Crimean Peninsula," Hinojosa said, pointing at the older man on the left. Two teenage boys wearing rebellious scowls were next to Murat. They were dressed in blacks shirts and holding AK-47s at port arms. Headshots for a recruiting poster. "These are Saqir and Amrat, the sons of Murat and Malik, respectively. They all live in the Sultan compound in Crimea. We've launched drones from our base in Bosnia and from Incirlik in Turkey. We will have redundant coverage. Another teammate will meet us at the airport."

"Did these . . . men," Harwood said, "help plan the attacks?"

Hinojosa pointed at him. "That's what we're going with. We'll work the intelligence en route. We can always wave off if things don't firm up."

"Defeat the enemy at its source," Harwood said. It was the new National Security Strategy. He liked the concept. Transnational terrorists that fought under an ideology instead of a flag had to be rooted out from their safe havens. Most famously, Al Qaeda had hosted with the protective defenses of the Taliban in the largely ungoverned spaces of Afghanistan. Other organizations were now copying the tactic. Ideology that spread through loosely knit individuals could take root in any living room or ranch. All they needed were a computer and an idea.

Harwood nodded.

"You good?" Hinojosa asked.

"As long as it's connected. There has to be a thread, like hot pursuit." The concept of hot pursuit maintained that if a friendly force was in contact with an enemy force and the fleeing enemy crossed into a protected area, such as say over the Pakistan border from Afghanistan, the pursuing force could continue within reasonable limits. Sergeants such as Harwood appreciated the deliberately vague guidance. But here, Crimea was part of Russia, albeit annexed via combat, and they were not in contact with the enemy. In fact, they were going to have to find them. Looking at the pictures, Harwood could see the menace in their eyes. But was that enough? Of course not. If someone were to use that standard and look at a picture of him when he was nineteen years old, they would have shot him on the spot.

But he wasn't associated with a gruesome attack on the families of the president's cabinet. He stared at the pictures, letting his gaze lock in every detail. The man on the right, labeled, "Amrat Sultan, Malik's son," had a scar beneath his left eye. A burn mark on the neck of the center person, tagged, "Sadiq Sultan, Murat's son."

"So we're going after the men under the assumption that they participated in the planning?" Harwood asked. "No women or children?"

Hinojosa stared at him. She looked at Stone, who said nothing.

"We will follow the intelligence where it leads us," Hinojosa said. "Right now, this is what we've got. The president wants this to be swift. To send a message."

The sound of rotor blades filled the air. Harwood recognized the whipping blades of a Black Hawk helicopter.

"Grab your go bags and meet me by the helicopter," Hinojosa said.

"What about identifying Samuelson's body?" Harwood asked.

Hinojosa looked away, thought for a moment, and then locked eyes with him. "I have a backup in mind. Your primary mission is to get moving."

Harwood nodded, walked through the makeshift operations center, nodded at Faye Wilde to say goodbye, and then grabbed his rucksack from the car. Standing in the parking lot, he watched the fire trucks hose down the apartment building, plumes of water arcing into the charred frame. As he turned, there was a group of three men talking near two black government cars about twenty yards away. One man was on a cell phone, pacing. The other two were speaking in low whispers. All of the men were dressed in dark suits. They were standing just outside a streetlamp's halo of light. The taller man quit speaking and turned toward him.

Harwood immediately recognized the director of the FBI, Seamus Kilmartin. A former college basketball player and rock star lawyer with a big K Street firm in Washington, D.C., Kilmartin had a reputation as a political climber. Harwood didn't normally pay attention to politics, but the last couple of years made it mandatory viewing. Whether it was for the reality TV aspect, pop culture, or genuine interest in the political fortunes of the country, there was no avoiding the twenty-four-seven coverage of President Smart, former senator Sloane Brookes, and the beleaguered Kilmartin.

Kilmartin stared at Harwood with unflinching eyes, which Harwood gave right back to him. It occurred to him that Kilmartin would be in Hinojosa's chain of command unless something extraordinary were happening, which was certainly possible.

For no particular reason, Harwood nodded at Kilmartin. He then jogged to the Black Hawk that had just touched down in the field between the apartment building and the ambush location. After boarding, the pilot lifted off, circled the ambush site as if to emphasize the importance of the mission, and then tilted the nose of the aircraft toward Fort Belvoir, Virginia, and its private military airfield.

Sitting in the seat facing Hinojosa, he asked her through the headsets they were wearing, "What's up with Kilmartin?"

"What do you mean?"

"He's in the parking lot."

She shrugged. "Wouldn't you be if the president's cabinet was slaughtered on your watch?"

Good point.

"Now, this is important." She spun an iPad around to him and pointed with a manicured nail. "One more family member. Intel says this is the mastermind of the ambush."

Staring back at him was an image of a young woman, maybe in her early twenties. The label beneath her name read, "Malina Sultan, Malik's daughter."

Harwood studied the face. Soft and beautiful. Raven hair, like her brother and cousin. Piercing copper eyes. She would be considered a knockout in any society.

"We good?"

Harwood stared as the lights whipped by beneath them. He thought of killing the seed of an entire family. If they had hard intelligence that this was the nerve center and everyone pictured was involved, then so be it. Sucked to be them.

"I'm good," Harwood said.

CHAPTER 5

The image of the young woman, Malina, hovered in his mind as he prepared to step from the back ramp of an MC-130 Hercules special operations aircraft flown out of Incirlik Air Base. Harwood watched through the back cargo bay of the aircraft as the experimental Zodiac boat rolled out the back with a cargo parachute to stabilize its descent.

At Incirlik, they had quickly rehearsed the plan to take observation positions on a ridge above the compound. Harwood, the sniper, would provide cover as Stone and Griffin Weathers assaulted into the compound, if necessary. During the flight, they acquainted themselves. Stone introduced himself as a former Navy SEAL turned military contractor, who lived in Virginia Beach where he had served with SEAL Team Six. He was single and had no children. Harwood wondered if Stone had taken a similar rapid reassignment or if his departure was for some other reason. He had an edge that Harwood couldn't quite place.

Weathers was former Marine Force Recon and lived in Jacksonville, North Carolina, where he had served with the Marine special operators. He was a dual sniper and assaulter, an expert at explosives, and a student of martial arts, mainly karate and judo. He had commented that the newfangled martial arts were just different names for the same basic punches and parries that he had perfected. Made sense. Weathers was divorced with two daughters who lived in Jacksonville with their mother.

Hinojosa flew on the airplane in a black cargo jumpsuit, but of course wasn't jumping. Their plan of entry was to land in the water a mile off Hruzovyi Port, an industrial liquid natural gas transfer point. The Crimean Peninsula was chock-full of gas and oil and a large part of Russian incentive to invade stemmed from Crimea's port access into the Black Sea and subsequently into the Mediterranean and Atlantic shipping lanes. From their entry point, they would use an airdropped Zodiac boat to motor into the port area. It was approaching midnight of the day following the ambush, which had made international headlines.

Two F-35 stealth fighters provided air cover as they whipped along the Black Sea at five hundred feet above sea level.

Harwood jumped, leading Stone and Weathers into the combat mission. The static line on Harwood's parachute popped immediately and his parachute inflated. Seconds later, he was splashing into the water where he quickly unlatched his canopy release assemblies, dispatching his parachute and its accompanying drag. Gaining his buoyancy, he retrieved his night-vision goggle and used it like a pirate scope to find the flashing infrared beacon they had placed on the Zodiac.

After turning nearly two-thirds of the way around, he saw the blinking strobe. It was about fifty meters away. He sidestroked toward the raft, hearing only the splashing of his movements in the water. As he approached the small rubber boat, he saw that

Stone and Weathers were already inside, which didn't surprise him given that one was a SEAL and the other a marine. He heard the engine cough and sputter.

"Hurry, Ranger," Stone said.

"Heard that," Harwood said, slinging his ruck over the rib of the boat. Weathers clasped his forearm and pulled him in.

"All good?" Harwood asked.

"All good," Stone replied.

He could barely hear the muffled engine in the high-tech Zodiac, kitted with a sound-suppressed motor and other options that could prove useful on egress. Stone stared at the horizon as they sped north toward the lights of Yalta on the eastern shore of the Crimean Peninsula.

Harwood did what any good sniper would do: check his equipment to make sure everything was operational after the jump. He removed his SR-25 rifle from its watertight pouch, slapped a magazine into the well, and charged the weapon. He screwed the sound suppressor on the muzzle and then laid the stock on the gunwale of the raft. Through his Leupold scope he could see thermal and infrared images. He spotted a fisherman and reported through the communications system, "Fisherman in a small boat. Ten o'clock. Four hundred meters. No activity."

"Shoot him," Stone replied immediately.

Harwood looked over his shoulder to see if Stone was smiling. He wasn't kidding. Stone's face was set, eyes on the horizon. Stone's hand pressed the small detent button hanging from his communications system.

"I say again, shoot the fisherman," Stone repeated.

"No sign of enemy activity or intent," Harwood said.

"We're not in Afghanistan, Harwood. You're not the Reaper here, bud. Weathers, go ahead and kill the douchebag."

"The fisherman?" Weathers asked.

Very funny, Harwood thought. No way was he going to shoot an innocent bystander. He'd seen enough senseless death and there could be more people in the boat. While the fisherman could report them, someone calling him may also alert the police if he didn't answer. Who knew? The mission called for killing those who had planned the ambush, which Harwood had euphemistically rationalized. Sounded a lot better than killing the family members in an eye for an eye fashion.

Weathers leveled his rifle, an M24 manual bolt-action sniper weapon. The suppressor poked forward from the gunwale. Stone had slowed the Zodiac to a near soundless crawl. The fishing boat was two hundred meters away, nearly parallel with them. Harwood continued to watch through his scope. The fisherman had bib overalls on and Harwood imagined they were the rubber kind that would keep a fisherman dry. There was a lantern hanging from the ceiling of the center console boat. The craft didn't look modern, rather, it looked like a wooden antique. The fisherman leaned over the edge and began pulling a net into the boat.

He was checking his nets. As the man pulled another length of net, he stood and looked in their direction. Harwood heard two taps on a buttstock and then Weathers's weapon coughed. The fisherman continued to stand, then doubled over and spilled into the water.

"Target down," Weathers said.

"Roger. See how it's done, Reaper?"

"You came close to him so we could kill him, Stone. Don't pretend to teach me about combat." What he wanted to say was, that was murder. But he checked himself. They had just started the mission.

"You think Luttrell would be a millionaire today if they had just shot the goat herders?" Stone said.

Marcus Luttrell was the lone survivor of a Navy SEAL mission

gone wrong in Afghanistan. Selling the rights to his story had gar-
nered him fame as "The Lone Survivor," which was actually an
extract from the Ranger Creed.

*Readily will I display the intestinal fortitude required to fight on
to the Ranger objective and complete the mission though I be the lone
survivor.*

"I think we might have just burned ourselves," Harwood said.
Another man appeared on the deck, frantically searching for his
fishing partner. Either he had been on the other side retrieving
another net, or he had been down in the shallow hold.

Either way, they were too far beyond the fishing vessel to stop
and go back. Or, if Stone chose to do that, he would risk making
a trivial risk the main thing, creating an even larger fur ball than
he had already done.

"Too late now. We're heading into the landing area. Prepare
to disembark," Stone said, seemingly unfazed.

The nose of the boat slammed onto the shore as Stone jacked
the engine up to avoid damage to the prop and shaft. Harwood
and Weathers jumped out and pulled the raft into a small alcove
beneath the towering bluffs of the Crimean Peninsula. The port
was a half mile to their north and the city of Yalta was a quarter
mile to their south. Harwood and Weathers pulled a camouflage
net over the Zodiac as they unloaded their gear.

"This way," Stone said.

Harwood walked trail, as they had rehearsed. He was responsible for rear security of the team. Every three or four steps, he
would spin in three hundred and sixty degrees, scanning through
his night-vision goggle, which he had affixed to the harness on his
scalp. A musty mixture of saltwater spray, a faint scent of petroleum, and Weathers's body odor filled his nostrils. The time was
0100 local. Their plan was to attack the target at 0300, or 3 A.M.,
which was the ebb of the human circadian rhythm. Even the most

dutiful guards had a hard time staying awake from 0300 to 0400. Once they could envision the dawn, the body could awaken, no matter how tired.

Like on all missions, Harwood resorted to his training and his ethos. He knew how to secure a patrol. He also knew that soldiers always fought for their buddies, not necessarily flag or country. While Harwood was a devout patriot, when the bullets started flying, it was teamwork on his left and right that would win the day in the name of that higher calling.

They stumbled rapidly up the east side of the bluff, following a minor trail filled with hard rock outcroppings. Soon, they were silhouetted by the half moon glaring down from a cloudless sky.

"Need cover," Harwood said. The infantryman in him was uncomfortable with Stone's apparent lack of concern for conceal-ment. Instead of a surgical ninja approach, such as Harwood preferred, Stone's style seemed to be the proverbial bull in a china shop. They eventually found a covered position on the west side of the ridge about a hundred meters beneath the peak, a terrain feature known as the military crest. It was precisely the type of location Harwood preferred. High terrain, but not silhouetted against the sky, as they had been. The landscape reminded him of Southern California. Dry hills with hidden crags along the sides. They were only about 800 meters above ground level, but the van-tage was a good one.

The Sultan compound sat just a quarter mile below them. It was 0200 hours, an hour before hit time. Through his scope, Har-wood studied the complex of buildings and fences. There was a large rectangular building that seemed to be the main living quar-ters. A few muted lights were on in rooms facing them on the northwest corner. The backyard was large with two small guest cottages. The homes appeared to be stucco with red-tiled roofs. The security fence looked to be about ten feet high but was no match for their vantage point. Harwood and team had clear fields of fire.

"Movement in the backyard," Harwood said.

A young man was walking from one of the guest cabins to the back deck of the home. A second man stepped onto the deck, this one much older.

"Confirm target," Harwood said. "Looks like Murat and one of the sons. It's thermal, but I think I can make out the scar. Must be Amrat."

"No need to confirm. This is the compound. All individuals are enemy combatants and are valid targets."

Valid targets. Team Valid. Harwood understood, now. What constituted a valid target remained to be seen.

Hinojosa's voice chirped in his ear.

"I'm watching through your scope. I confirm that is Murat and Sadiq Sultan, our two primary targets. Intelligence analysts are telling us that they are planners for a team that calls themselves Threat Zero. Like patient zero, I guess. Regardless, facial, gait, and voice recognition confirm. Valid targets." Harwood's scope connected to a satellite feed so that Hinojosa had full situational awareness of the mission.

"Roger," Harwood said. Then to Weathers, "I've got the dude on the left. Stone, you're spotting."

"Easy shot, Harwood. No need."

"Then make yourself useful and check our six," Harwood said. In his tactical element, he didn't care who was in charge of the mission, he had the combat experience to lead and survive on any battlefield.

"Fuck you. I'm watching for squirters," Stone said.

"I'm on target two," Weathers said.

The two men looked up. Harwood heard it, also. The faint sound of helicopter blades.

"On three," Harwood said.

Before he could count, Weathers shot and the man on the right spun and fell against the deck railing. Holding his aim steady, Harwood sent the SR-25 7.62 round into Murat Sultan's head as the man turned in his direction. He watched half the skull come off as the man stumbled, banging against the glass storm door, shattering it, and sliding down in a bloody mess.

The wood door opened, and a younger man stuck his head through the shattered storm door. Stone fired and missed. Weathers dropped the third man in the doorway.

Had to have been Amrat, Harwood thought.

The helicopter blades became louder.

"Stone, what have we got?" Harwood asked, scanning the target for Malina.

Flashes moved through the rear window, which Harwood figured to be the kitchen. Stepping over the dead bodies and onto the back deck was a young child, perhaps three or four years old. The child's arms were in the air, flapping like a bird, as if playing a game.

"Target," Stone said.

"Not valid," Harwood countered.

A woman dashed through the storm door, tackled the child and rolled off the deck into the yard. Racing to the far side of the deck, she lifted an assault rifle and began returning surprisingly accurate fire. She held the baby behind her in an artful move as she raced to the northeast corner of the main building.

She didn't make it that far.

Weathers fired and hit her center mass. The woman stumbled, her rifle spitting a final volley of bullets into the air. The child tumbled away, crying, and stood in the middle of the yard next to Malina Sultan, staring at the apparent mother. Harwood's mind was cycling. This is a baby. Her wide eyes looked up, as if knowing they had killed her mother. It was a little girl, he could tell now. She had a pacifier in her mouth. Long, curly black hair fell around her neck. Harwood jumped up and leapt onto Stone.

But he was too late.

Stone fired.

Harwood wrestled the weapon away from the former SEAL and shouted, "That was not a valid shot!"

He looked through Stone's riflescope.

Stone didn't miss this time. The child had fallen across her mother, dead, as if she intended to snuggle.

"That was not a good shot!" Harwood repeated. "Not fucking valid!"

He was breathing heavy, rasps of air escaping from his lungs.

"Not fucking valid, you son of a bitch!"

He thought of Monisha. This girl was maybe three. She had nothing to do with anything.

"Calm down, Reaper," Hinojosa said into his ear. "You need to extract. You've been detected."

Without thinking, Harwood tossed Stone's weapon away from him and it skittered down the hill. Then he pulled his knife and leapt toward Stone, who was ready. Their knives sparked as Harwood dropped his knife, grabbed Stone's knife hand with both hands, wrenched it to his left, twisting until Stone released his knife in obvious pain. Harwood kicked Stone's left heel out from under him and then put his knee in Stone's chest. He anticipated Stone reaching for his pistol and beat the SEAL to his own weapon, pointing the man's HK pistol at his face. His hands trembling, Harwood's mind flashed with images of Monisha, the Chechen, and Samuelson. If he murdered Stone on a mission he would be in jail. Who would take care of Monisha?

"Not valid!" he shouted in Stone's face.

The sounds of his voice were drowned by the humming blades

of a Russian Hind attack helicopter. Rockets peppered the terrain around them. The upgraded Hind had enhanced avionics and optics. They were sitting ducks.

"Bigger issues, Reaper," Stone replied. He smiled until Harwood smashed his mouth with the butt of the pistol.

The helicopter continued to zero in on their position, the rocket and machine-gun fire becoming more accurate by the second.

"You ladies can fight," Weathers said. "But we need to unass the AO."

Stone smiled at him through bloody and chipped teeth. "Just doing what the prez asked us to do."

Weathers tugged on his shoulder. "Need your firepower, bro. Leave this shit for once we've exfilled out of here."

Still reeling from Stone's ruthless murder of the child, Harwood stood, shook off the shock, grabbed his knife and SR-25, and focused on the slow-moving Hind. It was maybe a half mile away and closing. It slowed as it locked onto their position. The nose flared up, taking the pilots out of his view momentarily, then leveled, spitting rockets into the hillside below them.

His best shot was on the pilot in the starboard seat, one he figured to be the copilot. It didn't matter. He needed to create as much confusion as possible so that they could escape. His real desire, though, was to go into the compound and check on the girl. He scanned the area. It was either wishful thinking or his imagination, but the girl had moved. She was halfway up the steps, crawling over the dead men. A soldier seeking shelter from the beaten zone.

Police sirens now filled the air with their shrill warning. Harwood removed a parachute flare from his rucksack and laid it by his side.

He established a solid sight picture on the copilot and fired twice. At least one of the rounds struck the man.

"You got pilot, Weathers?"

"Roger."

Weathers fired and the helicopter began to flare upward, as if the pilot had manipulated a control to slow the aircraft.

"We've got an intercept that the fisherman you shot called you guys in. You need to exfil now," Hinojosa whispered in his earbud.

"Roger. Find a way to send an ambulance to the target. The child is still alive."

Hinojosa didn't respond.

"Do it!" Harwood said. "Or I blow the roof off this fucking op."

After a long pause. "Done."

"Tell them I'm marking it with a parachute flare."

Harwood grabbed the parachute flare, removed the top of the canister, placed it on the bottom, and slammed it against the rock. He angled the mouth of the tube at forty-five degrees to send it far enough to hang near the target location.

The helicopter spun wildly out of control and crashed at the base of the hill. The flare opened with a pop and hung above the backyard, highlighting the child crawling over glass inside the house.

"Don't you dare shoot," Harwood said to Weathers. He locked eyes with the marine, who nodded.

"We're moving now," Weathers said.

The three men retraced their route over the hill, and down to the boat, which wasn't there.

CHAPTER 6

"The Russian military is tracking you," Hinojosa said through the headset. "Improvise."

Harwood had been improvising his entire life. He didn't need some lady in an airplane twenty miles away to tell him what to do.

"You tossed my rifle, douchebag," Stone said. He reared up in Harwood's face, pouring stale breath on him. Harwood could bench about 425 pounds by now since he had been doing extensive rehab from his combat injuries. His hand lashed out like a cobra and grabbed Stone's thick neck, squeezing it in his vise grip.

"I don't give a shit about your rifle. You shot a defenseless girl, you coward. I'm in charge. Do what the fuck I tell you to do or I will absolutely slit your throat."

"Come on, guys," Weathers said. "We gotta move."

Harwood shoved Stone backward, feeling the hateful glare burning into his skin.

"Follow me," Harwood said. He picked up the pace at a slight jog, which was no problem for him, given that he ran daily with his rucksack on his back. Stone was laboring a bit, but Weathers seemed to be doing fine.

He found a dirt road that led north, toward the industrial port ten miles north. Keeping to the low ground, he navigated through shallow dry creek beds, always checking his magnetic compass to make sure they were on azimuth. Their exfiltration plan had been to meet an American fishing vessel in the Black Sea prior to sunrise. It was 0430 and the sun would be up within two hours. They had to move quickly.

Russian helicopters were buzzing around the hill from which they had ambushed the Sultan family. The first casualties delivered by the president's Team Valid. In Harwood's mind, it was an inauspicious beginning. He believed that every terrorist deserved to die a terrible death and personally wanted to be the one to deliver that final note.

He was the Reaper, after all. Thirty-three kills in ninety days. Always there saving everyone's ass. It was a team sport, but the Reaper might as well have been the quarterback, calling the plays, delivering the touchdowns. Killing the bad guys when it most counted.

After an hour of jogging through the scrub and washboard ditches, Harwood saw the lights of the port. They paused, sucking in oxygen. A light sheen of sweat covered Harwood's cut body. The polypropylene shirt wicked away the moisture, keeping him dry. He drank some water through his CamelBak tube.

"Need to cut it," Harwood said. He nodded at Weathers then looked at Stone, who glared at him. Helicopter blades chopped in the air behind them, circling their sniper lair. The air was moist and cool, a fresh breeze blowing off the Black Sea. Stone was wheezing from the run. Harwood felt fine. The conditioning delta between him and Stone seemed important to him and so he logged it away in the back of his brain.

Weathers used wire cutters to snip the chain-link fence. He pulled back the cut semicircle of fencing and used the pliers to bend a small loop into the metal to hook onto the standing fence and hold open the gap. Weathers went through first, sliding on his belly, followed by Harwood. Stone slipped under last. They huddled behind a four-foot-high mound of dirt and grass about fifty meters from the main port building and the steps to the piers.

They were in what looked to be a hybrid commercial and industrial port. About twenty fishing boats were haphazardly lined up against a concrete pier. Large pipes ran along a second pier. They appeared to be for fluid trans-load, such as liquid natural gas or fertilizer. At the end of the pier were two additional T berths where ships could anchor in the Black Sea and take on or discharge liquid through the piping.

"Security, ten o'clock," Harwood said. Two uniformed men were talking on radios, scanning. Almost certainly, they had been alerted. Both were armed with pistols on their hips.

From a low brick building a man walked up to the two security guards. He had on a black watch cap and a heavy waterproof parka. Stadium lights surrounded the perimeter and made any concealed movement within the port facility impossible.

They chatted briefly, looking around, as if one of them were saying, "There was a shooting and the suspects are on the loose."

Lots of head nods and urgent movement of hands.

"We need to kill them," Stone said, gritting his teeth.

Stone's answer to everything seemed to be slaughter. No finesse.

"What we need is a boat," Harwood said. "That might involve killing them, but we should be focused on finding an operational boat."

The helicopters patrolling the skies crept closer to the port, maybe a mile or two away. They were doing a classic grid search. By Harwood's calculations they had maybe another twenty minutes before there would be no escape.

"Wait a minute," Weathers said. "There's our boat. It's at the end of that T head."

Harwood looked through his scope and recognized the distinctive outline of the Zodiac. Saw the high-tech engine with its unique stealthy trapezoid shape.

"We can go in right here, slip across the water, get in the boat, and blow out of here," Weathers said.

"Roger. No match for the helicopters though," Harwood said. He pressed his push-to-talk button. "Any way to keep those helicopters off our ass?" he said to Hinojosa.

After a moment, Hinojosa came back with, "Negative. You have an hour to link up."

"Roger, out."

Their only option was to make a gun run for the transport in the Black Sea that awaited them. From there, they would have a decent shot at escaping.

"Okay, Stone, you go first," Harwood said. "Then Weathers. Then me."

Stone smiled. "Don't want me capping those assholes? You're such a pussy, Harwood. Reaper my ass."

"You're in lead because you're in charge of the boat. You're the Navy SEAL, I think. I'll be over watch until you're in the boat."

"You think?"

"Just execute. Quit bitching. Want me to toss your pistol? Your knife? You make a wrong move and *I will definitely* cap your ass."

The helicopters were closing in. The blades chopping less than a mile away. Mad at himself for letting his emotions get in the way of execution, Harwood shifted gears. He said to Weathers, "Okay, you lead. I'll follow. Then we'll see if Stone makes it in time."

"Fuck that," Stone said. "I'm lead."

Stone took the bait and low crawled around the berm. Harwood leveled his rifle at the three men, who were breaking their huddle. The man in the watch cap turned and walked back into the building. The two security men split, one walking in the opposite direction and the other walking directly at them.

Fifty meters wasn't a lot of distance to cover. Stone was in the water, moving silently toward the boat. They had no reason to believe it would still be operational, but it was the best option available at the moment. The boat ride alone would be thirty minutes to cover the ten miles they needed.

Harwood slid down behind the berm. The guard's boots crunched on the dusty shale just on the other side of the berm. He tapped Weathers, pointed at himself, dragged his finger across his throat, and then pointed at Weathers, and wiggled his fingers. Weathers nodded.

Harwood soundlessly extracted his knife from its sheath affixed to his outer tactical vest. He carefully locked the blade in place. Weathers watched him and then looked toward the water. The footfalls stopped on the other side of the berm, maybe five meters away. Harwood took deep, steady breaths. He was a sniper, true, but hand-to-hand combat was a Ranger skill that he had mastered. He cuffed the knife along his right forearm, blade facing out.

The man spoke in Russian, a language Harwood did not speak or understand. The tone of the man's voice was not rushed or excited. A spot report, maybe: *Nothing to see here so far, but there's this berm.*

In his periphery, Harwood saw Stone reach the Zodiac and slip over the edge. They were checked in place by the guard. As soon as he thought he might need to initiate the action, the guard stepped around the berm on the side nearest to Harwood, but he must have seen Weathers's prone body first, because he lifted his pistol and shouted, "Stop!"

The voice was guttural and harsh. The man stepped past Harwood, who was pressed into the side of the berm, some tall grass covering him. Focused on Weathers, the guard closed on the former marine.

Harwood sprang from his concealed position and simultaneously slipped his left arm around the guard's neck while slamming his fist into the man's right wrist, causing the pistol to tumble out of his grip. With the threat of a position-revealing shot minimized, Harwood jammed the knife into the man's larynx, then raked it toward him, using his positional leverage to pull the knife through the neck muscles and carotid artery. Blood sprayed across his sleeve as the man's head lolled to the side. Harwood lowered the guard's limp body onto the hardpan behind the berm. He nodded at Weathers, who returned the nod, as if to say, "Good job." Weathers was slithering toward the ledge that dropped into the harbor when Harwood took the man's radio from his shirt pocket.

"*Polozheniye del?*"

Harwood heard the question but didn't understand the words. He imagined it was a quick status check. Of course he couldn't be certain. Either way, they had less than a minute or two before the other guard became suspicious. Weathers was in the water and gliding toward the Zodiac. The guard was bleeding out. Harwood looked across the port and saw the partner guard stop walking and look back in his direction.

"*Polozheniye del?*"

No option. He slid his SR-25 rifle quietly up the berm and laid the crosshairs on the man's chest. The guard at his feet was not wearing any body armor. He would take the chance that his partner was also without protection. Harwood's mind cycled with the mission, the shooting of the three targets and then the little girl. But here, he had a bona fide Russian in his crosshairs. The Russians had been America's enemy for many years, decades even. Russia had invaded Crimea where they presently were attempting to escape a tightening noose of military and police. Solid with the morality of the shot, Harwood squeezed the trigger. For a moment he wondered if he had missed, which really wasn't possible at this distance, maybe two hundred yards. The man stood there, looked at his chest, looked back up at Harwood, fell to his knees, and then slumped forward face-first onto the concrete.

Harwood disassembled his rifle, stuffed it in his rucksack, then low crawled to the lip of the bulkhead. He found the hand rungs the others must have used and lowered himself into the water, which was cool at first. His adrenaline though kept him warm enough to make the fifty-meter swim rapidly. He didn't believe he was as quiet as the marine and Navy SEAL, but he did his best.

Stone had the Zodiac on idle as Weathers pulled Harwood into the boat.

"Go," Harwood said.

The Hind helicopter flew low and fast over them, banked, rose into the air, and started scanning the port area.

"No way we outrun that thing," Weathers said.

Stone kept the motor on idle and used his hand to pull them around the backside of the center concrete pier, providing them cover and concealment from the searching aircraft. They would almost certainly notice the two dead guards, Harwood thought. On cue, the aircraft lowered and landed near the far guard that Harwood had shot.

"Now's our best shot," Harwood said. "We either stay here and fight them with all their radios and calls they'll be making, or we slip out and try to get outside their immediate search arc."

Stone nodded, gunned the engine, which was drowned by the whirring rotor blades, and they shot into the open water. Stone kept the Zodiac near the protection of the pier until they reached its end.

They were in open water with ten miles to go.

"Go submersible!" Harwood shouted.

"Too soon," Stone replied.

The Hind helicopter lifted into the air, turned its nose toward them, and let loose a volley of rockets that whooshed overhead, leaving smoky trails. Wildly inaccurate, the rockets were the least of Harwood's worries. The Hind E could spit out high-volume 23 mm machine-gun rounds and deadly accurate tank-busting guided missiles, either of which would be lethal to their team. He didn't care if the team did another mission, but he did care about living to fight another day.

"Everybody lay down and activate the submersible, Stone," Harwood said. Stone's bearded face was set in rock, staring back at him. His hair whipped wildly in the wind as he kept his hand on the till of the high-tech engine. Harwood retrieved his pistol and said, "Solve a lot of my anger issues right now, asshole. I'm in charge. Do it."

"Come on, man, just take us down," Weathers said.

Stone smirked, pressed a button, and said, "Better get down."

A thin bullet-proof Plexiglas canopy began sliding from the titanium cockpit of the Zodiac. Jet wings expanded out from the pontoons, like an F-14 Tomcat. The nose of the Zodiac pivoted downward, catching water and pulling the Zodiac underwater. Harwood and Weathers were lying with their heads toward the bow while Stone's feet were near their heads. The cockpit sealed with rubberized receptors along the bow of the vessel, preventing leaks as the experimental watercraft lowered into the water. The engine was contained within the airtight lock that Zodiac had designed in competition to win a Navy contract for shallow water submersibles.

Machine-gun rounds plinked off the protective shield above them and more rockets sprayed wildly. The ninety-horsepower engine pushed them deeper into the water until they were completely submerged.

Stone pressed some buttons on the cockpit console that Harwood assumed were navigation aids. Through the canopy, he saw the bubbling trails of machine-gun rounds burrowing through the water. The Zodiac was now like a coffin, sliding soundlessly through the water. There had been some discussion about using a Mark VIII SEAL Delivery Vehicle for the mission, but given the discreet and ambiguous nature of the mission, whoever was in charge had opted to experiment with the Zodiac Sea Diver.

They plowed through the murky sea, reliant upon navigational devices that looked a bit like avionics. A radar pinged, showing potential obstructions or obstacles that might hinder navigation. After a few minutes of silence, the men looked at one another. The bullets had stopped for the moment. There was no evidence of enemy fire boring through the water. Harwood held his thoughts in his mind as if he were holding his breath beneath the water. The canopy was less than a foot from his face. Weathers lay next to him with Stone's boots in between them. Each of them was probably thinking the same thing: *I hope we make it*.

The Zodiac shuddered as it bore through the water. The cockpit and wings helped make the boat more aerodynamic, but still the designers had work to do on the vessel, Harwood thought.

After twenty minutes powering through the water at twenty knots, twenty less than above water max cruising speed of forty, Harwood said, "I'm showing us two minutes behind pickup time."

"Excuse the fuck out of me, Reaper, but I tried to keep us up above as long as possible to maintain speed," Stone said.

"I get that, but you didn't see the helicopter coming at us. I did. Now drop the attitude and let's figure out how to make up the time."

"How much time we got to link up?" Weathers asked.

When he spoke, Harwood could smell his stale breath. The confines were claustrophobic. Maybe SEALs and marines were used to this, but it wasn't Harwood's jam.

"Thirty-two minutes," Harwood said. "And we need to be at that point." He pointed at the radar screen that had a destination icon blinking in green. As he was pointing at the radar, an icon appeared on the top of the screen.

"Bogie," Stone said.

"Maybe, maybe not. As long as we're under water, we're fine," Harwood said.

"Got to get up and make up that two minutes. This is all about precision," Weathers said.

After the altercation in the sniper hide site, the leadership dynamic had changed. Stone and Weathers were deferring to Harwood, which was how he wanted it. He waited a few minutes and watched the icon on the radar.

"Okay, surface. Keep the canopy down. That will help with speed. Haul ass toward linkup and be prepared to go back under," Harwood said.

Stone pressed a button that elevated the nose of the Zodiac, pointing it upward and providing lift. The raft shot from the water, went airborne, and splashed down with a thud. The canopy cover remained in place. Stone opened the throttle and they skimmed along the sea's surface. They were twenty miles away from the shoreline now, in supposed international waters, but Harwood knew that meant little to the Russian Federation that had invaded and seized the Crimean Peninsula.

"Status of radar?"

"Bogey still headed toward us. Gaining," Stone said.

"Speed?"

"Forty knots. Pegged wide open," Stone replied.

A common threat had if not bonded them at least focused them on the task at hand: survival.

"I'm showing we're thirty seconds off," Harwood said.

"That's too much," Weathers said.

"Going as fast as I can," Stone defended. "Another bogey. Six o'clock," Stone said.

The radar showed a blip on the screen in front of them and behind them. Harwood hoped that one of them was useful. Without warning, a second icon appeared next to the original one approaching from the south.

"Three bogies," Stone said.

"One bogey, two friendlies," Harwood said.

"Not sure about that. Different image. Should be seeing something indicating friendly. Getting no squawk code."

The squawk code was an aircraft's signal as to whether it was friend or foe. All aircraft identified themselves, typically, so that they could warn off potential threats.

Lights flickered to their front. The canopy shield had a milky film on it from the constant spray of the sea.

"Link up in one minute," Harwood said. "Lower canopy."

"We'll lose speed," Stone replied.

"We need to see everything for this phase," Harwood replied.

"Roger that," Weathers seconded.

Stone pushed a button. The canopy retracted. The wind and

water blew in with force. Harwood, Stone, and Weathers slipped on their night-vision goggles.

"There it is," Harwood said. With the canopy out of the way, Harwood saw the Night Stalker Task Force 160th MH-47 special operations Chinook aircraft. It banked upon spotting them, pivoted in the air, and then began chopping away at fifteen knots as it lowered its ramp. The Zodiac gained on the helicopter, aiming at the gaping cargo bay, illuminated only by two infrared lights blinking on either side.

Stone shot the Zodiac up the ramp. They flew into the back of the helicopter, the engine sparking off the metal ramp. Stone had decelerated enough so that they didn't crash into the cockpit. The ramp slammed shut and the MH-47 nosed over and gained its max speed of nearly 200 mph.

The crew chief was dressed in an olive Nomex jumpsuit and wearing a space-age helmet and face shield. Two crewmen manned machine guns out the port and starboard hatches. The interior was pitch black, save the starlight seeping in through the porthole windows. Harwood knelt and held on to the Zodiac as the crew chief strapped them in and attached the straps to the floor of the aircraft D-ring with snap hooks.

"Two Hinds bearing down on us!" the crew chief shouted.

"How long to destination?" Stone asked.

"You do your shit. We'll do ours," the crew chief responded. "We have Apache escort."

Harwood did the math. The Hind could fly about 180 mph. The Chinook was faster at nearly 200 mph. The key was gaining enough distance to outrun the missiles the Hind could fire from miles away. And the Apache helicopter would not be able to keep up. Its max speed was about twenty miles below that of the Chinook, more in keeping with the Hind.

"Missile!" the crew chief shouted.

CHAPTER 7

Harwood stared across the barren conference room at Hinojosa. They stood on opposite sides of a gray metal table with two chairs. The fluorescent lights dangled from the ceiling on weak chains. Hinojosa was dressed in a black jumpsuit with her hair yanked back in a ponytail. Harwood was still wearing his sweaty mission attire of black polypropylene shirt, black cargo pants, and muddy outer tactical vest. He poked a finger at Hinojosa.

"Forget for a minute that we were nearly knocked out of the sky," he said. "I understand this team is expendable. But I'm not killing women and children. We go after valid targets! Authorized targets! Not kids!"

Hinojosa nodded. They had narrowly escaped the Hind rockets, but the Night Stalker pilots were the best. Spitting chaff and flying at max throttle they had dodged the Russian military. He had been surprised they had not scrambled jets, but with the Turkish military patrolling the skies, perhaps the Russians had played it safe.

"The president was clear. The families of the terrorists." Hinojosa crossed her arms.

"So where does it stop? Execute the ninety-five-year-old grandmother in a wheelchair? The newborn baby? Eliminate all the terrorist seed from the earth? Is that the thinking? That it's some kind of DNA thing?"

"Vick, stop it," Hinojosa said. She placed her palm out as if she were stopping traffic. "There is some moral ambiguity here, I know."

"Some? This entire mission is bullshit." His gaze never wavered from Hinojosa.

"And there's a new threat," she said. She slid a document across the table. Stamped on the top and bottom were the words: Top Secret/NOFORN. Top Secret was one of the highest classifications, while NOFORN meant that no foreign governments or personnel were authorized to view the information.

He read the short summary.

START/MALIK SULTAN CAPTURE AT DULLES AIRPORT REVEALS CONNECTIVITY TO PERZA FAMILY IN IRAN AND THE DAOUD SYRIAN WEAPONS CARTEL IN DAMASCUS. SULTAN FAMILY HAS OPERATIONAL EXPERIENCE AND IS CONNECTED TO RUSSIA. DAOUD PROVIDES WEAPONS. PERZA PROVIDES FINANCING. SAMUELSON IMPLICATED AS FOURTH SNIPER. WITH SULTAN CAPTURED AND SAMUELSON CONFIRMED DEAD, PERZA AND DAOUD REMAIN AT LARGE. CHATTER INDICATES A FOLLOW-UP TARGET. INTELLIGENCE ANALYSTS PRESENTLY ARE REVIEWING INTELLIGENCE

THAT INDICATES THE PRESIDENT'S DAUGHTER AND WIFE, THE VICE PRESIDENT'S FAMILY, AND THE FAMILY OF THE SPEAKER OF THE HOUSE OF REPRESENTATIVES MAY BE AT RISK. DEFENSE COMMUNITY TAKING APPROPRIATE SECURITY MEASURES. WE BELIEVE THAT THESE ASYMMETRIC ATTACKS ARE INTENDED TO NOT ONLY CREATE FEAR AND HAVOC, BUT ALSO TO IMPACT THE CHAIN OF COMMAND DECISION-MAKING ABILITY AS THE ADMINISTRATION FACES KEY DECISIONS ON IRAN, NORTH KOREA, SYRIA, AND RUSSIA. LIST OF VICTIMS KILLED IN AMBUSH ATTACHED IN SEPARATE CLASSIFIED DOCUMENT./*STOP*

"Samuelson shouldn't be mentioned in this report," Harwood said. "It's like all that unmasking bullshit from a couple years ago. When we show he's not involved, then the entire intelligence community will have egg on its face."

"The evidence is pretty strong against Samuelson, but we'll get back to that," Hinojosa said. "Have a seat."

They sat, and she retrieved another document from her folder. Metal chairs scraped against the concrete floor. The air was musty and dank.

Harwood looked at the piece of paper. It had twenty-two names on it. He recognized a few simply because they were well publicized. He had no friends or comrades on this list. They were twelve family members of high-level government officials. Not to be unsympathetic, but he had seen these lists before and felt more emotion than he was feeling now. That was because he had friends and battle buddies killed by improvised explosive devices, sniper rounds, and artillery. This was a heinous act, but then again, it was just another casualty list in an ongoing war. Still, twelve family members and ten law enforcement officers. As if the LEOs around the country hadn't been through enough targeting from radicals. None of it sat well with Harwood.

"So, we *are* getting revenge for the president while a threat goes loose in the United States. Makes no sense. We should go home," Harwood said. "Go after these guys." He pulled the intel report from underneath the casualty list and pointed at it.

"Not our call. There's another task force to go after the terrorists in country. Our mission is to cut it off at its source. Now, since you need convincing what we're doing is legit, there's this."

Hinojosa pulled a folder out of her briefcase and tossed it on the table. Opening it, she flipped glossy photographs of the family Team Valid had just ambushed: Malina and Amrat Sultan with their father, Malik, and cousin Sadiq. They were standing in the back of the compound that Harwood and his team had just attacked. Malina was holding a stick and pointing it at something on the ground as the others seemed to be paying rapt attention.

Hinojosa pulled another photo from the deck. It was a zoomed-in shot of the previous picture. Malina's stick was pointing at a mockup of Camp David and its surrounding area. The tip of the stick was precisely on the U-shaped bend in the road that had become the ambush location.

"You just killed three of the planners of this mission. The girl was collateral damage, but she lived. Lucky thing that Stone is a lousy shot. Winged her in the shoulder. She's young. She'll heal. There will be no mission to go back and kill her."

Harwood looked at the pictures then into Hinojosa's eyes. Felt a thrum of connection. She nodded at him.

"Okay," Harwood said. "You're in charge here, but once we

go tactical, I'm in charge. Stone is a boneheaded moron. Weathers seems okay. An operator. But Stone's out of control and you need me to rein him in."

"I'm good with that," Hinojosa said. "We have a problem, though."

Harwood said nothing.

"The rifle you tossed has been found by Russian military."

He had thought of that. He wasn't going to blame his actions on post-traumatic stress or traumatic brain injury, both of which he struggled with. He'd been rightfully outraged that Stone would shoot a child. Perhaps he should have handled it differently, but since adopting Monisha, he had an entirely new perspective on children. Instead of just thinking of himself and his teammates, he was the legal guardian of a human being. While being a squad leader of men in combat was important and challenging, he had been dealing with adults. He was surprised at the new depth that Monisha had added to his thought processes. Now, he was gaining clarity on his life's purpose and calling. Service, savior, and, yes, sometimes, sniper. Send it.

Send it. The spotter's clarion call that the target was valid.

Team Valid.

Maybe this was a valid mission, after all, Harwood thought.

"But they won't have my fingerprints, will they?" Harwood said.

Hinojosa shook her head.

"No. You've been erased from our database. The three of you don't exist."

"What about you?"

"My status is of no concern to you," Hinojosa said. "What is of concern, though, is our next mission, which begins tonight."

She removed another folder from her briefcase.

"While you guys were executing, I was building the next

target folder." She laid five photos on the table as if she were a poker dealer. "These are the family members of the Iranian member of the team. I have to get you into Ardibal Province, which won't be easy. We will have to take you through Kurdistan, into the mountains west of the Caspian Sea. There's a compound on Lake Sooha. The family lives there. It's well fortified, as you might imagine."

She laid a satellite image of a rectangular high-walled estate overlooking the Caspian Sea on one side and Lake Sooha on the other. Harwood's first thought was, *Where are these people getting all this money?*

"Why's everyone got a freaking compound?"

"Focus on what's important. I'm giving you some input here, Vick."

Harwood studied the pictures and pointed at two spurs jutting off high ridgelines less than a mile away from the structure.

"Okay, tactically, these are the two best hide sites. We can recon and determine once on the ground. What's our egress?"

"Either the van you use on infil or you find your own way out."

"Our own way?"

"No U.S. government involvement," Hinojosa reiterated.

"Yet, here we are."

She sighed. "The MH-47 was in extremis. This boat wasn't going to make it. They'll do your insert into the mountains for the next mission, but after that they're done. There is, however, a SEAL team that can be there in twelve hours. Preferred option is the van. The SEALs are on a training exercise in Turkey and they've got an alert to be on standby."

Harwood nodded. "Now back to the real issue. Three men, two women. All adults," Harwood said. "Who are they? Why not come in across the Caspian?"

"I'll go in reverse. The Caspian requires going through Georgia, Azerbaijan, and/or Armenia. The Iranians have spies everywhere in those countries. Oddly enough, we assess the lowest risk to come in through the tough terrain here."

She pointed at the map that showed jagged, steep terrain near Lake Urmia on the western border of Iran with Turkey, an area completely controlled by the Kurds.

"The Kurds can help us through here, but what about once in Iran?"

"We've got a driver who can meet you and get you to your drop-off point. We did a quick map recon and figured a good offset drop-off point was here," Hinojosa said. She pointed at the map about an inch away from the two locations Harwood had selected. Anyone who knew how to read a map could choose generic fighting positions. The real work began on the ground, once you were on location. Everything was different, lines of sight, suitability of fire positions, and routes of egress. The art form was finding the best sniper hide that could match the hard mathematics involved in sniping.

"We?"

She looked away. Harwood saw her eyes harden and fixate on something far away, not in the room, maybe not in this world.

"Command back in D.C."

"Who knows what we're doing?"

This time she leveled her copper irises on Harwood. "The president, the director of the FBI, and me. It's that clean. That simple."

Harwood nodded, knowing nothing was ever that clean or that simple, but didn't press the issue. He registered though, that if Hinojosa was telling the truth, either the director of the FBI or the president, or both, were involved in selecting and approving the targets. But still, there had to be an entire machine gathering intelligence and making recommendations. It was possible that the machine was operating as normal and Kilmartin was skimming off the top, feeding the targets to the president, who then approved them. He recalled locking eyes with Kilmartin in the parking lot of Samuelson's apartment building. Something was off, but he couldn't place it, yet.

"The next family?"

"Correct. The wife, a daughter, a son, and two brothers."

"So, direct family? Did they have anything to do with it? The satellite shot you showed me with the Sultans rehearsing on a sand table makes me feel better about this mission. That was legit. I get killing jihadists who plan attacks against us. So, what about these people?"

"We're working it. This is the Perza family. Basir Perza, one of the sons of Farokh Perza, we speculate was a shooter in the ambush and is unaccounted for at the moment. Basir has a twin, Laleh, a medical school student. They have an older brother, Rahim, who helps his father with the family business. They're into imports and exports. Rugs, supposedly. Farokh's wife is an ordinary housewife. We'll call them targets 'P-one' through 'P-four.' P-one is the sister. P-two the brother. P-three the mother. P-four the father. I think calling the Sultans by their name may have personalized the mission too much."

Laleh, target "P-one," was beautiful. She had distinctive Persian features. Swept, raven hair. Wide almond-shaped eyes. High cheekbones. She was twenty-four years old. A student at the Ardabil University of Medical Sciences.

"Everything is personal when you're killing someone, Hinojosa," Harwood said. "Laleh Perza? A doctor in training? We're killing her?"

Hinojosa nodded. "Don't be fooled. We have communications between Laleh and the Sultan family in Crimea. The Sultans planned and the Perzas paid. Imports and exports are the perfect cover for this operation. All it takes is one container of rugs to get into a port in the United States. The rugs have weapons hidden inside. The container is delivered to a nondescript warehouse. The ambush team is small and have legitimate passports."

"Is this reality or speculation?"

"A little of both. Max Corent was able to find some communications between the Sultan family and the Perza family. Mostly financial transactions but also some emails. They mention something called Team Zero. Our analysts are trying to figure out what that means. Some are saying it's like patient zero, you know, the original patient infected with a virus."

"This is the original threat?"

"Something like that. Still trying to figure out what Threat Zero or Team Zero means. Could be bullshit. Could be biblical. Could be something in between."

"Okay, back to Perza. You're solid on the intel? You'd make these kills?"

"I'm part of this, aren't I? I'm facilitating. I'm doing everything but making the kills."

Noticing she didn't answer the question, Harwood pressed ahead. Time was short.

"But we know Basir Perza was involved and by extension he had the support of his family. That much is true?"

"Yes. Basir was a member of the team and had the full support of his family. They provided logistics and financing. Think about it. A father and mother send their son to war. How is this any different for any American soldier?"

Harwood was an orphan, so he had no frame of reference to process her question but understood what she was saying. He thought instead about the term Team Zero. Threat Zero. Killing bad guys had been his business for the last twelve years. He loved the United States. Knew it to be the best country in the world. Eradicating a new threat was not only important, but exciting. The notion that this may be a mission beyond simple revenge was a relief to him.

Team Valid versus Threat Zero.

"Max is pulling the thread on this 'Threat Zero'?"

"Yes. He's got another lead in Syria, but we're still developing that information and it would be premature to say anything with any specificity."

"Okay. How many total?"

"They're thinking four. The Russian, Iranian, maybe Daoud from Syria. More to follow on him."

"Back to Samuelson."

Hinojosa looked away, then locked eyes with Harwood.

"Yes. I'm sorry," she said.

"Again, there's no way Samuelson has anything to do with this," Harwood said.

"Not the way it's looking, unfortunately. The media is interpreting the Facebook Live suicide to be a confession. Samuelson's fingerprints are on some of the debris from the IEDs used to kill the families."

"Not possible," Harwood said, shaking his head.

"I'm afraid so. Max has confirmed it. They found some pieces of the PVC pipe that had been used to form the explosively formed penetrators. Samuelson's prints are on there. Also, some video footage at Home Depot in Hagerstown shows he purchased six-inch pipe a week before the attack."

"What happened to the extra shell casing next door to Samuelson's place? The prints? The fake scatter pattern of the casings in Samuelson's room? There's enough evidence right there for reasonable doubt, don't you think?"

"The bomb destroyed everything in there. The cartridge and fingerprints show others were involved, but right now there's more evidence on Samuelson than on the others combined."

"Are you part of the cover-up culture in the FBI now?" Harwood snapped.

Hinojosa bristled. Her face pinched tight, she said, "Don't you dare."

Harwood nodded. "Okay, I take that back. You seem legit unlike those high-level weasels running your show at the FBI."

Samuelson had been struggling with post-traumatic stress and severe brain injury. He'd been left for dead on the battlefield in Afghanistan, captured by a terrorist called the Chechen, and then brainwashed. Harwood didn't want to believe that Samuelson could have been so anguished that he turned on his own people.

"They've also got a list of complaints that Samuelson sent to the Veterans Administration complaining about their care and lack of service."

"They suck," Harwood said. "Lock me up if that's the standard."

"Come on, Vick. I'm showing you the case that they're building here. PVC pipe, fingerprints, suicide, and motive—the VA. Sure, they suck, but the president is in overdrive right now. He's chomping at the bit to brag about what you guys did last night. He wants to send a clear message to the enemy that the United States has taken off the gloves."

"Or stumbled down from the moral high ground," Harwood said. "Have they made the call on Samuelson yet?"

"Being a U.S. citizen has complicated the matter a bit, so, no, they haven't. The lawyers are reviewing it, but it's not looking good. We've been told to execute on Perza. That's where we are. And there's more."

Hinojosa turned to the list of casualties from the ambush and pointed a manicured, unpainted nail at a name.

"It seems Samuelson had been communicating with Carly Masters, the daughter of the Secretary of Defense."

"As in General Masters? The Raider of Raqqa?"

General Lou Masters had rocketed to the top of the military brass. In less than five years he had risen from being one of the most revered military combat leaders to the position of Secretary of Defense. Having orchestrated the destruction of ISIS in Syria and Iraq, he had earned the trust of the defense community and the president's administration.

"Carly Masters was killed in the Camp David ambush," Hinojosa said.

Her face was ashen, as if she was overcome with grief.

"You okay?"

"Yes," she said. "I'm fine. This isn't easy for me, either. But I have a job to do and I'm going to do it." Then she added, "I was friends with Carly."

"And Samuelson was, too? Sammie didn't seem the type to walk in tall cotton with beautiful women," Harwood said. "Don't get me wrong. He was a good bullshit artist, but he had zero game. And a general's daughter? Can't see that."

"FBI Special Agent Bronson and Max Corent found some unopened snaps on her phone. They were from SammySam0123."

"Snapchat?"

"Yes. Corent confirmed it's Samuelson's account. Registered to him. No doubts there. And there were some others from FrogBuds2006. That seems to be more cryptic."

"A SEAL?"

"Well, that's our guess. They're tracking the accounts right now. Because Samuelson was on Facebook Live and is a primary suspect, they are focusing on him first."

"Anyone else of significance killed?" Harwood asked. "I saw the list and read the dossiers, but was more focused on Samuelson and then we were too busy getting inside the enemy's decision cycle and killing their families."

Hinojosa spun the list toward her and ran her finger down the names.

"I'd say they're all significant," Hinojosa said.

Harwood spun the list around and took a minute to read each name. Innocent men, women, and children slaughtered in cold blood. Yes, they were all significant. But were they material to understanding what had transpired?

As with the first time he'd seen the list, he recognized most of the last names. Saw Carly and Helen Masters. He didn't personally know either of the women but had read that Helen was the general's wife and that Carly had been his daughter.

"How did you know Carly Masters?"

"UVA Law School. Same class. Then had overlapping tribes in the D.C. area before I got reassigned back to Texas. I went FBI and she went to work on the Hill for a congressional committee. Think her dad hooked her up."

Something dropped in the back of Harwood's mind. He couldn't place it, but it was an important hunch. Like a tuning fork vibrating, the thrum was real but hard to distinguish.

"Which committee?"

"Senate Intelligence," Hinojosa said. "Why?"

"Ever think that there might be a motive here beyond terrorism? Did anyone want any of these people dead? Or just generally speaking did they want all of them dead to make a big impact?"

"The operating theory has been the latter. Ambush to kill the families of cabinet members. No one has tried to tear this thing apart looking at individual victims."

Harwood slid the three photos of the shooters from Hinojosa's file.

"These are the killers?" he asked.

"If you count Samuelson, yes. That's what Kilmartin is giving me."

"I saw that bullshit in the intel report. He's not a killer. Tells me he was setup. Tells me there's more to this ambush than we're thinking about. We're doing this mission to grind someone's ax, but ultimately there's more happening. Samuelson didn't do this. The question is, who set him up and why?"

Hinojosa shook her head. "Let's move on to the mission. I'm exhausted."

Harwood nodded. "I respect that. You should get some sleep."

"As should you," she said. "It's seven A.M. local. Pick a route so I can plan the logistics and you guys can rehearse."

"I prefer ground over water any day," Harwood said. "Take us through the mountains."

"You got it. I'll work this while you sleep. Once you guys are set, I'll get some rest."

Harwood eyed her. "Can't think straight without sleep."

"I'll be fine. Here's some new kit for you. Check it out." She slid a small bag across the table. Her eyes were weary, bloodshot. Once perfectly smooth skin a day ago had evolved into bags under her eyes. She was wiped. Nonetheless she stood and opened the door for him. As he was walking out, she gently touched his back, urging him forward. When he looked over his shoulder, he saw her eyes were downcast with tears streaming along her cheeks.

"You sure you're okay?"

"I'm fine. Just tired. This is exhausting for all of us," she said.

He turned around, stepped toward her, and laid a hand on her shoulder. She put her hand atop his and said, "Vick, no."

Vick.

Another step and he closed the distance. She was looking at him with weary eyes, her firm grip reflecting her conflict. He slowly rolled his wrist away from her hand and hugged her. She resisted at first but laid her head on his shoulder. His thick forearms framed her back and held her without pulling her any closer.

"I'm sorry about your friend," he said.

Her head nodded against his shoulder. "And I'm sorry about yours. Things don't always go as planned, Vick," she whispered. Her hand glanced against his cargo pants pocket as she hugged him. "But no matter what, don't think I'm a damsel in distress needing to roll my hair out of some medieval tower."

Disregarding what she was doing, he thought, *Samuelson*. This could all be about Samuelson. Or maybe even Carly Masters.

He stepped back and nodded.

"All right then. Let's execute."

She was wiping tears from her face, shaking her head in frustration.

"Roger that," she said.

Harwood spun and walked away, wondering about Valerie Hinojosa and who she might be. Whose mission was this? And why was he involved? Plenty of snipers out there aiming directly at him. The crosshairs were always on him.

He found his bunk in the old army barracks where they had a makeshift command post and inventoried his gear. They were going in overland to kill the family of Basir Perza. And yet, Perza was supposedly loose in the United States. They were taking the fight to the enemy in the most personal way.

The mission, too, was impacting him in the most personal manner as well. Samuelson, his spotter, was now implicated in the Camp David Ambush, as the media was now calling the slaughter.

He opened the bag Hinojosa had given him. Three arm sleeves that looked like an NFL quarterback's forearm playbook were inside. He toyed with one, found some buttons. Lights came on. The words *Sat Com* flashed until they held a steady beam, indicating perhaps a connection. A small map spun and zoomed in until it geolocated him, indicating his position in Turkey with a flashing blue dot. He pressed the Off button and the sleeve powered down. He didn't know what to make of the device. If they were off the books, why would some anonymous person or team need to be monitoring them? Perhaps the raid into Iran was a higher level of danger, requiring more immediate communications with the Navy SEAL team also in Turkey.

His speculation was going to do no good, so he thought about Monisha and hoped she was okay. He missed her smart mouth and them knocking out homework together. His mind drifted to Hinojosa. Why was she so conflicted? It was right there on her face. She had aged ten years in the last forty-eight hours. They were all stressed out, but what burden was she carrying? What was her secret? It wasn't all about Carly Masters.

Or was it?

He figured she would tell him in due time. Besides, he had his own secrets. Harwood was glad he was off the books and half a world away.

He reached into his pocket and retrieved a handwritten note with one word written on it.

BAKU.

He looked up, thought about what she might be trying to communicate.

Things don't always go as planned, Vick.

Before he could go ask her for clarification, Stone and Weathers were standing in the doorway.

"We need to talk," Stone said.

CHAPTER 8

Harwood knelt behind the large boulder with the Kurdish Pesh-merga guide, Monsoor. Behind them were Weathers and Stone, who had acquired a new SR-25 sniper rifle.

The men had rested and planned in their Turkish black site. Hinojosa, who had slept for three hours, efficiently organized the logistics and target folders for their next mission in a Tehran sub-urb. In addition to securing Stone a new weapon, the bag she had given Harwood included a TacSleeve Information and Navigation Systems, or TSINS, for each of them.

Wrapped around Harwood's thick, tattooed forearm was the flexible plastic communications device. He had rested and felt re-freshed, though he kept coming back to Hinojosa's reaction when talking about Samuelson. Hell, the entire situation ate at him. There was no way that Samuelson was a traitor. No way he would kill innocent civilians. But still, there was a connection he couldn't place.

And what was up with Hinojosa not being able to look him in the eye?

The MH-47 that had rescued them from the Black Sea had just delivered them to this ridgeline overlooking two valleys, one to the south in Iran and one to the north into what Monsoor called "Kurdistan." They were at the frontier between northern Iran and Turkey, only inhabited by Kurds. Anything beyond this point of departure was enemy territory. The plan was for them to link up with a white van where they would then infiltrate into their hide site by midnight.

Harwood took a deep breath. Thought about the mission. Three men, two women. All adults.

Did they have anything to do with the Camp David Ambush?

We're working it.

Work harder, he thought. He was glad the child in Crimea had survived. Gave him some confidence that these missions were legit. Waiting was always the hardest part of any mission for an operator such as Harwood and his two teammates. There was no telling what thoughts would stroll through the mind, mostly personal, like lost children finding their way home. Others were mission focused. Monisha. Hinojosa. Threats against politicians. The morality of killing indirect combatants, a euphemism for family members.

The silence buzzed with the distant rumble of an automobile engine.

The black firmament was filled with a million pinpricks of light. His breath escaped in a smoky vapor. Stone was staring into the distance, ostensibly securing their northern flank. His new sniper rifle pointed into the valley below them. Wearing his trademark do-rag, a kerchief wrapped around his head and tied with a knot at the back of his neck, Stone looked every bit the arrogant operator that he was. On the contrary, Weathers's high and tight glistened in the starlight. His black formfitting shirt and pants hugged his muscular frame. Even the outer tactical vest seemed to be Marine-organized with its ammunition pouches evenly spaced, like small nylon boxes.

Harwood whispered into his microphone.

"Target, one o'clock."

The Peshmerga guide nodded and stepped into the street, raising his AK-47. The man was dressed in baggy outer garments and traditional brown vest, which also served the same purpose of the more formal outer tactical vest U.S. soldiers wore. Harwood lifted his night-vision monocle to his eye and saw the two infrared blips emanate from the device secured to the AK-47.

Instead of a return infrared signal, the dingy white van kept driving, the driver perhaps not wearing his night-vision goggles. Fifty meters away now, the van continued without slowing down. Monsoor remained standing in the road. Harwood leveled his SR-25 at the driver, could see him clearly through his sight. His bearded face and hollow eyes looked determined, almost biblical.

Harwood thought, *Suicide bomber.*

"Status?" Weathers asked, most likely seeing and thinking the same.

"Don't like it," Harwood said.

"Cap him," Stone said.

Harwood laid the crosshairs on the man's temple. The bouncing van made for a difficult sight picture, but nothing he couldn't handle. The time distance was the problem. He had only a few seconds to make a decision. Hinojosa had briefed them that the guide would take them to the precise location for their next mission. While she had uploaded the latitude and longitude of the sniper hide site into the TSINS sleeves, the route was fraught with danger. Manned checkpoints. Army bases. Helicopter overflights.

Geopolitical tensions at an all-time high since the Shah was deposed in 1979 with 52 Americans held hostage in Tehran.

"I have the shot," Harwood said. The van was twenty meters away. If it was a vehicle-born improvised explosive device they were already dead men. As good as technology was, they truly needed the human intelligence on the ground. Killing the driver was not optimal, unless, of course, he was a madman. Not out of the question here. The crazed driver gripped the steering wheel with white knuckles. Leaning forward the man must have spotted Monsoor, because his eyes grew wide.

Harwood had the crosshairs on the bridge of the driver's nose. Easy shot.

The van slowed.

Monsoor said, "No!"

Harwood kept his sight picture.

"Take the shot," Stone said. "Fucker looks crazier than Norman Bates."

Keeping in his zone, Harwood said, "Monsoor? Two seconds."

"Don't shoot," Monsoor barked.

Harwood had already squeezed about a half pound of trigger pressure. He was closer to shooting than not.

Stone adjusted and leveled his rifle at the vehicle.

"Don't fire," Harwood said. The driver slowed, a look of confusion on his face. Not your typical suicide bomber reaction. After multiple combat rotations, Harwood knew the distant gaze, clenched jaw, and white knuckles of those who had already transported themselves to a place beyond this world. This was a confused driver with a dangerous mission, who had most likely been driving all night after being told last second to get on the road. Harwood finally saw what he needed to see. Through his night-vision device, he saw the wink of a small piece of infrared reflective tape.

The driver's eyes flitted from Monsoor to Harwood, though

Harwood was totally concealed. Stone was now standing above Harwood, saying, "Die, motherfucker."

Harwood rolled into Stone as the SEAL sniper squeezed the trigger. The bullet smacked the windshield's top right corner. Stone stumbled back, said, "What the fuck?" And then aimed his rifle again.

Harwood stood, his back to the van and Monsoor, faced Stone, and snatched his SR-25 with a powerful sweep of his forearm. Stone actually squeezed off another round before Harwood could disarm him completely.

"Want me to toss this one, too?" Harwood's voice was granite. His chest was flexed. Could feel his pectoral muscles tighten, his usual response to the fight-or-flight instinct. Always fight. Harwood had never fled from danger. Just the opposite.

Monsoor said, "Quick. We must hurry. This is the man."

Weathers stood and stared at Harwood and Stone.

"Stone, you better get your shit together. I don't think the Reaper's going to give you a third chance. Steady, bro," Weathers said.

Harwood and Stone squared off until Harwood said, "We've got to get moving."

In the background, Monsoor was talking Farsi to the driver, most of which Harwood did not understand. Monsoor rushed toward them, pushed on Harwood's shoulder, indicating for him to kneel. They knelt behind the rock that had been their cover at the small defile along the ridge.

"This is Farza, your driver. I go no farther. He will take you to your location," Monsoor said.

Harwood and Monsoor did the hand-to-forearm warrior clasp as he noticed the van conducting a Y-turn behind him.

"This trail takes you past the border control checkpoint, through a dry riverbed, and into a valley that goes into Ardabil

Province. It's about two hundred miles. You should make it before daylight. I don't know your target, but I do know these people. Farza will be loyal. He is Iranian Kurd. He's nervous, so you may need to coach him."

"Roger that," Harwood said. It would be impossible to coach him, though, from their hide site inside the floor of the van. "Before daylight works, but we'll miss our midnight target time."

Monsoor nodded and said, "Good luck. *Inshallah.*" Then he walked over the ridge toward the hidden truck they had used to ingress from the MH-47 drop-off site to this location. Harwood led Stone and Weathers to the back of the van where Farza had lifted the corrugated metal floor, which gave way to a false bottom.

Weathers climbed in first, lying flat on the bottom of the sheet metal, his head toward the cab, feet toward the rear.

"This is going to suck. Been five years since I did this," Stone complained.

Stone laid supine on the opposite side of the floor, leaving a small gap for Harwood. For a moment, Harwood considered riding shotgun, but that had not been the plan. The driver was good enough to get to their location without incident and therefore, Harwood figured, could get them to their sniper hide site.

Farza lowered the metal floor on top of the three elite operators. A socket wrench clicked in rapid succession as bolts were tightened. There was exactly an inch of space between Harwood's nose and the underside of the floor. His head was near the rear bumper. He hoped they wouldn't die from exhaust fumes. Cradling his SR-25 to his chest and palming his Sig Sauer pistol, he closed his eyes and began to rehearse the mission in his mind.

The van ambled down the road, Harwood visualizing the direction from which it had come. Shortly, though, he felt them slow and turn off the main road onto a bumpier secondary route. Two hundred miles.

Stone said, "Fuck."

Weathers remained silent, as did Harwood. He would entertain himself with his TacSleeve, but he didn't have the space to lift his arm. At some point, he drifted to sleep, his dreams vivid and harrowing. A small girl with a bullet hole in her forehead. His rifle bore wafting smoke like a leering ghost. He snapped out of his nightmare when the vehicle stopped.

Had they already gone two hundred miles? It was possible. But he recalled the maxim, no plan survives first contact with the enemy. Voices dueled above them, one inside the van and one outside. Perhaps they were at a checkpoint. The TacSleeve had an interpretation function but again he couldn't access it and wouldn't risk the dim light shining through a seam in the flooring.

The conversation became more heated. Farza was tired, Harwood knew that much. He didn't look like much of a fighter but looks could be deceiving. A shot punctured the conversation. The conversation ended. The door opened, weight shifted. Was someone getting in or stepping out? Harwood tried to sense what was taking place by reading the movements. Door pushed, not pulled. Van rocking out first. Both indicated that Farza was initiating the moves, but there was no way to be certain.

The back doors opened with a click. The ratchet spun in four locations. Harwood had his pistol ready, sure Weathers and Stone did as well. The floor lifted above his head. His view was upside down and backward.

It looked like Farza, who said, "Quick. There is a checkpoint ahead."

Harwood pulled himself out of the van, grabbed his rucksack from the floor of the van, and helped Stone and Weathers out.

"How far up the road?" Harwood asked.

"A kilometer. A soldier tried to stop me and take money. Happens all the time. When I paid him, he insisted on looking in the van. I didn't want to run the risk. Shot him and dragged him into the ditch. Your drop-off location is less than five kilometers from here. An extra three miles to walk."

"They heard the shot. They'll be here fast. Where are you going?" Harwood said.

"There is a cave a kilometer in the other direction. I'll go there. After your mission, I will meet you there. My instructions are to wait twenty-four hours and then forget you existed."

Harwood checked his watch. It was almost 1 A.M. local time. They had planned their ingress to take two hours. Another five kilometers would add another hour, at least. They needed to be set up by sunrise, which was less than six hours away. The night was cool, but comfortable. The breeze carried the whiff of salt water from the Caspian Sea.

Harwood powered up his TacSleeve and dropped a pin on their location, then powered down.

"Okay, I've got this location pegged. One kilometer to the west is a cave. We will see you there before midnight. If we're not there by then, like you said, forget we existed. Go about your business."

Farza ratcheted the floorboard into place. Harwood led Stone and Weathers to the side of the road, powered up the TacSleeve again, and used the map function to identify their route. They were only nine kilometers from their hide site, but the terrain was jagged and steep. It would be a difficult traverse.

The van spun around and disappeared up the road. Harwood and team walked briskly into the narrow defile to the north, found or made a trail, and began the climb toward their hide location.

Behind them, shouts in Farsi echoed off the valley floor. Within fifteen minutes, the Iranian army was on location. Helicopters were another fifteen minutes behind them. The search focused on the location of the dead soldier, expanding outward. As they climbed, Team Valid distanced themselves from the melee below.

Stopping occasionally to check the TacSleeve, Harwood knelt after three solid hours of walking.

"Drink water," Harwood said. The team had hydration systems in their rucksacks with rubberized tubes so that they could hydrate on the move.

"Distance remaining?" Weathers asked.

"Just two kilometers, but it's rugged," Harwood said.

"Can't be any more rugged than what we just walked," Stone whined.

"Never say that it can't get any worse," Weathers said. "Because it always can."

Each man faced outward, scanning for threats as they spoke. Like a basketball team running a play, these operators intuitively knew what to do and when to do it as they conducted their long-range insertion.

"Hate these things," Stone said, pointing at his TacSleeve.

"For some reason, Hinojosa wanted us to wear them. She's in charge," Harwood said.

"Oh, fuck off, Reaper. You just want to tap that shit," Stone said.

"Enough," Weathers said. "Stop the bullshit."

Harwood resisted comment. They needed to focus, not get distracted by Stone's antics.

"Okay, let's move," Harwood said.

As they stood, Harwood's TacSleeve vibrated against his forearm. In dim LED lighting, *VH* lit up on his device.

Valerie Hinojosa. A text message appeared just the way it would on an Apple Watch.

ACTIVITY AT THE COMPOUND. MOVE FAST.

As they climbed the sheer granite walls over the next hour, Harwood wondered if the Russians had made conclusions from the weapon he had tossed. American sniper rifle. Family of terrorist dead. Other families might be in jeopardy? He hadn't followed up with a question about the type of activity partly because he didn't trust the device. If she could communicate with him, so then perhaps could others. He was geolocated at least by this device and whatever satellite Hinojosa and the president were connected to.

They were fifty meters from the first hide site Harwood had selected. Weathers and Stone were grunting behind him. Harwood's rehab from Afghanistan injuries had led to him being in the best physical condition of his life. That he could outpace a Navy SEAL and a Marine Force Recon team member was testament to his conditioning. His body ached though. The last cliff was nearly vertical.

He placed his fingertips in a small crevice and pulled himself up, his hand muscles the only thing keeping him from sliding fifty meters down onto his teammates. His face scraped against the rock, which felt like one-hundred-grit sandpaper. Blowing out carbon dioxide, Harwood lifted himself onto the ledge, sliding his right leg over the lip. He rolled, balanced, and immediately scoped his surroundings. He was on a flat rock with a high wall to his west and east, like a small tunnel. He low crawled to the north, flanked on either side by granite, and fifteen meters later found a sheer drop. The map had been accurate, but also deceiving. While it was a good firing position, the route of egress would be exactly the way they came in, which was not necessarily the preferred course of action.

Harwood opened his rucksack, retrieved sixty feet of coiled nylon rope, tied a bowline around his waist, and then low crawled back to the lip of the cliff. He secured his heels against a minor rise in the rock, fed the rope over the lip, and leaned back. He felt a tug, like a fish striking an artificial lure, and then braced against the heavy weight of either Weathers or Stone. After a minute of climbing, Stone flipped over the edge, saying, "Fuck me to tears, Ranger."

"Shut up and establish security," Harwood said. He had no patience for Stone's bullshit.

He fed the rope back over the cliff, felt Weathers tug on it and leaned back as the marine climbed the rope.

"Good job, Reaper," Weathers said as he rolled onto the lip.

It was nearing five in the morning. The sun would be up by six thirty. The first hint of gray was edging toward the northeast.

"Target's there, almost exactly a half mile," Harwood said.

"Vehicles moving," Stone reported. He was looking through his Leupold Mark 4 spotter's scope. "Count three coming in the compound."

Harwood set up his SR-25 with PAS-15 Thermal Scope FLIR sight. Pressing his eye against the rubberized boot, he switched on the sight. After a second, his reticle filled with the high-definition images of vehicles moving with haste into the facility. The door to the main building of the compound, which he had been told was the primary residence, was open. A woman stood in the doorway and while he couldn't be sure, she looked very much like target P-one, Laleh Perza.

"A little early for everyone to be up and about, don't you think?" Weathers asked.

"Agree. The Russians probably figured out the Crimea hit and are giving a heads-up to the Perzas."

Three Suburban SUVs idled in the open courtyard of the compound. They had made U-turns and were aimed toward the exit.

"Okay, I've got the bitch," Stone said.

"Don't kill her yet," Harwood said. "She's getting everyone outside."

Stone pulled the trigger. Laleh's head exploded, a green and black splatter array splashing in all directions.

Two figures stopped at the doorway. Harwood fired on the bearded man, who he assumed was Farokh, the father. Weathers apparently added an insurance bullet. Farokh's body spun, hit the door, and slid down atop his daughter. Harwood shifted to the woman who had been following Farokh, but Stone fired and she fell to her knees and then across her husband.

Stacking them like cordwood.

A man darted into the picture from inside the house, knelt next to the woman—maybe his mother?—looked up as Harwood placed the reticle on his forehead, firing.

Four down. Father, son, daughter, wife. If all were kill shots, and they certainly looked to be so, they had accomplished the mission.

Shifting to the three SUVs, Harwood said, "Watch the exits. Kill the drivers. Then we're out of here."

The three vehicle drivers began to scramble in the backs of the Suburbans, each withdrawing weapons. They huddled for a moment, unsure of the direction of the attack. They looked toward the house, the Caspian Sea, and then the mountains, where they pointed. Harwood fired two shots, felling two of the drivers. Weathers followed suit, killing the third.

"Okay, pack up," Harwood ordered.

Another man ran from the house into the courtyard. Harwood was pushing himself up but stopped. He placed the scope onto the man, who looked like a male version of Laleh Perza, her twin, Basir.

But Basir was alleged to be a shooter. No way could he be back in Iran in such a short period of time. The dragnet placed at all U.S. airports and seaports would have snared him. Basir Perza stared up into the mountains, as if he knew Team Valid's position.

Harwood shot him in the neck and followed up with another shot to the torso.

"A squirter?" Stone called out over his shoulder.

"Something like that," Harwood said.

They collapsed bipods, each man low crawling in reverse through the tunnel of rock to the far side of the ledge. Harwood had kept the rope tied around his waist and he resumed his position as base man. Stone was first to scale down the rock face onto the more navigable ledge. Next was Weathers, who paused and said, "Easier coming up than going down. You okay getting down, Reaper?"

"I'll be fine. Let's go," Harwood urged. They had just killed eight people before the sun rose. He wanted to get back to the van before the Iranian military figured out what had happened. Their egress plan was sketchy enough, the last thing they needed was to spend a full day on the ground in Iran with the entire world piecing together that two of the Camp David attackers had their families slaughtered.

Harwood felt the rope go slack. Weathers was on the platform. He glanced over his shoulder. An orange hue was nudging up over the horizon, ready to start a new day and erase all of the protections of a night infiltration. Somewhere in the valley below the wildlife was already sensing the feast that awaited in the courtyard. Keeping the rope tied around his waist, he slung his rifle over his back and lowered his legs, spun, and clasped the beveled edge of the cliff he had been using as a brace to maneuver his team up and down the cliff.

His face scraped the rough rock. Fingers felt the pressure of his entire body and all of his gear—about three hundred pounds altogether—pulling downward. Every tricep and bicep exercise he had ever done in his life paid off at this moment. His right boot found a firm node to ease some of the pressure. From memory, he searched with his left boot and found the stairstep he had used to climb up.

"Twenty feet," Weathers said from below.

He could jump, but the landing area was small and occupied by Stone and Weathers. The incline was about seventy degrees, nearly vertical. Harwood slid his hands along the rock face until he found two minor ledges where he could use his fingers to lower himself another five feet.

"Bogey," Stone said. A vehicle engine rumbled, coughing diesel as it bounced along the road two hundred meters below them.

"More than one," Weathers said.

Harwood was vulnerable with his back to the approaching convoy. Farza and his truck were a mile to the north in a cave. The driver was most likely sleeping. This wasn't Farza, especially if two trucks were approaching. After another five feet of lowering himself, he felt hands on the underside of his boots.

"I've got you, Reaper," Weathers said. Harwood let Weathers absorb his weight, while managing his descent onto the small flat area from which they had begun the ascent a few hours ago.

"Two trucks moving slow at nine o'clock," Weathers said.

"Tough angle, but we can get the driver," Stone said.

"No, there's most likely infantry in those trucks," Harwood said.

Helicopters chopped in the distance as the brakes squealed on the trucks. Men began to dismount. The morning darkness would evaporate in less than an hour. Harwood looked up and saw the outline of a Chinook personnel helicopter followed by its more lethal escort, a sleek attack helicopter of Iranian design, the Shahed 285. Lethality was relevant, though. While the attack aircraft carried missiles, rockets, and machine guns, the Chinook carried personnel who could dismount and close with them. The presence of a Chinook initially confused Harwood. It was a distinctly American powerful twin-engine personnel aircraft that Boeing sold to the Iranians. Harwood had both parachuted and fast roped from the back of a Chinook.

"We're fucked," Stone said.

The three men knelt on the outcropping as they assessed their predicament. There were a few parallel trails running to the north, but they would be treacherous in the dark and visible in the day.

"We were good up there," Weathers said. "How do they know where we are?"

Harwood had thought the same thing. Their execution was flawless, almost. For a team that had operated together exactly once, they had pulled together and accomplished the kill portion of the mission. Now, they needed to exfiltrate. No mission was complete until every soldier was safely inside the wire, and they were about as far away from the wire as they could possibly be.

Harwood looked at the piece of plastic on his arm as it vibrated. A message from Hinojosa read: POTENTIAL COMPROMISE. ZERO TACSLEEVES.

He responded in the affirmative and said to his team, "Zero out the TacSleeves now. They've been hacked. That's how they know where we are."

"Son of a bitch," Stone said.

Harwood pressed the "Zero" function on his sleeve, removed it, and crushed it under his boot. Stone and Weathers did the same, grumbling as they did so.

"Plan?" Stone asked.

The Chinook helicopter landed on the ridge above them, not far from where they had conducted the ambush. The Shahed 285 was an angry hornet looking for someone to sting. It hovered, dipped, and turned, doubtlessly scanning for the intruders.

"No way to fight and climb at the same time," Harwood said. "Let's focus on the truck first, then the helo."

The three snipers scratched out positions from which to fight. "Stone, you watch those aircraft. Once we light up this truck, it will be on us."

"I can do both," Stone objected.

"Cover the flank. Helicopter is a big target. You can hit it," Harwood growled.

"What the fuck does that mean? I nailed that little bitch at the last target."

Harwood had no time for Stone's aggressive bullshit. Soldiers were dismounting from the truck, eyeing the steep climb. The engine continued to idle, spitting exhaust. Strange Farsi words floated upward with the diesel fumes. One man was giving directions as others helped uniformed men with weapons and gear disembark from the truck.

"Okay, have it your way. Max firepower on the truck, then you shift to the helicopters, Stone. Wait until it looks like everyone is off," Harwood said.

After another minute, there were about fifteen soldiers huddled, talking in hushed tones.

"Okay, Stone you take the left side. Weathers, you take the right side and I'll hit the middle. Fire at will. Look for squirters and kill them first."

Stone immediately fired. The silenced weapons were anything but quiet in the still air, but the continued thrum of the truck engine and the whine of the helicopters overhead masked the ratcheting of the weapons and the ping of expended brass on the rocks.

Harwood aimed through his thermal scope and shot the man in the middle of the circle who was issuing the orders. If you kill the alpha, the followers will be confused. The man dropped from a shot to the temple. Harwood had three more targets down before he heard the Chinook flying slowly overhead.

The chopper hovered, and commandos were sliding down thick fast ropes.

"Fast ropes!" Harwood shouted. He spun to his back and fired up at the men descending on their position. Stray rounds were sparking off the helicopter fuselage while door gunners were spitting machine-gun fire generally in their direction. "Two on the helicopter. Weathers, you keep the truck."

Harwood counted ten men sliding down the fast rope. He believed he had hit four and maybe Stone had hit a couple, he wasn't sure. They were taking fire from the ridge and from the Chinook. The Shahed 285 appeared over the ridge. Harwood and Team Valid were the center of a triangle with the truck, Chinook, and Shahed all representing encircling points.

He took a deep breath and steeled himself for what he was about to do. He took his sight off the fast rope and aimed into the cockpit of the nosed-over Shahed 285, what he considered to be the biggest threat with its advanced avionics and lethal firepower. The aircraft yawed in his direction, exposing the glass bubble of the pilot on the port side.

Harwood fired. The pilot's head kicked back. The windscreen splintered and he lost visibility. The helicopter rocked in the air but stabilized quickly. The copilot must have taken the controls. The Shahed buzzed past them and banked hard before passing the Chinook. Shouts above their position gave no doubt that Iranian infantry were on the ground. They were surrounded. Stone had silenced the starboard door gunner with a good shot. For the moment there was minimal fire exchanged in either direction.

"Status?" Harwood demanded.

"Truck has at least two still alive," Weathers said.

"Avoid the gas tank. Might be our only option out of here," Harwood said.

"Roger," Weathers replied.

"Stone?"

"We've got about three bogies above us. Hard to spot."

"Okay, you keep on them. Weathers, you stay on the truck. I'll stick with the helicopters."

Begin morning nautical twilight was upon them, replacing the black of night with a gray hue. Still the west slope of the mountain was dark, the light just seeping over the edges. Harwood wanted this wrapped up in five minutes. They needed to move. No doubt the Iranians would be sending a larger force now that they knew they had a fight on their hands.

Stone fired twice and reloaded, dropping his magazine on the ground and slapping a new one into the well. Harwood tracked the Chinook as the loadmaster appeared to be pulling in the ropes. Harwood put a bullet through the man's crew helmet. He tumbled, slid down the ramp, and fell a hundred feet into the rocks. If he wasn't dead before, he was now. The pilot yanked the aircraft in response to the crew chief's fall, placing the starboard pilot, typically the copilot, in Harwood's sight. He leveled the SR-25 and squeezed off two rounds. The Chinook flared upward, as if it was doing a wheelie.

The starboard pilot must have been controlling the aircraft, because it nearly did a backflip, lost altitude, and slammed into the rocks just fifty meters to their south. The explosive shock wave licked at their faces and pieces of rotor blades whizzed past them like a million ninja stars.

Fire erupted from the crash location and fuel sprayed everywhere, running downhill into their location.

"Fire!" Harwood shouted. "Weathers, are we clear to head down?"

"Does it matter?"

Team Valid picked up and began racing along the goat trail

they had taken up the mountain. Random shots pinged off the rocks as they scampered down the steep incline. Reaching the bottom of the hill, they found the truck still idling. Weapons up, Stone turned to cover any enemy from the hill. Harwood focused on the cab of the truck. Weathers worked his way to the rear, firing twice.

"Two down. Don't see anything alive!" Weathers shouted.

"Watch for the attack helicopter. Gun run any time now," Harwood said.

On cue, the Shahed 285 zipped along the ridge, spitting fire at the Iranians still up in the mountain.

"They don't know who they're shooting. Let's get in the truck and roll," Harwood said.

"Big-ass target," Stone countered.

"It has seventy-millimeter rockets that typically can't hit a barn and some machine guns," Harwood said. "Let's go as far as we can before we dismount and link up with Farza."

"If he's still alive," Stone said.

"Weathers, lay in the back and plink at the helicopter if it figures us out," Harwood said.

"Roger that."

"Stone, you drive. I'll shoot."

Stone stared at him in the diminishing darkness, grinned, and said, "Roger that, Reaper."

The truck moved along the dirt road in the direction Farza had departed. After a minute of driving, Harwood heard the buzz of helicopter blades.

"Lining up on our ass!" Weathers shouted.

Rockets smoked overhead, predictably high, and burst into the side of the narrow passage they were traversing. Rocks tumbled down and shrapnel sprayed the windshield. The machine-gun rounds were more accurate, stitching the side of the truck.

"Emptied a mag on it, but no luck. They know we are the target!" Weathers shouted.

Through his night-vision goggle, Harwood saw the road made a sharp turn to the west about a hundred yards ahead.

"Get us to that turn," Harwood said.

He untied the rope from his waist and slid into the well of the cab near Stone's foot. His boot was on the pedal as the truck bounced along the washboard cut in the road. With his teeth rattling, Harwood tied the rope to the top of the gas pedal and then looped it through a U-bolt cargo tie down against the engine well. He ran the rope around the gearshift a couple of times and said, "Okay, when we make this turn, jump out. Tell Weathers to jump, also."

"Helo coming in for a second rocket run!" Weathers shouted.

Stone turned the truck. Rockets whizzed past the rear, this time far more accurate, one cutting through the canvas covering the ribs of the cargo bay.

"Jump out!" Stone shouted over his shoulder.

With Harwood in the well, Stone opened his door and leapt. The vehicle was doing no more than thirty miles per hour. Harwood tightened the rope, tied off two half hitches against his round turns, and felt the vehicle speed along the road. Grabbing his rifle and rucksack, he opened the door and jumped into the narrow gorge, slamming into the side of the rocks. His head took a hit he could ill afford, but thankfully he was wearing a helmet.

Momentarily confused, Harwood remained motionless as the Shahed 285 turned the corner and unloaded a pod of rockets at close range into the truck bouncing along the road. The truck exploded into a fiery ball as the helicopter pulled away and began to circle its kill like a vulture.

CHAPTER 9

Former Virginia senator Sloane Brookes looked at her longtime employee, Chip Ravenswood, with a smirk. He was standing on the porch of her riverfront mansion near Reedville, Virginia, wearing a tight-fitting blazer over a sweater that hugged his muscular frame. His blue jeans were cut fashionably above his burgundy chukka boots. The plantation-style home sat astride nearly three hundred feet of Potomac River frontage. Giant oak and maple trees dotted the thirty-acre estate and compound.

That her ancestry dated back to the original Jamestown settlers had made her as close to royalty in Virginia as anyone could be. Her family property was a chunk of land along the Chesapeake Bay in between the mouths of the Potomac and Rappahannock Rivers. Hills, rock formations, and floodplains combined to create a beautiful site for a compound worthy of a king. High walls with turrets at the four corners were the distinctive features of the outer perimeter. The home was a classic Virginian mansion with white columns and red bricks. The parlor looked out onto the Bay and on a clear day, Brookes could see Tangier Island.

Having just flown into her helipad from a meeting at Washington, D.C.'s new trendy Wharf, Brookes looked fetching in a light blue sleeveless dress cut just above the knees, her four-inch Jimmy Choo stilettos that accented her toned calves and six-foot height, and her modest diamond earrings. Her blond hair fell loosely on her shoulders, making her look ten years younger than she was. Her actual age was a matter of great speculation among the Washington, D.C., glitterati.

"Took you long enough," she said to Ravenswood.

"You have a helicopter. I have a motorcycle. You win that race every time," he replied.

"I win every race, every time," she replied.

The evening air was filled with the thrum of insects with the occasional sound of a large animal growling, most likely a black bear.

"Well, except the last one," Ravenswood ventured.

"Three House terms and one Senate term. I can still be president," she replied.

"That's why I'm still around," Ravenswood said.

"Yes, me too. Now tell me what you know," Brookes said.

Ravenswood swiveled his head, eyeing the rockers on the full-length covered porch.

"Here?"

Ravenswood was a former marine and still shaved his scalp every day. She didn't know if he did it to hide a balding pattern or to look more badass, but either way, it worked. The hairless scalp, pinched eyebrows, and multiple tattoos on his arms and body—she had slept with him—combined to sinister effect. Rarely had he protested about the crazy hours she imposed upon him, but she didn't care whether he had grown accustomed to her late evening calls or not. He would come to her when she needed him. That was their arrangement and she paid him a nice, fat six-figure salary to be at her fingertips.

"The boathouse," she said. "I'll see you there in five minutes."

She closed the door in his face and walked through the labyrinth of her house to her bedroom, where she changed into boat shoes, blue jeans, a lightweight sweatshirt with the words *Dream Team* on the front. The term had no meaning to her. She simply liked the sweatshirt. She holstered a Ruger LC9S on her hip, slipped the edge of the sweatshirt over the weapon, and walked through her parlor, dining room, and kitchen, then paused as she considered taking the private tunnel from the basement. Deciding against that route, she opened the back door, walked through a screened porch, and then stepped outside. She followed the flagstone path to the wooden walkway, which led to the pier in the Potomac River. At the end of the pier was a house every bit the size of a small Cape Cod, perhaps two thousand square feet.

Stand-up paddle boards and kayaks were hung in the rafters. Two large speedboats were tied off on either side with smaller jet skis next to them, looking somewhat like pilot fish.

She sat on a padded seat in her Riva 63 Virtus powerboat and leaned over to flick on the radio.

"Have a seat, Chip," Brookes said. "Now, how about a status update?"

Ravenswood stepped onto the gunwale, the boat's sturdy frame shifting only slightly in the water as he lowered into the seat.

"Raafe Khoury is no more," Ravenswood said.

Brookes nodded, relieved. It was turning out to be a good day. Khoury was the information technology manager she had hired to manage her networks, including her campaign servers, Senate emails and communications, and personal networks. He had made some fatal errors that had perhaps even put in motion much of what was happening. But she was dealing with it as she knew how.

"We don't talk about him anymore," she said.

Ravenswood nodded. "Okay, then what's the emergency, boss?"

"What went down at Camp David?"

Ravenswood shifted uncomfortably.

"It appears that twenty-two people were killed. Twelve family, ten Secret Service. No survivors. A former Army Ranger named Sammie Samuelson is the prime suspect. He did a Facebook Live event, which authorities are seeing as a partial admission of guilt. His apartment building was destroyed, and I assume along with that, any evidence he might have left behind."

Brookes nodded again. Things were looking even better. "I saw the Facebook thing. Who was this Vick guy he mentioned?"

"Vick Harwood. Also known as The Reaper. Samuelson was his spotter in combat."

"The Reaper?"

"Best special operations sniper in the business."

"What's his status?"

"He has disappeared," Ravenswood said.

"Nobody disappears. I'm hearing the president has a special team hitting the families of the terrorists."

Ravenswood arched his eyebrows and leaned forward.

"Now that would be insider information, Senator."

"Only information I work with," she said. "But if you check Twitter there are the usual conspiracy theorists who are already fantasizing about plots and subplots."

Ravenswood smirked. "Sometimes they're right."

"But we usually shut them down, don't we?"

"Almost always," he said.

"Look at this," she said, handing him her iPhone. "Maximus Anon needs to be shut down ASAP." The tweets were consecutive and listed chronologically with numbers the way some of the Twitter researchers and pundits liked to do. Maximus Anon had over one million followers and had all the hashtags associated with the current presidential administration such as #besmartvote smart. They read the tweet together.

1. **MaximusAnon:** I think I'm onto what happened at #CampDavidAmbush. There were 22 ppl killed, one of which was the @SecDef daughter, #CarlyMasters. Masters worked for the intelligence committee & had taken a week of vacation.

2. **MaximusAnon:** Hear me out. Masters had indicated through a text to a friend that she had found something significant on a former member (don't ask me how I know, but this is 100%). The info she had related to previous presidential campaign.

3. **MaximusAnon:** Apparently this candidate had significant classified information stolen by, or worse, sold to foreign agencies. Masters alerted her friend, Corporal Samuelson, former Army Ranger sniper, who is being touted as assassin.

4. **MaximusAnon:** There is NO WAY Samuelson committed the ambush. Forensic evidence points at him, but he was framed. If you watch the FB live video in real time, he bats his eyes in Morse code, like POWs used to do.

5. **MaximusAnon:** His message is: I didn't do this. The government did. We have to now find out the connection between @sloanebrookesusa and the government.

"This is total bullshit, but can we shut him down before he gets any further?" she asked.

Ravenswood retrieved his phone and sent a text. He waited a minute, staring at his phone the entire time.

"Okay, refresh your feed and try to go to Maximus Anon," he said.

She swiped down with her thumb, watched the Twitter feed refresh and then typed in the handle.

"Account no longer available. Tweet no longer available." She smiled. "Good work."

Despite the fair winds and following seas of helpful social media icons that wanted her to win, Brookes had narrowly lost her presidential bid by less than one percent of the popular vote to the iconic businessman Bob Smart, who ran on the slogan, *Be Smart, Vote Smart*. Brookes, though, was young, beautiful, intelligent, and ambitious. She wasn't concerned. The country considered her a lock for president either six or two years from now, depending on whether the economy tanked and whether any international crises billowed out of control. One could hope. Something had to give, she believed. And she was a given for the party nomination this next cycle, despite some nascent challengers. Her support of abortion, increased gun control, free college tuition for all students, tax increases on the wealthiest two percent, and single payer universal health care anchored her hard-core leftist base. She even gained some Bernie Sanders supporters who saw her as a more viable candidate. As a former prosecutor and commonwealth's attorney, she was viewed as tough on crime. Her father had served in the Marines during Vietnam and had earned the Purple Heart, which gave the illusion that she had a soft spot for the military. She frankly saw that seven-hundred-billion-dollar budget as a target that could be shredded by a third, but knew she would have to keep up at least semi-hawkish appearances. She could say

whatever she wanted on the campaign trail. Once she was in office was a different matter.

Now, she just needed an edge beyond the help of the tech
giants with their favorable algorithms and offensive/defensive cy-
ber capabilities to shadow ban social media pundits whose findings and research might take root. Yes, she needed all that and
something more.

The president seeking a personal vendetta against the family
members—noncombatants—of terrorists? Now that was something more.

She could have a field day with that, if done properly. She
would have to walk that fine line, which she was capable of doing,
between showing empathy for the families of those slaughtered at
Camp David and disgust for the president's tactics. Though, she
had to admit, it was a Machiavellian move he was doing by attacking the families of terrorists. She was disappointed she wasn't
in office so that she could have thought of it first. Or had she? Con-
fident that the majority of people would find the president's actions appalling, she would nudge the right people to pursue the
legal angle. Congressional demands. The FBI could kick in a few
doors and seize computers. Leaks to CNN and MSNBC to get Fox
News spun up defending the president. Get a full-on media war
going.

"You want me to take your information to the press," Ravenswood said. Not a question. He knew his boss. She was not going
to leave a fingerprint, human or digital.

"Yes. Our guy at CNN. Rocky Campagne will eat this up. The
public has a right to know that noncombatants are being targeted,"
she said. "I'm concerned that we're losing the moral high ground.
We are a nation that welcomes the oppressed and stands up for
the little guy. Not one that slaughters women and children."

"Save it for the stump, boss. I'm not wired. Loyalty is my

middle name," Ravenswood said. "Who in Congress should we touch?"

"Well, in addition to Rocky, I want the appropriate lawmakers to know what is happening. They *deserve* to know. The intel committees. Armed soldiers. There are already reports that the Sultan family has been murdered," she said.

Ravenswood let out a slow whistle. "In less than twenty-four hours we capture Sultan at Dulles and now have killed his family? Sends a strong message."

That was her concern. People's immediate reaction would be that this was some kind of display of strength. But over time, she could obscure the issue. Find ways to muddy the waters by highlighting the women and children, who were either killed or left as orphans.

"How is it strong to kill innocent families?" she snapped. "And do we know Sultan was involved?"

Ravenswood held up his hands. "Easy, boss. That was my gut reaction. As a Joe Six-Pack out there, you need to know that there will be a lot of people on board with this eye for an eye."

"It's not legal. Even the team conducting the raids is called Team Valid. They've got three men and one woman. They're in Iran right now attacking the Perza compound."

"You're scaring me, boss. This is intel about a deep black operation against terrorists we haven't even found yet. How do you know who the Perza family is and that they were involved?"

"I've still got my sources, Chip. In fact, you should be telling me this, not the other way around."

Ravenswood looked away.

"That's right. You're slacking off. You're still on my payroll. You've got your fancy Wharf condo and slaying all the women you want. Well, earn it," she said.

"What do you need me to do?"

Exactly where she wanted him.

"Expose this thing. Campagne and Congress. Tonight."

Ravenswood nodded, but faltered. "If we expose this now, it could get field operatives killed."

Brookes shrugged, careful about her response.

"They're killing innocent people, Chip. Are you okay with that? This Team Valid is in violation of every principle we have in this nation. There's a greater duty here." After a pause she added, "I can always get someone else to do this . . . and everything else."

With that threat, Ravenswood stood, brushed off his pants as if to sweep away his conscience, and said, "I've got it."

Brookes nodded and stood, keeping her hand near her hip and the pistol.

"I'll let myself out," Ravenswood said.

"If they never make it back, that would be just fine," she whispered. Some Kenny Chesney lyrics enveloped her words, but she saw him nod. "I'll expect to wake up to the morning news of major scandal breaking."

Ravenswood nodded, stepped onto the dock, and walked into the darkness. She watched him disappear into the night, heard his car start, the gravel crunch, and the tires squeal. Headlights cut through the night like beacons until he was out of sight.

Brookes pulled out a burner phone she carried and dialed a number.

"Are we in business?" the voice answered.

"Yes. It's your turn," she said.

"Roger," the person replied.

Brookes hung up the phone and stuffed it back into the pocket of her blue jeans. She breathed in the musty smell of spawning fish and muddy water. Insects buzzed around her. Fish smacked at the surface of the river. Something swam in serpentine fashion in the water next to the boat, perhaps a moccasin. There were certainly plenty of those here. And to think, she'd moved to her ancestral land to get away from all of the snakes in Washington, D.C.

The presidential loss still stung, she had to admit. She had believed there was a chance. The résumé was perfect. To bolster her pro-veteran image, she had founded a development company that also did community charity work for veterans. Brookes, Inc. had rebuilt and gentrified much of downtown Richmond, Virginia, which she oversaw in her two terms as a member of the Virginia House of Delegates. Then she had handily won the First Congressional District of Virginia, a conservative bastion; she had won as a Democrat on a centrist, pro-business platform. The "October Surprise" scandal her candidate had endured certainly put some wind behind her sails, flipping her in the polls from down three percent to up four percent. From there it was smooth sailing into her senatorial bid and wins. Twenty-two years of elected public service and she was still a young woman. She ran, swam, and did yoga every day.

Now two-plus years into a new administration, she was in full prep mode to take on the incumbent. *Better with Brookes* was her new campaign slogan. Her advisors had said the alliteration of the *B* would subliminally work on voters. It was all bullshit, of course. Most voters did so along party lines and the real fight was for the independents. Could she reach them in greater numbers than before? She thought so. She needed an edge to draw in more of the base that was toying with socialism, while also digging into that independent core enough to get across the finish line. The truth was that any national race today was a fifty-fifty toss-up. It was all about promoting your positives, suppressing your negatives, and doing just the opposite to your opponent. True, she was focusing on her speaking engagements, board of directors work, and nonprofit leadership, which in the end meant nothing. It was *all* about finding that insider edge, which she might have just discovered.

She had never married, speculating rumors about her sexuality. She knew it would enhance her chances if she married, but she hadn't found that man yet. While a politician, she did have some personal principles to which she adhered. Technically not too old to have children, she had resigned herself to the strong possibility that it might never happen. She did want them, desperately, but again, she wasn't going to sacrifice her personal happiness and marry the wrong man.

Brookes *was* desperately searching for a solid male running mate, preferably one from Pennsylvania, Florida, Wisconsin, or Ohio. She needed a defense hawk and possibly a governor who had executive experience, as opposed to simply legislative chops. Brookes was a bona fide liberal and wanted someone the conservatives could look at and say, "I could support him." She could give it time, though. She knew she would have challengers from those states and she wanted to see who performed best in the debates. Among party elite, there was little doubt that she would win the nomination again. There was grumbling, though, that if she couldn't beat him the first time, why would people believe she could win a second time?

Because this time she had found an angle, which she didn't have before. While not a novice, she had believed that good old-fashioned hard work and retail politics would propel her to victory. Disavowed of that foolishness now, Brookes knew she needed something else. She had scouts in each government agency and even a few in the White House. The FBI was a particularly easy mark, given the politicization of that organization over the past several years.

Her tip on Team Valid was solid. Better than solid. It was

ironclad. Her contact there would make a good high-level appointee in her White House when she destroyed Smart. She had one mole in the FBI, one in the Director of National Intelligence, the former CIA director, and a prominent journalist. Should she win, she would gladly repay the favor.

As far as leaving the members of Team Valid out in the cold, possibly exposing them, well, that would be on the current administration. There was no tracing this back to her. By dawn tomorrow morning the world would be breaking wide open with fresh allegations about the president's private hit squad out for revenge against innocent women and children. The president would be accused of major violations of international law. If he had covered his tracks, then he would hang the Secretary of Defense or some general. But still, the damage could be insurmountable. Benghazi-like but worse and more damning. Provable of positive action taken by a president, as opposed to speculation of passive inaction not taken. Same result, sure, but it was the path that mattered.

The entire country was *Better with Brookes*.

Except, maybe, Team Valid.

CHAPTER 10

Harwood, Stone, and Weathers hugged the rock wall. The Shahed had not spotted them yet, but it was only a matter of time. The sun was definitely over the Caspian Sea, but the mountain range still cast a dark shadow over the valley and gorge where they hid.

"We're done, man," Stone muttered.

"One thing I know about helicopters is they need gas. The question is can we live long enough until they're gone," Harwood said.

"He's hovering," Weathers said.

The helicopter was stationary, the pilots perhaps believing that they had killed the invaders. Its fuselage was nearly at a perfect ninety-degree angle to Harwood's line of sight.

"Stand still," Harwood said. He slid his rifle over Weathers's right shoulder. The thermal optic gave him a perfect view of the pilot's head, covered by the aviator helmet. The crosshairs held steady and Harwood squeezed the trigger. The muzzle flashed. The bullet cracked the windshield. The pilot's head kicked to one side.

Harwood switched to the copilot as the aircraft began to descend. He tried to lead, firing two rounds that missed their intended target. The helicopter banked hard and lifted into the air, preventing a crash into the jagged terrain to their front.

"We're burned now," Stone said.

"Hold tight," Harwood replied.

"Don't blow out my eardrum, man," Weathers said.

As the copilot leveled the aircraft, Harwood took one final shot. This time hitting the neck of the copilot, who must have instinctively swatted at the wound, because his hand came off the controls and the helicopter bore into the ground. There was no explosion. Rather, the rotor blades kept turning until they were sheared to nubs by the granite walls of the crag into which it had fallen.

"Good shot, bro," Weathers said.

"Let's move. Not much time," Harwood ordered. He led them into the road and began jogging. They passed the exploded and still burning cargo truck, its heat licking at their faces and feeling pretty good in the cool morning air. After another mile of moving quickly, they found their drop-off point.

"See these tracks? This is where Farza dropped us. He said he would be another mile up the road."

They continued moving until they found the turnoff and small cave into which Farza had parked his truck. Stacking with their backs to the wall, Harwood was taking no chances. He looked at the tired faces of Weathers and Stone. They were running on fumes, having been in the bullet car wash all morning long. It sucked to be shot at. Naturally it was worse to be hit. So far they had literally dodged the bullets. A few scrapes and cuts were okay, part of the business.

"Just like the battle drill," Harwood whispered. He was referring to the squad-level task of entering a building and clearing a room. Each man had done a variation of that drill/task a thousand times.

Both men nodded, their tired eyes more evident in the morning sunlight. The dawn of day was only a soldier's friend when it was freezing and the "big heat tab in the sky" warmed his icy body. There were no other advantages to daylight for these men.

Fortunately, there was enough darkness in the cave where they could swing in using flashlights and remain somewhat obscured. The ambient light from outside the cave would backlight them, but if they moved swiftly to the flanks, if there were flanks, they would be okay. Harwood's mind buzzed. Something wasn't right. Multiple combat rotations ingrained in him a sixth sense, an ability to determine if trouble was afoot.

He looked at the sand leading off the two-track road upon which they had traveled. Tire marks went in, but not out. Good enough. But he also saw multiple boot prints on the tire tracks. Looking back at Weathers and Stone, who were so close he could smell them, he motioned at the prints. Counting at least three sets of boot prints, he held up three fingers then motioned that he would go left, pointed at Weathers to go right, and Stone to watch the entrance. Stone used a hand to lift the body of a stun grenade off his outer tactical vest, in essence asking, "Do we want to lead with this?"

Harwood shook his head. He didn't want to risk damaging the only means of transportation out of the valley and back to the Kurds. He mouthed, "Follow me," and stepped into the cavern.

Peeling left, Harwood held his SR-25 sniper rifle at the ready. His rail-mounted flashlight poked a strong beam into the darkness. There was the truck. No driver. He was able to move left out of the funnel of the cave mouth. Weathers was moving to the right, his flashlight providing more light in the darkness.

No sign of Farza.

The cave seemed deep, like an abyss. The light ended before any cave wall could be seen. Harwood sensed other humans, though. Smelled them. To his left, he saw the beady eyes of a man crouched low. The flashlight caught the glint of a weapon barrel. He wasn't able to distinguish whether the man was Farza or some nameless enemy, but the movement of the weapon toward him was reason enough for Harwood to snap off two rounds into the man's face. Harwood's first thought was that Farza was disposable as long as the truck worked. Though he hoped he hadn't just killed their guide.

A fusillade of gunfire peppered the cave wall behind him. Weathers fired from the opposite side and Harwood returned fire at the sparking muzzle flashes deep in the recesses of the cave.

This was definitely an ambush.

Stone collapsed into the cave and crawled into the cab of the truck. Harwood shouted, "Crank it!" He continued charging to the back of the cave, returning fire, with Weathers on his flank, hanging in his periphery.

"One down!" Harwood shouted as he shone his light on the Iranian soldier.

"Two down!" Weathers replied.

Three sets of boot prints. Where was the third man?

Pistol fire erupted in the truck. Harwood shouted, "Cover the rear of the cave!" He ran to the back of the truck and saw Farza with his throat slit lying in the back, blood pooling around his body. Another man was on his back, Stone standing over him with pistol drawn in a two-handed grip. His head split a canvas curtain that separated the cab from the cargo bed of the truck.

"Bitch almost got the jump on me," Stone said.

"Farza's dead. Let's go," Harwood said.

Weathers collapsed into the back of the truck. He helped Harwood drag the Iranian body out of the bed and dump him on the cave floor. Harwood snatched the keys from Farza's pocket, along with the man's wallet and identification.

"I know like five words of Farsi," Weathers said.

"Five more than I know," Harwood countered. They dumped Farza's body in the cave. Harwood said, "Cover from back here. I'll take the right flank in the cab."

Weathers laid down and extended the bipods on his SR-25. Harwood crawled through the curtain into the cab of the truck and said to Stone, "Let's go. Make a left and let's get as far as we can."

Stone nodded, cranked the engine, and they began bouncing out of the cave and onto the road. They rode in silence for about an hour, the road straight and narrow. The general sense was as long as no one said anything, then everything would remain the same. No detection. Escape and evade. Mission almost accomplished.

With every mile, every minute, the tightness in Harwood's throat eased a fraction, but just a tiny bit because they were a long way from home. They had just ambushed a wealthy Iranian family and fought both the Iranian military and air force. There was no denying that they were deep in enemy territory without any assistance to exfiltrate out of there. No magic Chinook helicopters. No Navy SEALs would be coming to their aid.

They were Team Valid. Off the books. And in Harwood's mind, about as *in*valid as they could be. But still, they pushed ahead. When he wasn't thinking about the task at hand—crossing the border into Turkey—his mind drifted to the righteousness of their mission.

Were they killing the right people? Was their mission, in fact, valid?

The sun was at full bore. Just by looking out the window, Harwood could feel the pressure brought on by the rising sun. The

morning haze was burning off and the sun was a stage light following their every move. The deep ravine through which they had
been traveling eventually leveled out into a widening riverbed, or
wadi, as Harwood and his Ranger buddies called these washouts.
Stone drove fast, but with control. Personality conflicts aside, the
man could operate. High-risk operations tended to blight even
the most adversarial relationships in favor of survival. The truck
slowed almost to a stop as Stone navigated through a deep wash-
out in the road. Each tire fell into the rut and then Stone acceler-
ated out, spinning up the opposite side of the ravine. This was
nothing but a trill with a little flow of water, but enough to carve
away much of the road. Once up and on the other side, Harwood
nodded.

"Good job. About ten miles to the border," Harwood said,
checking his GPS. Whether they should have crushed the Tac-
Sleeves or not remained to be seen. Certainly, navigation would
have been better with them, but if they had indeed been compro-
mised, then they had made the right decision.

Stone nodded, focused, eyes on the road, hands gripping the
steering wheel at ten and two o'clock, one foot on the accelerator,
the other on the brake.

"Vehicle, six o'clock," Weathers shouted.

"Dammit," Harwood said. Though he knew their luck wouldn't
hold, that they would have to fight at some point in time, there
had been a small glimmer of hope blossoming in the back of his
mind.

"Two trucks. Techs. Fifty cals on the back," Weathers shouted.
Harwood stepped through the curtain, saying, "Keep driving and
let me know if you need help up here."

Lying next to Weathers, Harwood popped the bipods on his
SR-25, looked through his scope, and assessed the situation.

"No shots?"

"Nothing yet," Weathers responded.

The two tan pickup trucks were about a half mile away and had men wearing checkered scarves and flowing white robes. Dust clouds rose behind them like jet contrails in the sky. At these speeds, they could make it another couple of miles before they had to engage. If they could kill early they might be able to prevent any significant reporting to higher headquarters that could muster larger forces. The good news was that so far they had not seen any further aviation since the initial confrontation. The bad news was that could change any second.

"Bouncing too much for a clean shot," Harwood said.

"Agree. Better to wait. Maybe a turn somewhere and get stationary," Weathers muttered.

Through the scope, Harwood's sight picture bounced all over the place. The trucks were in the picture, then out. Dust plumes billowed as Stone spun the wheels through sandy patches. The engine roared at varying pitches. Nothing sounded good. Everything was hanging by a thread. Should they press ahead or should they stop and shoot?

The truck made a sharp turn and began to climb. This was a good sign. They were entering the mountainous area from which they had descended last night on their infiltration route. The cover and concealment would be more plentiful in the mountains, also. Through the back of the truck, Harwood's view was blocked by a jagged rise in the terrain as Stone's ascent along the road continued. Soon, he was able to look down on the road again and could see the trucks.

They were approaching the trill with the water and the deep cut.

Harwood jumped up and crawled to the cab.

"Find a spot here. We've got two techs on our trail and we're going to plink them at the cutout we just went through."

"Low on gas and low on time, man," Stone countered.

"Just do it. Then we'll haul ass."

Stone nodded.

The Iranians in the pickup trucks slowed at the trill. Stone pulled over and nosed the vehicle to the west to give Harwood and Weathers better shots.

"Thirty seconds, then we're moving," Harwood said.

"I've got good field of fire and good sight picture," Weathers said.

"You take the right and I'll take the left," Harwood directed. "Send it when ready."

"Roger."

Harwood studied his vehicle target. It had pulled behind what was now the lead vehicle as they approached the deep wadi. The individual manning the .50 caliber DShK machine gun in the back was watching the deep cut and was holding on to the grips of the large weapon. Considering him the most immediate threat, Harwood led the man's head with the retina in his scope and waited for the moment he remembered. The lead vehicle's front wheels dipped into the cut, causing the vehicle to stop. The trail vehicle paused momentarily, as well.

"Now," Harwood said.

Weathers and Harwood snapped off single shots. Harwood's target was down and his scope was immediately on the passenger in the cab, who had a radio handset to his mouth. Harwood sent a 7.62 round through the open window, into the handset against his ear, and ultimately into his right cheekbone.

The driver began spinning his wheels to back the truck out of the ravine. The truck swerved, turning horizontal to the slope. As the driver shifted from reverse to drive, Harwood used that fractional pause to squeeze off two rounds.

With the three occupants of his vehicle dead or severely

wounded, he scanned with his scope to the lead vehicle and found three dead occupants.

"Good to go," Weathers said.

Harwood scrambled back to the cab and said, "Threat eliminated. Let's roll."

Stone pressed on the clutch, grinded the manual gear into first, and gunned the truck out of their temporary fighting position.

"Just a few more miles," Harwood said. Stone remained silent. In anticipation of moving quickly at the linkup point, Harwood shouldered his rucksack and clipped his SR-25's three-point sling into the snap hook on his outer tactical vest.

As they made the turn toward the pass where just last night he and their Kurdish guide, Monsoor, had watched the truck approach, Weathers tapped Harwood on the shoulder.

Harwood was watching the ridge. There was a man near the mountain pass. He was barely distinguishable, but it had to be Monsoor.

"What you got?" Harwood asked.

He turned toward Weathers, who said, "This."

Harwood barely had time to block the knife thrust into his rib cage. He rolled away as Weathers retrieved his pistol and aimed at Harwood, who chopped down on Weathers's arm. The pistol skittered onto the bouncing truck bed. Weathers planted a kick to the side of his leg.

The Reaper rolled away, fighting the momentum of the uphill climb. It was too much, though, as Stone gunned the truck, nearly popping a wheelie. He flipped off the back of the lurching truck. Two shots rang out as he continued moving.

What was Weathers doing? They were Team Valid. Teammates.

He slid off the side of the road, clutching his SR-25, found a large rock, and huddled behind that for cover. Two more shots kicked shrapnel into his face. He didn't return fire, as the truck kept moving.

Looking over his shoulder, he saw the two pickup trucks in the wadi. Up ahead, Stone continued driving the Iranian cargo vehicle toward the linkup point on the Turkish border.

Behind him, he saw a convoy of trucks moving toward the wadi.

Worse, the violent chop of helicopter rotor blades sang through the air, unmasked by the silence left in the wake of the diminishing speck of his getaway ride.

CHAPTER 11

Sloane Brookes rolled over in her thousand-count Egyptian cotton sheets, no pet, no man, no bother. Just how she liked it.

The sun beamed through the east-facing window that looked out over the boathouse where she had met Ravenswood last night. She felt a tickle of anticipation at the back of her mind. Had everything she wished for been put in motion or not? As she reached for the remote, the sheer negligee rubbed against her nipples, sending a frisson of pleasure through her body. Still, she kept her hand's momentum toward the remote instead of the nightstand drawer.

Flipping on the eighty-inch television on the wall opposite the foot of her bed, a newscaster's grim face dominated the screen. The crawl read, *In wake of Camp David Ambush, president allegedly put in motion efforts to assassinate Muslim family members in foreign countries . . .*

That's good. She hadn't really thought through the Muslim

angle. That should help with the media pit bulls going after the president, who had taken a thousand cuts for alleged anti-Muslim beliefs. Unmuting the volume, she listened as Rocky Campagne, rising star at CNN, laid out the most salient points of what needed to be conveyed.

"High-level sources in the intelligence community have disclosed that the president has personally authorized a mission to kill the family members of those believed to be involved in the Camp David ambush. Already we have reports of an attack in Crimea and a developing situation in Iran near the Caspian Sea. Initial reports indicate that even though the primary suspect is a former Army Ranger named Corporal Sammie Samuelson, the president wanted to divert attention that a white male might have planned and executed this terror incident to shift the blame to members of the Islamic community."

She watched Rocky's handsome, square-jawed face and copper eyes, thought about the last time they'd slept together, got a little turned on, punched the mute button, and said, "Perfect."

Brookes slid out of bed, pulled on her exercise clothes, and walked onto her porch. The morning air was cool, buzzing with everything coming alive in May. There were few pleasures like springtime in Virginia. Just dope up with whatever antihistamine worked best and enjoy the splendor of azaleas and dogwoods blooming brightly, creeks and rivers flowing fully, and everything in sight growing.

She ran her hands along the smooth spandex of her running outfit. It was black with yellow flames shooting upward from the ankles. The pants were also functional, reflecting light during the hours of darkness. Touching her nose to each knee as she stretched, Brookes felt her hamstrings tighten. She punched in her Spotify running playlist, which included Snoop Dogg, the Eagles, and Bob Marley, among others. She checked the time—7:16 A.M.—and knew she had to hustle. Lastly, she clipped her trusty Ruger holster on a wide riser belt she wore under her lightweight windbreaker, a souvenir from when she was a pacer for the Marine Corps Marathon in Washington, D.C.

Stepping off the porch she ran toward the boathouse and then turned north along the river, following a game trail that she had worn into a bona fide running trail over the years. Approaching her fifteen-foot-high compound wall, she pressed a small fob in her windbreaker. The metal gate door opened and she continued running as the gate closed behind her. Keeping an eye for moccasins and copperheads, she darted at a seven-minute-a-mile clip for nearly three miles. The trail zigged and zagged and started to climb into a hilly, rocky area. She slowed as she dipped over a ridge into a small hollow framed by large rocks on three sides.

She drew her pistol and stepped behind a large gray chunk of granite. A copperhead snake lurched to her right about ten feet away.

"No need for the pistol, Sloane," a voice called out.

"If we were texting, I'd send you an 'LOL' right now," she shouted.

"Well, nothing funny about anything that's happening," the man said.

"Fox News is calling you the most dishonest man in the country," she said. "Based on that, I think arming myself is warranted."

She heard a twig snap around the corner of the rock. Another footfall rustled some damp leaves. She slid her finger inside the trigger housing of the Ruger.

"I'm actually back here," the voice said. Josh Henry, former CIA director, previous bureaucrat in the Department of State, and longtime political party operative, was standing directly behind her. The copperhead had most likely responded to his movement,

Brookes thought. And more to the point, who was on the other side of the rock?

As she turned to confront Henry, she felt a presence behind her.

"You didn't think I'd come alone, did you?"

An arm chopped down on her hand, knocking the pistol loose.

"Hey!" she snapped.

Brookes cracked a sharp elbow into the ribs of her rearward assailant. She spun away and landed a roundhouse kick to the man's face. Wishing she had steel-toed boots instead of running shoes, Brookes cradled the man's head and slammed her knee into his face. The man's nose made a loud cracking sound as blood splattered everywhere.

She stepped away and spun one more time, placing the heel of her shoe in the man's temple. He had been leaning over, holding his hands to his face, but now was tumbling to the ground in the fetal position. Brookes picked up her pistol, spun and aimed it at Henry.

"Good job," he said. "You nearly killed the president's briefer."

Henry was aiming a pistol at her, also. By the looks of it, the handgun was a Sig Sauer P210.

"This pantywaist?" she said, tossing her chin over her shoulder. "I've had better fights in Gymboree with my niece."

"Neither of us wants to pull the trigger here," Henry said. "Why don't we just relax."

"That's where you're wrong. I'd shoot you in a heartbeat. Just like I didn't hesitate on your patsy here. You wanted the meet. Here I am. Let's meet. Put your gun away first and then I'll consider holstering mine."

Henry was dressed in khaki pants, golf shirt, hiking boots, and an unzipped lightweight blue jacket. He slid the pistol into a holster on his left hip.

She stepped back so that both men were in her field of view. She took a brief glance to her left to make sure Henry hadn't brought along any other guests. Brookes then looked at the briefer, who was huddled on the leaves and trail wearing shiny brown loafers, dress slacks, a button-down shirt, and blazer. His glasses lay broken next to him. His coiffed brown hair was askew.

"It's your dime. I've got a workout to get in. Tell me why I'm here," Brookes said. Fully aware that either man may be wearing a wire, she measured her words, placed the onus on Henry.

"I intended to have Miles Everett here brief you on some developments with Team Valid," Henry said.

"I'm sorry. I don't know what you're talking about," Brookes said. "Further, if Everett is the president's briefer, he works for the director of National Intelligence, not you. Where's your buddy General Dillinger on all this?"

"Dillinger is aware that we are here talking to you," Henry said.

"Excuse me? You asked for this meeting and you tell Dillinger, you might as well be telling Jeff Bezos and the *Washington Post*."

Henry sighed and ran a hand over his bald scalp. All of this was an act for Brookes. She went into every situation believing that someone could be wearing a wire.

"Come on, Sloane. Dillinger is on board. He's got as much to lose as anyone."

Brookes paused, looked down at the briefer, who was now on one knee.

"You broke my nose," he mumbled through a bloody hand.

"You stained my new running outfit. We're even. Get over it," she countered.

"I brought Everett here to discuss what we have in place."

She pointed at Everett. "Wearing a wire, Everett?"

"No," he said.

She pointed at Henry, "Wearing a wire, Josh Henry, former CIA director?"

"No, and we've discussed this."

"Okay, talk," she said.

Everett stood and leaned against the rock she had originally been hiding behind. He pulled a handkerchief from his pocket and held it against his nose. His face was already swollen and bruised.

"Let me try to start while Everett gets his composure," Henry said.

"If somebody doesn't say something useful in about ten seconds, I'm going to keep running and call the cops that I've got intruders on my land," Brookes said.

"Team Valid is officially cut off," Henry said. "Everett here was in the briefing at five this morning. He updated the president on the dossier that the FBI is building on Corporal Samuelson. He appears to be the ring leader, but a new theory is emerging that he might also be a lone wolf."

"Really?" she asked. "What about the others?"

"The 'others' are still in play. But Samuelson is sticking. The president seems interested in him."

She stared at Henry for a long moment. Studied his features, seeing years of State Department meetings etched into the soft crags. Absent from any of his comments was any reference that the briefer had actually told the president about Team Valid. The "new theory" was part of their plan. This meeting, she supposed, was an update to tell her that everything was going according to plan. They could have done this via secure chat, though they were trying to have the smallest footprint on communications.

"Okay, so why the meet and greet here?"

"Well, you needed to know. You've got a lot at stake here. If this president goes down, we are counting on you. The vice president doesn't have the flair to energize the opposition base that the current president does. So we need to give you a personal heads-up that Samuelson's family is going down, along with the others."

"A personal heads-up," she said under her breath. "Why do I think it's more than that?"

"There's nothing more," he said. "Obviously none of this can be discussed on email, text, phone, and so on."

"And we recovered *your* MacBook," Everett said through bubbling spit and blood.

Brookes snapped her head toward the briefer. He had a leering grin on his face, as if he had been waiting to say those words out loud. Perhaps he already had, to someone else?

"That's right. It was in Samuelson's apartment," Henry confirmed.

Dropping her need to be circumspect, she asked, "What was it doing there?"

"For some reason Carly Masters trusted him," Henry said.

"Where is it now?" she asked. Until she had it back, the MacBook was still a liability. Recovering the computer wouldn't completely cover her ass, but it would go a long way to making her life easier. The cloud had complicated things, but she believed she had taken care of most of that.

"In a safe place," Everett mumbled.

"Safe my ass. Give it to me, you little twerp," Brookes said.

"Sloane, just relax. We've got it locked up until the storm passes," Henry added.

She looked from Everett to Henry. They weren't carrying any backpacks or satchels that could hold a MacBook. Satisfied they were telling the truth, she asked, "So what's the trade?"

"No trade, Sloane. We hold on to that until everything is

wrapped up. Then we either destroy it or give it back to you. The worst place for that thing right now is in your possession."

"It's my computer. I'll be the judge of that," she countered.

"We know what is on that hard drive. Your work with Raafe Khoury in the Senate Intelligence Committee resulted in some transgressions. We have your back."

"You have my back?"

"Yes. Samuelson is good for the ambush. The Sultans and Perzas have been eliminated. Khoury is dead. You're covered."

She thought about Raafe Khoury, her former information technology chief. The Pakistani man was an IT genius. Apparently too smart, though. He had made possible everything she needed done. This was all good news though. Perza family dead. Check. Sultan family dead. Check. Khoury dead. Check. Now her big secret resided with a few loyalists who wanted plum jobs when she became president. She was happy to trade the power for protection.

"And the president will be revealed with Team Valid when they go after Samuelson's family."

Presidential scandal with bite. Check.

"Who are they?" she asked.

"Who is who?"

"His family. Who's going to be killed?"

"Samuelson's only remaining sibling is a woman formerly known as Valerie Samuelson," Henry said. "His parents have gone off the grid."

"Never heard of her. Formerly?" Brookes said.

"Actually, she doesn't go by her maiden name. She's an FBI agent," Henry said.

"An FBI agent? The president's going to kill an active agent?"

This was even better than she could have imagined. When the agent was dead, she'd slip that info to Rocky Campagne and it would be his big scoop. They had discussed him being her press secretary previously. This would make it a lock. Of course, it was unlikely that President Smart knew anything of the attacks.

"The instructions are to kill every family member of the attackers," Everett interjected.

"Her name?"

"Valerie Hinojosa."

CHAPTER 12

Harwood low crawled in the heat of the afternoon sun. His face was white, covered in sand and dirt. His mouth was dry as cotton as he sucked hot water through the hose of his hydration system.

The crack of rifle fire snapped overhead. He didn't know if his two teammates were in a fight with the advancing Iranian military below his position or if they were both targeting him. Stunned that Weathers had surprised him, Harwood was just now coming to grips with the reality that Stone and Weathers were leaving him for dead. Was it his conflict with Stone? His argument with Hinojosa? Had she instructed them to ditch him?

Hinojosa's text about the TacSleeves being burned was clear enough. Someone had hacked into their communications system. If she was going to dump him, why would she warn him and the team? Had something changed in between killing the family and their labored exfiltration?

He thought about the slip of paper.

Baku.

She knew something might go wrong.

The puff of dust in his face and the echoing of machine-gun fire focused him back on the mission at hand: staying alive. Thankfully he had his SR-25 three-point sling snapped into his outer tactical vest. He had his pistol, knife, and rifle. His hydration system was about one-third full and he had an MRE pouch in his cargo pocket. Slim pickings for someone dumped in the mountains of Iran.

As he sought cover, he found a sheer cliff that fell forty feet into a ravine. The small gorge had the twinkle of water at the bottom. Probably not drinkable, but definitely good cover and concealment. He slid over the lip of the rock formation and did his best to lower himself using toe- and fingerholds. He was exhausted, though, and his concentration wasn't perfect. His boot slipped on a narrow wedge of rock and he was suspended by his two hands, fingers holding over two hundred pounds of gear and his body. His feet scraped for purchase as he chanced a look over his shoulder. He had twenty feet to go and there was no telling the surface at the bottom. Could be rocky. Could be muddy.

His fingers gave way and he bundled into a tight ball, executing a parachute-landing fall, keeping his feet and knees together. The bottom of the ravine was in between rocky and muddy. Just like after every parachute jump, Harwood did a quick inventory of himself. No broken bones. Maybe a bruised hip. Weapons intact. Rucksack okay and probably saved him from a broken back. Good to go.

He studied the small trill of water and decided to follow its flow, which perhaps would lead him to the Caspian Sea. That body of water couldn't be more than ten miles away. He could do ten miles on the MRE and the limited water. From there he could improvise, provided the Iranians didn't cut him off. They would presume he went west, toward the Turkish border. Instead, he began a light jog, splashing through the mud and rocks to the north, toward the Caspian Sea and hopefully Baku, the city Hinojosa had mentioned to him, and whatever fate may hold for him there.

After two hours, the ravine opened to a meadow. The sun was setting to his back behind the mountains from which they had fought this morning. A large body of water lay a mile or so to his north. The Caspian Sea.

He found a good camouflaged location and waited for sunset. He ate his remaining ration, a bland-tasting spaghetti and meatballs. Harwood wasn't a food snob. Rather, he viewed food as fuel. He sucked his hydration system dry and watched the shadows grow long as the sun set. Using his sniper scope, he studied the small village on the shore. There were fishing boats tied to a wooden pier. A few men on the boat farthest from the land hauled up a net and dumped a bevy of fish onto the dock. Two men jumped out and began cleaning the fish, tossing the remains into the water. It might have been his imagination, but he thought he could smell the guts and blood from his location a mile away. The breeze was off the sea toward him so it was possible. There were about twenty buildings in the village, fifteen of which looked like residences and the rest shops or maybe a restaurant. Harwood was familiar with fishing villages. They were simple operations. Enough homes for the fishermen and their families. Stores to purchase basic provisions, especially netting and lines. A pier to tie off the boats. And a major highway artery to move the goods to the big cities where the restaurants needed their product. It was all there.

Harwood was banking that the town would shut down early and he would be able to secure one of the boats and make his way to Baku, which his memory told him was some fifty miles to the northwest. It would be the first big city he got to. Once there, he would figure out a plan.

The last of the fishermen cleaned up well after dark, but Harwood was patient. When he saw the lights go out in the last of the houses, he collapsed his bipods and removed his scope, stuffing it into his rucksack. While the meadow was open, he was able to move swiftly through some tall grass until he reached the two-lane asphalt road. To his right was the road rising into the darkness. On the horizon he could see lights like a halo over some city he would never visit. To his front was the Caspian Sea, its waters lapping gently at the muddy shore thirty meters away. To his left was the village; the first building appeared to be a general store, as he had guessed. The rest were weatherworn and sagging one-story shacks, most likely the homes of the fishermen, passed down through decades if not centuries of mining the sea.

A boat would be their most prized possession. The only way to feed their family, to survive. Harwood thought about the morality of stealing a peasant fisherman's boat to survive. While not happy with the internal debate and the repeated outcome—it's not right—he could think of no other option. Most likely the fishermen were wholly disconnected from the Iranian government, their military and their support of terrorism around the world.

This mission was filled with dilemmas. Killing the family members of terrorists. Stealing a peasant's boat.

A noise from the sea broke his reverie. He scanned through his scope until he found the dim white light of a boat. It was a low vessel with a covered console and machine gun on the deck, definitely more modern than the fishing trawlers that inhabited the pier. As the vessel turned toward the docks, there were two armed men on the deck laughing as they held a woman by her long black hair. Her head was turned up in defiance and her hands were bound behind her back. She was wearing a brown peasant's dress that appeared ripped and wadded near the hem. The men wore olive uniforms and had AK-47s strapped to their chests. The men's laughter and voices tumbled over one another, drowning out the woman's sobbing. The tears and contorted mouth were all Harwood needed to see. Images of his favorite foster sister, Lindsay, escaped from their locked compartment and floated through his mind. Abused, used, and ultimately killed by a sexual deviant, Lindsay had encouraged young Vick to run as far as he could from their foster home in Maryland. Tired of seeing his sister pimped out by scheming foster "parents," Harwood had gone into the barn that fatal day. The old man was trying to rape her, and as she resisted, the man shot her.

Harwood's instinctive reaction had been to grab the pitchfork as he emerged with rage from his hiding spot. The next thing he knew he was standing over the man and the pitchfork was pinning his throat to the dirt floor. Blood was everywhere. He checked on Lindsay, who was dead. He looked back at the man, who was also dead. Then he ran. At sixteen, he didn't know where he was going, but he knew one thing.

The Reaper had been born. And he was on the run.

A light came on in the third shack from the general store. Harwood took a step back and assumed the prone position, aiming his rifle along at the pier. A man stepped from his front door and ran toward the pier. He was carrying something in his hand, which Harwood guessed was a pistol. Harwood moved the scope back to the boat. The man's footsteps rang loud as they slapped onto the pier. The letters on the side of the boat were written in Farsi or Arabic, Harwood wasn't sure. But it was clear this was a government ship of some type.

The boat was docking at the T-head of the pier. Harwood counted the one man at the helm and the two guards outside of the control room. The vessel didn't appear to have any space belowdecks, but he couldn't discount it. There were three antennae poking from the ship and as the boat crabbed next to the pier, the mounted DShK machine gun became more evident. Harwood guessed this was a coast guard patrol ship.

The man stopped on the pier when one of the guards held up his rifle and the other put a knife to the young girl's throat. From the house, a door slapped against the frame sounding like a gunshot. A quick glance showed a woman pulling a robe around herself and looking at the pier.

Mother at the house. Father on the pier. Daughter on the boat.

Harwood put his crosshairs on the man with the knife, his head like a pumpkin in the scope. He squeezed the trigger. The weapon coughed, louder than he wanted, but the silencer helped dampen what would otherwise be a bellowing echo down the valley and onto the sea. The man dropped the knife and fell inside the boat.

Quickly, Harwood was on the second guard, who was holding the rifle. He shot center mass and scored a hit in the man's chest. Double tapped him to make sure. The rifle fell with a splash into the water.

The apparent father turned and looked in Harwood's direction. He was invisible, concealed beyond recognition, unconcerned about detection. Harwood already had his crosshairs on the door, waiting for the man to step outside. The window was open but did not provide a good shot. Human instinct and curiosity being predictable, the man came running out with his weapon up. He stared at the two dead guards.

Harwood exhaled deeply, squeezed the trigger and delivered a bullet to the man's forehead. He waited five seconds for any further reaction from inside the boat. He knew he had a small window of time to move.

The daughter was trembling, her mouth open in a silent scream, as her father rushed toward her. The pain and anguish on her face caused Harwood to look up from his scope, look away. He'd seen too much pain and agony in his life. Why did it continue? He was doing his part, he considered, to stop it where he found it.

The father rushed forward and lifted his daughter over the boat's gunwale. The mother ran toward the pier. Lights were coming on in the tightly packed community. Harwood was up and running toward the pier. His rucksack felt like it had a concrete block in it. The SR-25 swung awkwardly in one hand as he pumped for speed with the other. As he passed the main street into the village, people were stirring in their homes behind curtained windows. The police state might work to his advantage, keeping the downtrodden villagers in their homes for just a minute longer.

His boots slapped on the pier as he raced toward the family. Moonlight was the illumination. The pier had some naked bulbs hanging from wooden poles and connected by black electrical cables, but they were either turned off or nonfunctioning.

The man lifted his pistol and shouted at Harwood, who spoke no Farsi and understood a few words. He was dressed in a thin white T-shirt, dark slacks, and brown shoes with rubberized soles. He had black hair with flecks of gray. His face was broad and wizened, eyes narrow and suspicious.

Harwood stopped, feeling the peering eyes from behind the curtains a hundred meters to his rear. The father held his daughter close with his left arm and leveled the pistol at Harwood's gut. He eyed Harwood's SR-25 then looked over his shoulder with a quick glance. The wife held tight to her husband. Harwood could only imagine what the family was seeing: a grimy, black man wearing black cargo pants and shirt with black rucksack pulling at his shoulders. A rifle in his left hand and his right hand free to either draw his pistol from his hip like an old-style Western gunfight or draw the knife attached to the webbing of his outer tactical vest.

He held his right hand up, palm out, the universal signal for stop, listen, or don't do what you're thinking about doing.

The man's eyes flicked from Harwood to the village. Something was happening behind Harwood but he didn't chance taking his eyes off the father. Harwood said, "We have to hurry. They were going to hurt her more." He pointed at the boat.

The father nodded, as if he understood. He seemed to go through a series of quick mental calculations that Harwood suspected included *saved my daughter, risked his position, three dead Iranian government types, trouble for the village.*

"Quick," the man said. He kissed his daughter on the top of the head. She was maybe fourteen now that Harwood got a closer look at her pained countenance. Then he switched positions with the daughter, handing her to the mother. He said something to the mother, who nodded. The girl's eyes remained fixed on Harwood. "With me," the father said as he tucked the pistol in his belt. He waved his hand at Harwood and walked quickly to the boat, which had remained adjacent to the pier, despite having no lines tied. Harwood followed the father over the gunwale and stepped over his fresh kills. The boat deck was slick with blood, causing him to almost slip. Once he was in the back of the boat, he looked at the mother and girl, who had turned to keep her frozen stare on Harwood.

She mouthed the words, "Thank you," as her father fired up the boat.

Harwood nodded. The girl carefully lifted her hand and opened and closed her palm, extending her fingers in a muted wave goodbye.

After ten minutes of heading due north into the Caspian Sea, the father said, "Where?"

Harwood thought about the note again. Baku was the place, but where in Baku? He wasn't sure he wanted to give away his destination to someone who could be captured and tortured by the Iranian police.

"You speak some English," Harwood said. "I don't speak Farsi."

"It's okay. Some English. Where?"

"Baku," Harwood said.

"Azerbaijan?"

"Yes."

The man considered it, looked at the gauges, and then at Harwood.

"It's a long way. Over two hundred kilometers," the man said. He paused, looked at Harwood and continued. "You saved Fatima. It's okay."

Harwood nodded. "Thank you."

The father played with the gauges for a bit as Harwood began collecting weapons and information from the Iranian government officials. Each man had an AK-47 and Makarov pistol. They carried identification, which Harwood pawed through more out of combat instinct than needing any useful information from Fatima's captors.

"No. Don't touch," the father said. "Here. Steer boat."

Harwood switched places with the father, each understanding that trading names was not a good idea. Looking through the windscreen, Harwood saw the black expanse of the evening and ocean spread infinitely before him. The boat's hull slid smoothly across the glassy sea. He rested his hand atop the wheel but felt it correct on its own. It was on autopilot. The GPS was not unlike Google Maps or some other map function save the Farsi characters as opposed to English he was accustomed to. The destination wasn't precisely Baku, but some point close, according to the map and the charted course, which was displayed by a single straight line. The boat was traveling at thirty knots.

The noise behind him distracted him enough to cause him to look. The father had a large knife out and was slicing open the abdomens of each man, working his hand way up inside the chest cavity. He came out with a large organ and tossed it over the side like chum.

"Lungs. Make them sink," the father said, looking up at Harwood, who nodded.

The father was a hard man. A fisherman, used to a hard living. He wanted no trace of him or the guards left behind. He was repaying a debt to Harwood and would then disappear, Harwood surmised. When the father was done removing the lungs of each man, he tossed the corpses over the edge. The man found a broom and began sweeping the blood into the well.

When he was done, the father stepped up and nudged Harwood out of the way.

"This is Zolfaghar. Fast," he said, then pushed the throttle all the way down until it was pressing against the housing. "Seventy knots."

Standing inside the control room of the vessel, Harwood placed his right foot back and braced himself against the frame. The bow lifted into the air and the boat spat a giant rooster tail as it rocketed north.

Harwood used the smooth ride and apparently trustworthy father as time to focus on personal maintenance. He first found a portion of the deck not covered in blood where he stripped and cleaned his weapons. He dug through his rucksack and reloaded his magazines with 7.62 mm ammunition. He emptied and repacked his rucksack, making everything tighter. He found the scraps of a bonus MRE he had stashed in the bottom and wolfed it down. Lastly, used some moist wipes to clean the grime off his body where he could. He stuffed the wipes and MRE wrappers in the MRE bag, rolled it, and jammed it into his rucksack. His hand hit something circular and small. He studied the tracking device and tossed it overboard. Then he fell asleep.

He dreamt of firefights in Afghanistan with Corporal Sammie Samuelson lying next to him, saying, "Send it." His unblinking focus on the target. Samuelson's reliability, albeit new to him as a spotter after the Chechen had killed Joe LaBoeuf. Long conversations about nothing and everything as they lay motionless for hours, sometimes days, in the same hide position, waiting for that one shot that would make the difference. Lots of conversations. Some professional, most personal. Samuelson was from Texas. His parents divorced when he was young. He'd lived with his father. Wasn't close with his mother, but they visited some. In the divorce apparently Samuelson's parents had divided property and children, because Harwood's mind pulled out a memory about a sister and ran it through the dream filter. The parents were standing tall above the children, who were staring at each other. As they began to speak, Harwood's dream floated to his own childhood. He was a spectator on everyone's family because he didn't have one of his own. A foster kid who had run away and joined the army, which had been exactly the right thing to do.

The boat slowed and shifted so that Harwood awakened. He cradled his rifle as he leaned against his rucksack. He'd slept maybe an hour.

"Here. Quick," the father said.

Harwood stood and let his eyesight adjust from the back of his eyelids to the early morning darkness. Scattered lights sprinkled in the distance. To his right was the sea, but to his front and left were buildings etched against the night skyline, black on black.

"City that way," the man pointed across the bow. "Out now."

"Roger. Thanks," Harwood said, staring into the man's eyes. The father nodded. They were even. Harwood hoped he made it back to his daughter. Surely, he'd have to refuel and then ditch the boat somewhere before he got back to Iranian waters. Not his problem.

The boat shimmied to the side of what looked like an old T-head pier for offshore oil or liquid loading and unloading. Harwood disembarked onto the narrow concrete platform and the attack vessel silently slipped away into the night. Harwood followed the three-foot-wide maintenance walkway across nearly two hundred meters of water before reaching land. He found a low ditch paralleling a north-south road. By his calculations he was three miles south of the city to the north, which he assumed was Baku. A few oil rigs pumped rhythmically with their cantilevered arms in the distant foothills. The area had an unnatural smell of salt water and industrial by-product that he couldn't quite place.

Picking his way along the ditch, the occasional car would rumble toward or from behind him, whereupon Harwood would lay prone and motionless until he was convinced he could proceed without detection.

Unclear on where exactly he was going once he got to Baku, Harwood replayed his last conversation with Hinojosa in his mind. They had not discussed CIA safe houses, the U.S. embassy, or any other logical meet-up locations. She'd slipped the paper into his pocket without mentioning it to him, meaning that she was worried about others listening in on their conversation. Perhaps it was something coded?

They had discussed the Sultan raid and the legitimacy of the Perza raid. After some back-and-forth, she had informed him that Samuelson was a key suspect in the Camp David Ambush. Then they'd discussed Carly Masters and what, if any, role she'd played in this matter. After some tense words, they'd then hugged when she slipped the paper into his pocket.

The conversation had flowed logically from one topic to the

next. He'd been preoccupied thinking about Samuelson, but he remembered there was an anomaly in the conversation. Something about a damsel in distress. It didn't fit with everything else they had been discussing.

Won't be rolling my hair from some medieval tower.

It was the only thing he could think of, the only seemingly misplaced comment. Her voice had seemed tense and her demeanor uncharacteristically awkward. Even the hug. It felt . . . forced. She needed to be close to him to whisper in his ear and slip the paper into his pocket.

The only geographical reference in the conversation other than target locations had been a medieval tower. Was there one in Baku?

Convinced that Hinojosa had been too precise and professional in her conduct and communications to have a random statement slide into the conversation, he continued along the most covered and concealed route to the city. The tall buildings etched against the skyline hinted that the city was not some former Soviet Republic backwater, but a modern metropolitan area. The road ten meters to his left was elevated, affording him an avenue of dead space in which to walk without being spotted by drivers. To his right was the Caspian Sea. He knelt to get his bearings near a bundle of washed up driftwood. He disassembled his SR-25 and carefully packed it in his rucksack. Transitioning from soldier on the run to "peaceful hiker" was probably his best option. He scraped through the driftwood and picked up a four-foot walking stick that was maybe three inches in diameter. He lifted the edge of his black polypropylene shirt over his pistol, giving it a nudge for reassurance now that the comfortable heft of the SR-25 was in his ruck. He removed and stuffed his outer tactical vest beneath the top flap of his rucksack.

He soon came upon a sprawling beach with chairs and umbrellas already in place for a May beach day. The road veered away toward the inner city, giving way to a series of hotels and restaurants above the seawall. Harwood scraped his left shoulder against the wall, and continued forward, poking the stick in the sand on every other step of his left foot. Scanning now, he was more alert for threats, despite his exhaustion. The hour or so of sleep he'd managed helped, but not much. The sun was probably two hours from nudging over the edge of the sea to his right. He was at his circadian rhythm ebb and he knew it. The soft sand was inviting, for sure. He could lie there, take a nap, and let the sun serve as an alarm clock. He had no idea about the homeless population in Azerbaijan or Baku specifically, but considered that as one disguise option.

Voices to his front caused him to stop. He retrieved his night-vision goggle and held it to his eye like a pirate searching for land. About twenty meters to his front was a male and female couple having sex on a blanket in the sand near the water. The man was on top, holding the woman down, her legs wrapped around his back. Probably some nightclubs just closing down in the area.

He pressed ahead, betting they were both too inebriated and consumed with desire to bother with him. He was right. Their voices faded in the background as he continued another half mile by his own pace count. The lights from the hotels and commercial district were bright enough to cast a skidding yellow reflection off the Caspian Sea, which was lapping against the otherwise uninhabited beach twenty meters to his right. As he walked, the beach transitioned to bulkheads and industrial port facilities. He had to dodge a couple of fences and walk a few tightrope-like concrete piers until he passed a dormant amusement park on his right. The city was an eclectic mix of resort and industrial.

Was there a medieval tower?

The night was blessedly in that temperature range that was

both cool and warm enough to be comfortable. Still, he was sweating and another hour into his fatigue when a rank smell pushed outward from a culvert at the base of the wall. Had to be a sewer of some type. The fetid odor propelled him forward until he found a staircase, which he climbed to the point he could see over the lip of the boardwalk and road beyond. A few cars sped in either direction. The boardwalk was empty save a few bums sleeping on scattered benches. The amusement park's towering structures seemed out of place behind him, though, as he studied a series of canals and roads that separated the city from the sea.

He studied the city. Bright lights everywhere except one location to his two o'clock, which he figured to be northeast given his axis of advance. The darker area intrigued him. Park? Historic area?

Something medieval?

Harwood had studied the Caucasus only in relation to his combat actions in Iraq and Afghanistan, and accordingly only knew that they were a secular, modern government that was almost ninety percent Shi'a Muslim. How they pulled off that feat, he would never know, but he assumed it was similar to the Balkans where the Muslims had been exposed to the liberties of freedom. The extremism of their religious beliefs had been dampened by the exposure to capitalism and democracy.

He quickened his pace along the beach until he popped up again on the boardwalk, still uninhabited at almost 5 A.M. The activity was picking up, though. The street now had protective fencing on either side and was humming with a not yet steady flow of fast-moving cars and Vespas, the European cross between a moped and a motorcycle.

To his right he saw the center of the dark area framed by bright lights on either side. A modern European hotel rose into the sky

five stories high with rounded turrets of luxury rooms overlooking the sea on each corner. The darkened structure looked like a
watchtower and it was ancient. Perhaps medieval?

Harwood lowered himself and studied the boardwalk and
beach. The water was close to the bulwark and the farther east he
went, the less beach he had to work with. The boardwalk was
starting to have a few scattered wanderers appear. He needed to
make a decision. With nothing more to go on than instinct, he hurried across the expansive boardwalk and then through a brightly
lit tunnel with blue backlighting. The tube was a passageway over
the now rushing traffic as the sun nosed over the vast Caspian Sea,
Turkmenistan too far in the distance to see any land.

He passed a couple of slow walkers and then took the steps
down to the wide sidewalk and was staring at a watchtower. He
swung to the left and entered the grounds of what was an old
city downtown. It had been preserved. Brown bricks and well-
manicured trees and shrubs held in stark contrast to the machin-
ery of a functioning metropolitan downtown. Restaurant owners
lifted protective steel doors and flipped closed signs to open. The
scent of bread baking wafted into the air. Cars buzzed behind him.

He saw a woman standing in the shadows of the tower. Long,
dark hair fell off her black shirt. She was wearing olive cargo pants
and boots. Too far away to positively identify if she was Hinojosa,
but she fit the basic contours.

Above him to the right, a window scraped open on the top
turret balcony of the fancy hotel, no more than fifty meters away.
He turned toward the noise. Saw a face peering directly at him.

The muzzle of a rifle appeared.

Harwood ran into the darkened recesses of the old city, feeling the hot jet wash of a missed shot.

CHAPTER 13

Sloane Brookes piloted her boat into the north channel of Tangier Island in the middle of the Chesapeake Bay just below the Maryland-Virginia border. She idled, reversed, and slipped to the right, threw her bumpers over, and then shut the engine as she tied the fore and aft lines to the cleats on the pier.

Normally, she would have one of her ship captains take her, but not today. Jeremy Jessup had strict rules about who was allowed onto his property and when they were allowed. He made an exception for Brookes because she stood a good chance to be president and he wanted to help her, that much she knew.

It was almost 10 P.M. and the nighttime ride had been unnerving as she remembered the "red, right, returning" rules of ship captains and navigated the shallow waters around Tangier. Jessup's house was on the north island and situated on the channel. Ingress and egress was relatively easy and she'd made this trip a few times before. In many respects, Jessup was the key to so much of her success in the past and Brookes knew that he would be crucial to her future in politics.

She breathed in the musty smell of the shallow tidal waters and listened to the sounds of nature. Water lapping the shores, crickets in harmony, and bullfrogs croaking. She walked up the wooden pier toward his house and Jessup stepped outside, easing the screen door against the frame. He watched her approach, then looked over her shoulder.

"Everything's shut down. Thanks for coming so late," he said. Jessup had blond-red hair and a full beard of the same color. He wore a partially buttoned short-sleeve surfer's shirt, board shorts, and OluKai sandals. He stood a few inches over six feet, which made him barely taller than Brookes.

"Well, I try to play by your rules as long as you play by mine," Brookes said.

"I think we're good to go on that one."

He turned around and walked inside of the wooden house on stilts. He had fresh, raw oysters laid out on ice and a bottle of wine.

"Is this a date?" Brookes laughed.

"No. She just left," Jessup countered.

Brookes paused, looked around, saw nothing that indicated someone else had been there. No second used wineglass. No second snack plate.

"I'm joking," Jessup said. "You drove a long way. You like oysters and this is your favorite wine."

"I've never told you either of those things," Brookes said.

"Seriously?"

She paused. Jessup was the American version of Julian Assange. He lived in the deep web and was a special government employee on the FBI, CIA, and Director of National Intelligence payrolls. If they needed something hacked, he could do it, and often did. His presence on Tangier Island, surrounded by salt water, sometimes wreaked havoc on his systems, but he preferred being remote and isolated, Brookes assumed.

"So you've been spying on me?"

"I'm protecting you as a confidential informant. Isn't that how it works nowadays?"

She smiled. "Good one."

Brookes sat on one of the barstools along the kitchen counter and slurped down a couple of oysters while Jessup opened the bottle of Stags' Leap Chardonnay and poured two glasses.

"Follow me," he said, carrying the glasses between his fingers in one hand and the bottle in the other.

Brookes grabbed the tray of oysters and carried them onto the screened porch. The sounds of nature carried through the mesh and Jessup turned on some music that competed. On the porch was a high top table and bar with two barstools. He placed the wine and glasses on the high top and sat on one of the stools as she chose the other, sliding the oysters onto the table. Jessup walked behind the bar and brought his Ethernet-connected MacBook to the table, opened it, and began talking.

"These four screens show you everything you need to know. Top right is Team Valid in Baku going after the Reaper. Top left is the president's briefer sitting at home in his study shitting razor blades. He's a weak sister and we need to do something about him. Bottom left is your buddy from the CIA Josh Henry. He too is in his study up late at night. Maybe he's looking at us, who knows? Well, actually, I know. He's not. He's watching porn. Trannies. Different strokes. And the last box at the bottom right is the president. He's tweeting, it seems."

She studied the live video and wondered, "I thought Team Valid was a done deal?"

"Well, they dumped Harwood, Samuelson's buddy. But he survived. Thankfully, we've got a tracker in his rucksack. I've hacked into the Baku security systems and am tracking through Interpol. He's got an APB on him and he's not going anywhere if they don't get him first. Azerbaijan has their secret police on the case and has assured us discretion."

"Too many people involved," Brookes muttered.

"Just look at Crossfire Hurricane. Shit. Over a hundred people involved and they almost pulled it off."

"'Almost' being the operative word," Brookes said. She leaned back and grabbed her wineglass, took a sip, thought, and then took another sip. Harwood had dashed into the black hole of the old city of Baku. "Remind me why I care about this guy? He wasn't even a factor before. How did he get involved?" She pointed at the quadrant that had shown Harwood.

"He knows Samuelson. Samuelson knew Carly Masters. Carly Masters figured you out and confided in Samuelson. We don't know what Samuelson may have told him."

She nodded. "Huh. The Reaper. Army Ranger trying to be famous like all the Navy SEALs. That's good enough for me."

"Well, he's a pretty driven guy and he has enough shade in his background to make him good for the Sultan and Perza killings. Allows us to leave Stone and Weathers out of it."

"But we needed him captured by the Iranians. Wasn't that the idea? After the Sultan and Perza problems were handled, of course."

"Yes. Those were the instructions. American Ranger captured in Iran. Almost certainly the Iranian government would go public with it and then the president would be on the bubble having to both explain what had taken place and try to deal with the hostage situation."

Brookes's phone chimed.

"President has tweeted again, it seems," she said. She had a special ring tone to alert her every time the president tweeted to his over fifty million followers. "Here it is. 'We must denounce the brutal and savage murder by Islamic terrorists of my cabinet family members. They illegally infiltrated this country to commit these crimes. I'm closely watching the investigation and will take appropriate action ASAP. Please pray for the families.' It took him twenty-four hours plus to send that out. Wonder why?"

"Probably has to balance what he can say with what he wants to say."

They watched the quadrant showing the president. He put down his phone and walked into his chief of staff's office. They chatted briefly.

"They both look exhausted," Brookes said, visualizing herself in the Oval Office.

"Secretary Masters's daughter is dead. The cabinet members' families have been slaughtered."

"Led by a mentally disturbed former Army Ranger who was angry at the Veterans Administration and Carly Masters, who had recently rebuffed his advances," she said.

"Precisely."

"And all of that seems to be taking hold, correct?"

"So far it looks good. We fed some info to Maximus Anon who seems to be nibbling at it."

"Thought we shut him down?" she asked.

"Twitter shut him down for a few weeks, but the outcry is pretty overwhelming. I always plant a sentence or fact in their tweet stream that is no shit classified, which allows us to suppress them longer. Under the previous administration they'd be arrested, but not so much today."

"Huh," she muttered. "Never thought of that. Just knew you guys were doing what needed to be done."

"Well, we are good," Jessup said. "You pay for the best; you get the best."

"No mistakes," she said.

Jessup looked offended, then ignored her comment.

"Back to this. The Sultan that they have in custody is pleading ignorance, which of course is very authentic. Claims he was just here for a business meeting. FBI is being hard on him, but he's got nothing to give."

"Okay, so what's next?"

"You met with Henry this morning. He's talking to his man at the FBI, who will make sure everything is good on our end."

"Okay. Sounds good. We're on track then," she said. After a pause she tapped the screen where the briefer was lamenting in his home study. "Can you blow that up?"

"Sure." He pressed a button that enlarged the quadrant to display on the entire screen. "What are you looking for?"

"That's my MacBook that Masters stole." The silver MacBook Pro had a miniaturized *Better with Brookes* campaign bumper sticker centered above the Apple logo. A quarter of the laptop was visible beneath a leather satchel that lay open. The letters *B-e-t-t* were visible. No question it was hers.

"Yes, they recovered it from Samuelson's apartment."

"Why didn't they give it back to me instead of this pinhead?"

"Stone had it and Deke Bronson shook him down before the establishment of Team Valid."

"I love it when you talk passive voice," Brookes said.

"You don't want me talking active voice here, because you know who established Team Valid."

"I do. And we're good. I just want my Mac returned to me. That's all."

"I've checked and there's nothing on there that you have to worry about. I deleted everything that could possibly be an issue for you. Most of it was in the iCloud. I was able to remotely enter your MacBook, also. I'd let them think they have leverage over you and play their game. You have nothing to worry about."

"Says the man who lives in the middle of the Chesapeake Bay."

"You have to admit there's a certain charm to these rather Spartan digs."

"No. Actually, I don't. I don't see the charm other than being able to dig your own oysters, but who wants to do that?"

"Well, I do. And I've already moved the monthly stipend from your bank account to mine. We should really vacation in the Caymans sometime."

"Is that a pass, Jeremy?" she asked.

"Think of it more as an invitation. I live a decent life. I'm counting on you to become president so I can get some fancy title. I know you'll be off-limits then, so I thought I'd throw an invite out now. Nothing ventured, nothing gained."

"I'm flattered," she said. And she was. He had been entirely professional and helpful as she navigated the conspiratorial waters of tipping the scale in her favor for this next run. She needed an edge and Jessup was proving that he was reliable. She found him handsome in a rugged way. The beard didn't do much for her, but she could probably convince him to shave.

"I'll take that under advisement," she said with a smile.

She pushed back, placed a hand on his shoulder, then turned and walked out the door.

On the trip back to her Reedville estate, she navigated the waters using the GPS in her Riva 63 Virtus boat until she was nudging into her boathouse. On the trip she thought about Jessup. He was a close confidant. Had helped her win her Virginia Senate campaign. Had a long history of Democratic politics in his family. His father had served as the chief of staff to three different Democratic governors and Jessup himself had been the chief of staff to the Virginia Senator Brookes replaced after he had retired due to some accusations of sexual misconduct. Jessup had nearly completed the full six years with her, but had stepped aside to help prepare her presidential run.

They'd come close, losing by the slimmest of margins. Jessup, a natural at mining the deep and dark webs, had stepped aside as campaign chairman and actually took over the role of digital marketing, a euphemism for plying the fertile fields of Twitter, Facebook, Google, and media outlets in an effort to sway the all-important independent vote. Every poll had showed her leading Smart by two to four percent until the last few days, and even then, no poll showed her losing.

Jessup had done all he could, legal and perhaps illegal, to swing the vote. She had told him not to give her the details and just do what needed to be done. With the aftershocks of Operation Crossfire Hurricane and the unveiling of the corruption of the FBI, CIA, and DNI, she had to tiptoe lightly. But still, she counted on the people believing that lightning indeed couldn't strike twice in the same spot, that the necessary checks and balances had been put in place. Also, she needed those assets to help her, yet she wanted to keep a firewall between her and them. That was where Jessup came in handy. He was constantly scrubbing her emails, cleaning her cloud, moving money, illicit or not, and managing practically her entire estate. She paid him one hundred thousand dollars per month and figured that $1.2 million a year wasn't chump change. Wasn't going to make anyone rich, she thought, but a solid salary in this day and age.

She walked along the flagstone path from the boathouse as she checked her phone, watching the president's tweet get retweeted and liked thousands of times over. She had to admit that it was an effective way of pole-vaulting over the media, which was unreliable at best. Even as a Democrat she was feeling the pendulum swing against her in the wake of the blowback from mainstream media collusion and convictions after the bungled campaign spying operation.

She absently wondered if she'd had a spy in her camp, having worked her way through everyone associated with her campaign and coming up empty every time. No, it was a one-sided deal. People wanted her to win. She had come close and she would win this time, no question.

As she approached her back deck, she felt a presence move swiftly alongside her. She retrieved her Ruger and spun as she aimed it directly at Ravenswood.

"Hey, hey!" Ravenswood said, holding up his hands in mock surrender.

"Fucking, Chip, don't ever do that again!"

"We need to talk. Did you see this?"

He lifted his phone that was open to a tweet stream from someone called BluePillProgress2020.

#Breaking An inside source with knowledge of the Camp David Ambush states that President Smart has assigned a black ops team to kill the families of the suspected terrorists. A member of Team Valid is active duty Army Ranger Vick Harwood. #TeamValid #ValidTarget #ImmoralAct

"Twitter? That's what you've got for me? Where are CBS, NBC, ABC, and everyone else? This should be breaking wide open," Brookes said.

"They've all got it. Both Harwood and the president are now exposed. This is like kindling. A one-off spark that will start the fire."

She looked onto the river a hundred yards beyond her sloping manicured lawn with giant oaks and maples. That was about right. At least he had used finesse. Then she thought about Jessup and wondered if he did it or if Ravenswood had followed through as she had instructed him. He was certainly capable. This was all part of the plan, which she wasn't supposed to know about.

"Okay, well, where are we on getting my laptop back?"

"Still working it," he said.

"Work harder. Somebody's got it. I need it back. That's your next task. If the newspapers and television cable shows and networks aren't on fire with this by midday tomorrow, we need to apply more pressure."

No way was she going to burn Jessup or make Ravenswood think that she had another source of intelligence. She kept Ravenswood compartmented from Jessup. Of course, Jessup was all knowing. Jessup was big league, a general in the fight. Ravenswood was an infantryman, a pawn in her tactical skirmishes.

"Out a little late for a boat ride, don't you think?"

She leveled a hard stare on Ravenswood that was not lost on him in the moonlight.

"Think is right. Go out into the river and sit there and think. No phones, no Twitter, no Internet, just my brain. And my brain is telling me that you are spending too much time here and not enough time doing what I pay you to do. You can take that tweet and shove it up your ass if it doesn't get things moving."

Ravenswood said nothing.

"Am I clear?"

"Yes, ma'am, all clear," Ravenswood said.

She gripped the Ruger tight in her hand. There would be a time for cutting her losses but that time was not now. With Jessup as Wizard of Oz, all knowing and all seeing, and Ravenswood the tactical operator, she had the means to provide a major broadside to the president.

"Oh, and make sure they know that an American citizen is being targeted by Team Valid. A family member."

Ravenswood raised his eyebrows and nodded, then left the way he had most likely arrived, around the side of the estate.

She smiled as Ravenswood blended into the darkness. The president would never see what was coming or where it came from.

CHAPTER 14

Harwood vaulted over a low brick wall that separated the guard tower from the sidewalk where he had been standing.

Who was shooting at him and why?

He had expected pressure from the police or military, but not some random shot from a hotel window. Sprinting through what appeared to be a well-preserved ancient city with low single-story square homes made of black bricks laid out like a small subdivision, Harwood felt the movement behind him. He zigged and zagged to avoid any shots that might have been coming his way, but he didn't hear or sense anything other than a single person following him. Reaching the back side of the old city, he did his best pommel horse imitation and pushed up over the long brick wall, landing in some shrubs adjacent to a sidewalk on the opposite side. Traffic zipped along the roads now that the sun was up and it was probably approaching 7 A.M. local time.

He saw a gap and darted across the busy highway, reaching the other side with the echo of blaring horns chasing him down an alley. After a series of turns through increasingly busy streets, he found a small park amid the modern towering skyscrapers that poked into the sky. Feeling vulnerable, he moved north toward what appeared to be a more residential section. Still sensing a presence behind him, he cut across traffic again only to see the woman who had been at the tower.

It was Hinojosa.

"Vick, stop!" she shouted.

Harwood stopped on the sidewalk next to a six-foot-tall concrete wall. He didn't know what was on the other side, but he could scale it if he needed to.

"You've got ten seconds," Harwood shouted.

Hinojosa ran toward him. Harwood gripped his pistol but didn't remove it. He scanned the skyscrapers where millions of people could see them. He felt exposed, a sharp contrast to the mountains of Iran.

"Hurry," she said as she approached. She darted past him and he turned to follow, wondering if she was the rabbit leading him into an ambush. She seemed to know where she was going, checking her phone every block, every turn. She was probably using GPS, Harwood figured, which made her trackable by whomever might have been shooting at him.

They ran into a hostel, up a flight of stairs and into a room. Two bunks, one made and one unmade, were on either side of the small room. The room smelled of dirty laundry and stale sheets with a lingering odor of rotten fruit. A gray dividing curtain was pushed all the way back to the window along a steel pole that ran the length of the ceiling. They were on the third floor. Thirty-foot drop out of the windows, if they opened, which seemed questionable.

Hinojosa grabbed him by the shoulders. They were both breathing hard from sprinting through the morning streets of

Baku. Her brunette hair fell around her shoulders. She looked at him with wide, questioning eyes. Her grip was firm.

"What the fuck, Valerie. You have me dumped in Iran? What did you tell Stone and Weathers?"

"I didn't tell them anything. They got an independent message from somewhere to do that," she countered. "They're here. They just tried to kill me."

"They shot at me!" Harwood said.

"That was my room. I booked it yesterday when you left for Iran. I need to tell you something," she said, still panting.

"So tell me. They're chasing us, I'm sure."

"Me, too. I'm Sammie's sister. I'm a target of Team Valid. They're trying to kill me because the president has ordered them to," she said.

"What?"

"Didn't Sammie ever tell you about him going with Dad and me going with Mom after the divorce?"

That was all the verification he needed, because Samuelson had told him that. While the information was probably easily obtainable, there was no reason why she would lie to him and make herself a target.

"Okay, I'm processing this. Yes. He mentioned that. But you're an FBI agent. The president can't just have you killed," Harwood said.

"Come on. You're the Reaper. You know that you guys can kill anyone. Foreign or domestic if it's in the national interest."

Something caught in Harwood's mind but then slipped away. Everything was moving too fast. "Okay, where do we go? How do we get out of here?"

"I paid for this room as a backup when I got to town, knowing that they could probably trace my credit card reserving the room near the Maiden Tower. Stone beat my door down and came after me. I was prepared and dashed out of the room before he knew what was happening. Of course, Weathers was in the lobby, so I escaped out the back and ran across the street when I saw you."

"Okay, we're alive. So what's your plan?" Harwood asked, feeling time slip away.

"I've got one," she said. "We just need to get to the BP headquarters. From there we can hitch a ride."

There was the slightest creaking sound in the hallway.

Harwood retrieved his pistol and stepped in front of Hinojosa, putting himself in between her and the door. He pulled her to the wall that would give him a clear shot the second someone pulled at the door.

The door opened swiftly, and a couple came stumbling into the room, obviously drunk from a long night. Harwood lowered the pistol as they fell onto the bed without noticing, or at least commenting on, Harwood and Hinojosa. Harwood kept his eyes trained on the door and the hallway beyond. He saw a shadow falling toward them, pushed forward by a flickering bulb twenty meters away beyond the stairwell.

Harwood closed the door as a bullet splintered the wood. He twisted the useless button on the doorknob, grabbed the sheets from the bed, and tied a quick square knot connecting the sheets and wrapped one around the frame of the bed. He pried open the window, using his knife to break free the jamb that had been sealed shut by paint and years of disuse.

The window was large enough for him to scan the exterior. The sheets would get them halfway down. From there it would be a well-executed parachute-landing fall onto what looked like a back alley behind the hostel. Across the street an adjoining road split the backs of other buildings, as if this were a garbage truck run. He tossed his rucksack to the ground and turned toward Hinojosa.

"Hey, man, what the fuck," the man said in a thick east European accent. "Can't a guy get laid?"

Harwood turned his pistol on the couple and said, "In five seconds a murderer is going to come crashing through that door. Either come out with us or take your chances." Then to Hinojosa, "Go, now."

He helped her out the window and watched as she shimmied down the sheet, which pulled the bed frame all the way to the wall. She suspended herself from the end and let go, falling to the street and rolling then popping up as she retrieved her own pistol. She swept left and right and nodded at Harwood up above.

The door splintered open.

Stone. Standing there with his outer tactical vest laying atop chicken plate body armor. He was breathing hard. Quick eyes scanned the room, most likely assessed the couple frozen on the bed to be no threat, then focused on Harwood, who was halfway out the window. He had his feet wrapped around the sheets like a performer at Cirque du Soleil, which freed up his hands to snap off two quick, but loud, pistol shots at Stone. The back of his mind was scratching with the question, *Where is Weathers?* The shots burned holes in the tactical vest and seemed to knock Stone back a notch. He was sliding down the sheets using one hand, keeping the pistol and his eyes aimed upward.

He saw a shadow lean over the windowsill and squeezed off two more shots as suppressive fire. Soon he was suspended with one hand from the sheet, his left deltoid feeling the pull of his body weight. He pushed his feet and knees together and released. The ground caught him and he rolled, popped up, and scanned to find Weathers leveling a silenced M4 rifle at them. Harwood fired two more shots, scooped up his rucksack, and raced across the street to where Hinojosa had already found protection. She leaned around the corner and fired two rounds at Weathers and then two at Stone in the window.

Weathers had come from another location. If he had been set up, they would be dead. Harwood had seen him shoot and he was lethal. They had been lucky to be one step ahead of Weathers and Stone. He watched Stone turn his head toward Weathers, which meant he was moving toward them, he presumed. Firing two more suppressive shots at Stone, he grabbed Hinojosa by the wrist and slung his rucksack over his shoulder.

"We have to move," he growled.

In a flash, they were racing around the corner of a narrow gap between two homes. Brick mortar sprayed into his face as one of the Team Valid members fired again. They raced fifty meters, turned left and angled away from the two assassins.

"It's either you or me, but one of us has a tracker somewhere," Harwood said through rapid exhales. He was in good physical condition and could run for miles with his rucksack. He always trained with two twenty-five-pound weights in his ruck, among other things. The weight today was about the same, though he had no plates in his ruck at the moment.

After fifteen minutes of zigzagging through the dilapidated homes of the northeastern part of the city, they entered a barren, fenced lot that had some dirt pushed up at the end. Grass was growing from the construction lot berms and the land looked unused for weeks if not months. A rusty bulldozer was parked to the right, its blade resting on the ground like a slack jaw.

Harwood led them behind the berms, opened his ruck and assembled his SR-25 in record time, popped the bipods, snapped the scope into place, and aimed toward the gate.

"Go through everything you've got. Phones, watches, your little backpack, everything and check. I cleaned out my ruck on the way up from Iran. Found one and tossed it. I don't think it's me."

Hinojosa slipped a small black backpack off her shoulders, dumped it and pawed through the contents.

"Money, passports, identification, chick stuff, headphones, and some protein bars, nothing else."

"Check the pockets. You're looking for—"

"I know what I'm looking for, Vick." She was frustrated, worried.

"Okay, then find it."

"Nothing," she said after rummaging through the pockets.

Harwood thought. "Why did you bring headphones?"

"Always travel with them. Bose noise-canceling." She stopped, unzipped the container, retrieved the headphones and played with the battery well.

"Oh my God."

"Keep looking to see if they put a backup somewhere else. Doubtful. The more they put on you, the greater chance you'd find it. But it's kind of like checking for ticks. Might be everywhere."

She spent another five minutes going through everything and repacking her bag.

"Okay, I've got it."

Harwood removed some fishing line and C4 explosives from one of the outer pockets of his rucksack. He rigged a tripwire, stuffed a blasting cap in the explosives, put the tracker on the berm, scraped a thin layer of dirt over it, tied the fishing line to the chain-link fence behind them, and said, "Be careful. You trip that line it'll pull the baseball card out of the clothespin. The clothespin has two thumbtacks that will send current through this copper wire and battery to the blasting cap. The blasting cap will ignite and detonate the C4. Might not kill you, but could take off a limb."

Hinojosa was in the prone. The fishing line was a meter to her right. Harwood stepped over her back, lined up behind his rifle, saw no movement to their front. It would only be a matter of time. Harwood guessed that Stone and Weathers would steal a couple of Vespas and home in on their location in minutes if not seconds. He retrieved a pair of wire cutters from his rucksack and some work gloves.

"Use this," he said, pointing at Lindsay, his rifle. Hinojosa slid over, and looked through the sight. "I'm going to cut a hole and we're going out the side."

Harwood low crawled to the chain-link fence twenty meters away from the berm. Using the work gloves and wire cutters he had a three-foot-by-three-foot hole cut in the fence, lifted the cut out and snagged an open piece of wire over the chain link above the gap, holding the cutaway portion up. Vegetation crawled up the fence, effectively providing a screen in either direction. He cleared the leaves and twines from the gap he had created, stuck his head through. There was a row of homes across the street. The cut opened directly onto a sidewalk that was maybe four feet wide. The route of egress would be precarious, but it was better than nothing. With the sun shining brightly, there was no concealment upon which they could rely.

He low crawled back to the berm. "Anything?"

"Nothing."

"Good. Go crawl through that hole and I'll cover you." He cinched his ruck tight and said, "Take this, please."

Always reluctant to separate himself from the tools of his trade, Harwood wasn't going to waste any time getting to the fence once Hinojosa was through. She hefted the ruck on top of hers and did a half duckwalk to the opening, knelt, dropped his ruck, slid through, and then pulled his ruck through the gap. She was beyond the fence and presumably securing the opposite side. He collapsed his bipods and ran sideways with his weapon at eye level, spied the fence in his periphery, and lowered himself through the hole.

He crawled backward into the gap, pulled his rifle through, and then reached up and pulled the lip of fence down and secured it to conceal the cut.

Hinojosa was waiting.

"Quick, this way," she said.

Harwood turned and followed her, grabbing his ruck as he ran. They went left and then turned behind the fence, winding up maybe thirty meters from the berm. There were three dilapidated homes that appeared vacant, their backs abutting the fence. Harwood held a finger to his mouth. The high-pitched whine of the Vespa echoed down the streets from opposing sides. Harwood climbed the side of the flat-roofed home, crawled across the muddy roof, and set up his rifle. He didn't have a clear shot through the fence because the vegetation was dense and had overgrown the top of the razor wire to provide an effective screen. Still, he caught bits and pieces of the berm they had hidden behind.

He did have a view of the opening at the far end of the vacant lot. Anyone coming through would be in his crosshairs. But he knew that Stone and Weathers weren't stupid. There was no way they were going to step into the ambush. With that thought, he turned and whispered to Hinojosa, "Up here."

Reaching over, he lifted her up and they centered themselves on the rooftop. No less than a minute later, Harwood caught a flash out of his periphery. Then it was gone.

Stone's voice said, "Cutting a hole in the back now."

Hinojosa tensed. Stone was one house over working the wire

cutters on the fence just as Harwood had only minutes before. They couldn't hear Weathers's response because they were most likely using earbud push-to-talk radio communications. Harwood and Hinojosa remained frozen in place, listening as Stone worked the wire cutters.

Across the empty lot, Weathers came into view. He was crouched low, holding his rifle at eye level, sweeping and scanning in a 180 arc. He found refuge along the fence in a small depression where he set up overwatch for Stone breaching the fence. Harwood knew if they didn't move Weathers was unlikely to see them. He steadied his breathing, not daring to shift his bipod and make a noise that might alert Stone to their location. He had the tactical advantage of surprise at the moment and wanted to maintain that.

Stone popped through the gate and rolled to one knee. He was just in Harwood's field of view.

"No joy this side of the berm. Still tracking them here?" Stone said. His voice carried over the fence to the rooftop. Stone was still low crawling, unable to see on the opposite side of the berm. Weathers must have reported that his side was clear, even though he was still twenty meters away.

Harwood exhaled and moved his head slightly to begin adjusting his eyesight to the scope. Stone was standing up and walking now, holding his rifle at eye level, scanning much the same way that Weathers had from the opposite side.

Which was why he didn't see Harwood's improvised explosive device. The explosion was like a mini nuclear weapon. Stone yelped and actually flew a few feet into the air before landing on his back. There was blood. Weathers was frozen in place for a moment, which allowed Harwood to draw a quick bead on him center mass and squeeze off a double tap from the SR-25. Two bullets center mass. He remembered that Stone had been wearing body armor and assumed Weathers was also when he saw the man stumble, look down at his chest, grimace in pain, but break into a full sprint. Harwood let him and fired two more shots, one which appeared to hit Weathers's leg. The former Marine Force Recon sniper spun, fell to one knee, lifted his rifle, and snapped off a fusillade of rounds in Harwood's direction.

"Time to move," he said to Hinojosa. He slid backward to the far edge of the roof, lowered himself down and grabbed his rifle from Hinojosa who nudged it to him. She was next and safely on the ground. Police sirens wailed presumably in response to the explosion. If the Team Valid members were detained and exposed, that was okay with him.

Four police cars sped past them three streets over, the seesaw sound of the European and Asia emergency responders like a shrill bomb warning.

"Let's go," Harwood said. "The oil company, you said. Get us there or tell me where they are so I can."

"Follow me," Hinojosa said.

Stone's pained howling echoed through the streets. He was hurt. Harwood had no idea how badly but began following Hinojosa with the satisfaction that he had wounded both men who were trying to kill them. If he had gotten lucky and nicked a femoral vein on Weathers with the leg shot, then so much the better. He would bleed out and neither would likely pursue anytime soon.

Hinojosa rounded the corner onto a busier street. She was running with a purpose in mind, knowing where she was going. A left, then two rights, never breaking stride, and then finally she darted into an open courtyard that fronted a low-slung brick office building. Behind the building though was a large corrugated metal warehouse. She dashed through an open gate, which led to the side of the building. As they turned the corner to the back, there were a dozen blue trucks backed up and off or onloading packages by way of a long loading dock. The cabs were truncated, not like the extended cabs with sleeping sections Harwood typically saw in America. Taut blue canvases were tied on either side of each truck, allowing the vehicle to operate as a flatbed or a fully enclosed cargo carrier. Sliding warehouse doors were up, twelve open mouths being fed by men shuttling boxes back and forth. The basics of logistics. Product in and product out. Exhaust fumes billowed, smelling sweet and noxious. Men shouted in a strange language. Everyone was focused on their task at hand.

They ducked behind the raised cement loading dock.

"Airport?" Harwood asked.

"Yes. If we can get there, I have a contact."

"I think we bought time regarding Stone and Weathers, but not sure about who else is chasing us."

"We don't have much time," Hinojosa replied.

Harwood said nothing. He nodded and thought. She was telling him that the U.S. government had communicated to Azerbaijan that she and Harwood were enemies of the state. The Team Valid mission was a liability now, he presumed. Something somewhere must have gone wrong. Maybe it was the tossed rifle in Crimea, or perhaps it was the giant cluster in Iran. Or maybe it was none of those things; it could be something different altogether. There was an apparent attempt to blame the Camp David Ambush on Samuelson. He would bet his entire paycheck that Samuelson didn't have anything to do with that operation. That he was used as a pawn. Sammie's traumatic brain injury had never fully healed. His connection to Carly Masters, who was murdered in the ambush, might be a clue, he didn't know. Then there was the missing laptop. So much to unwind and he was driven to get back to the United States and figure it all out. Clear Samuelson's name and protect Hinojosa, his only sibling.

"That truck. I'm seeing a lot of FedEx boxes," Harwood said.

He pointed at the nearest vehicle. "They've finished loading. The driver is getting out to lock his ramp door."

Hinojosa nodded in agreement, though she seemed hesitant.

"Need to move now," Harwood said. The driver exited his vehicle on the side opposite them. The loader had turned his back and was walking into the warehouse. Harwood dashed to the passenger side door of the truck. Hinojosa followed. He opened the door and they both tumbled into the tightly confined space. There was no room to hide. The driver would be back in seconds and Harwood's only option was to draw down on the man. He retrieved his pistol and handed it to Hinojosa, who handled it easily. Harwood removed his knife and pushed back into Hinojosa, creating as much room as possible for him to maneuver.

The driver's door opened. The man opened and ignited a Scorch Torch butane lighter and held it to the tip of a half-smoked cigar. He puffed a few times and cigar smoke billowed all around him. He shut the flame and dropped the lighter into the pocket of his blue work shirt. He was wearing black dungarees and brown square-toed work boots that would serve him well in a street fight. He looked down and lifted his left foot onto the platform before hoisting himself into the truck in a well-practiced move. He was a stocky man with thick forearms and a wide neck. His eyes focused on his foot placement then the steering wheel. His large hand reached out and gripped the wheel as he pulled himself into the driver's seat in a smooth move that had him slamming shut the driver's door with his left hand simultaneously. He puffed on the cigar, smoke filling the cab now.

His head snapped to the right and he shouted something that sounded like, "Sam kimsan!" He reached for the cigar, grabbed it and tried to stab it into Harwood's face, but Harwood's hand was a cobra striking. His left hand clasped the man's considerable forearm, the orange tip of the cigar inches from his face, and his right hand thrust the knife toward his neck. Harwood pushed the driver's hand back toward his own face and before the cigar tip reached him, he dropped it into his lap and the tip slid into his crotch. The man's face contorted in pain as he stood up and the cigar rolled beneath his ass onto the seat. Harwood forced the man down, as Hinojosa reached over and grabbed the cigar, tossing it from the window.

"Drive," Harwood said. His voice was calm, forceful. The man's eyes bulged out and flitted from Harwood to the windshield. "Drive," Harwood reiterated. He tapped the steering wheel with the knife and then pointed it straight ahead, indicating the direction he wanted the man to drive. Hinojosa's hand shot forward with a wad of cash. The top bill was yellow and purple with the numbers and letters: 100 MANAT. There appeared to be at least ten in the stack. One thousand manat? Harwood had no idea how much that might be. Judging by the man's wide eyes, it was a decent chunk.

"Manat. One thousand," Hinojosa said.

After some hesitation, the man moved his eyes from the money to Harwood and reached out as he had most likely done a million times to crank the engine, shift the gear, pump the clutch, and press the accelerator pedal. The truck lurched forward with a jerk. Harwood pressed the tip of the knife against the man's neck and said, "Drive!"

He had no idea if the driver understood any word he said, but the intent was obvious. The truck began rolling smoothly forward along a feeder road away from the busy warehouse. Another truck passed by them from the opposite direction. The oncoming driver was too busy navigating the narrow lanes to notice Harwood and Hinojosa.

"*Harada?*" the driver said. His eyes were set in the distance.

It was a question and the only question he could possibly be asking, Harwood figured, was: Where did they want to go?

"Airport," Harwood said.

The man seemed to understand as he nodded and kept the truck rolling toward the gated entrance. Harwood's throat tightened when he saw the guardhouse with a uniformed man on the opposite side, checking the incoming vehicles. There was no truck in front of them in the exit lane and Harwood had no idea if the driver was typically required to stop and provide a bill of lading or invoice. He had done enough moves in the military to know that the paperwork was always triple checked despite the fact they still lost half your stuff.

"Drive," Harwood said, pressing his back against Hinojosa and the rear of the cab. In case the guard came to the exit side he wanted to be coincident with the line of sight. Also, he wanted Hinojosa to have a clear shot at the guard, should he climb up the platform and look in.

The driver slowed at the narrow passage lane that, once they were beyond the gated entrance, would provide them some freedom of maneuver. He continued slowing. Harwood repeated, "Drive. One thousand manat." The man slowed some more. He reached onto the dashboard and retrieved some papers, nodding at Harwood, holding them up as if to say, "Just let me drop these off like I'm supposed to."

Hinojosa lifted the pistol over Harwood's shoulder, aiming it at the man. He felt her arm resting on his shoulder while the hand with the money rested on his leg. The man glanced at Harwood to show him the papers again and his face froze when he saw Hinojosa aiming his pistol at his face. For a second, it appeared he would drive the truck into the guard shack.

"Drive!" Harwood said.

The man focused, corrected, and slowed some more. The truck came to a stop. The man handed the papers over through the window to an outstretched hand. Normal transaction. Done a thousand times a day. Nothing to see here. Still, Harwood pressed the knife into the man's throat just beneath his jawline. Some words were exchanged. The knife pressed deeper.

The man rapped the door twice, causing Hinojosa to tense. He felt Hinojosa's forearm go rigid and her body jump. Harwood hoped the door knocks were the standard signal that everything was good to go. The driver carefully turned and pushed the gearshift, easing through the gate. Harwood's stomach unclenched with every revolution of the wheels, every shift of the gears, and every increase in acceleration.

They were on the highway, blending with other cars and trucks, heading east. Harwood always had a good sense of direction ingrained in his DNA. Even as a kid on the foster farm, he studied the sunrise and sunset, comparing summer to fall to winter to spring. Etched in his hard drive were the cardinal directions and the ability to wake up and automatically know his north from south, east from west. When he had run away after killing Lindsay's attacker in the barn, he ran south, then west into the mountains, and finally found a lady willing to give him a ride. He didn't have a gun or cash to pay the woman, but she seemed kind enough to drop him in Hagerstown. From there he slipped into Harpers Ferry, West Virginia, where he caught a train to Cleveland, Ohio. After that, he rode with a group of college kids to Chicago where he lived in a homeless shelter for two years, attended high school, and graduated with his GED. He never heard from his foster mother. She had either buried the man on her property or called the cops and they couldn't find him. His guess was that she dug a hole big enough for Lindsay and her assailant and used the tractor with some chains to drag them both into the grave, covered it up, and planted some seed on top. Foster kids were common run-aways and so Lindsay wouldn't be missed. It made Harwood sad to think about her forever interred with the man who tried to rape her and then killed her.

Blue signs with airplanes on them began appearing on a regular basis. They had been on the road for twenty minutes. Harwood had kept his eyes on the driver. He had made no sudden moves to get his cell phone, press an emergency signal, or secure a weapon. For all Harwood knew, the airport was on his route and he was going to make an easy one thousand manat.

"Where do we want to go?" he asked Hinojosa over his shoulder. "We're getting close."

"Arco Petroleum. I have a contact. They have a milk run to Dulles every other day," she whispered.

Harwood had mostly flown in military airplanes, often jumping out of them onto runways similar to the one here in Baku. The ground sloped away from them as the road followed a peninsula away from the big city of Baku to a more remote area full of prairie grass and sand-colored dirt. The road upon which they were traveling fed into the typical airport road network. Rental car returns. Arrivals. Departures. Some signs had English words on them. The runway was long with a single axis, from north to south, the prevailing winds most likely coming off the Caspian Sea.

"Over there," Hinojosa said. She was pointing at the big green-and-yellow sign near the south end of the runway.

In the rearview mirror a motorcycle raced alongside the truck. The driver looked to the right with curiosity, or perhaps hopeful that it was the police. A quick glance told Harwood that it was Weathers. There was a blood-soaked bandage wrapped around his left leg and a rifle strapped across his chest. Brazenly zipping through the streets of Baku, Weathers appeared hell-bent on killing Hinojosa and him. The mirrored face shield on the helmet prevented confirmation that it was Weathers, but the leg wound appeared to be from a shot and not a blast, which should have done much more damage.

And it meant that there had to be a redundancy tracker somewhere on either him or Hinojosa. There was an off chance that the gate guard at the warehouse called the police and Weathers intercepted the call, but then they would have seen police vehicles, also. This full-court press to prevent his escape first from Iran and now Azerbaijan meant that he and Hinojosa knew something that Stone and Weathers's superiors, whomever that might be, had to keep secret at all costs.

Weathers lifted his left hand, which held a pistol, and fired it. The passenger window shattered along with the mirror, which was their only way of detecting his location. Harwood was already in the process of switching seats to protect Hinojosa when the glass blew into his face. He shook his head and leaned out of the window to return fire.

Weathers had fallen back and looked like he was going to change lanes and attack the driver's side. Harwood fired three rounds, center mass of the motorcycle, which Weathers was using for protection by leaning over, chest parallel to the fuel tank and helmeted head just above the handlebars. It was a big-engine racing bike, though Harwood couldn't tell which make or model. All that mattered was it was working for Weathers.

He saw his shots create some sparks before the motorcycle disappeared behind the truck, which was doing about 50 mph. They were two miles from their destination and would be necessarily slowing down soon. He had to shake Weathers, so he leaned back across Hinojosa and the driver, who shouted something unintelligible.

Weathers was coming up tight on the driver's side, left hand aiming the pistol at Harwood's head, right hand revving the throttle to gain on them. The driver let go of the steering wheel and pulled his arms from underneath to overtop Harwood as Harwood was one-third out the window steadying his pistol. The grip was warm in his hand. His aim was steady. He squeezed the trigger just as Weathers fired two shots at him, both pinging off the steel cab next to his face. Harwood's shots hit the motorcycle gas tank. Fuel was spraying everywhere. Harwood fired into the machine, trying to create a spark or have the hot lead ignite the gas, but those tricks only worked in the movies.

Still, the gas was all over Weathers. Remembering the cigar, Harwood leaned back in and snatched the lighter from the driver's shirt pocket. He snapped it open, locked the flame in place, and leaned back out as Weathers was roaring toward them. The lighter was heavy, solid steel encasement. They were doing sixty miles an hour and about to hit heavy traffic coming into the airport. Weathers's gun was up and firing.

Harwood tossed the lighter, calculating Weathers's speed, their speed, and the slipstream of the truck. The lighter hit the handle-bar, flipped into the air like a field goal hitting the goalpost cross-bar. Weathers's helmet moved just enough for Harwood to know that his opponent saw the danger he was in. Weathers used his pistol hand to swat at the lighter. He connected and it skittered into the street.

A spark of flame, though, caught on his hand and began to climb up his arm, as if he were a Hollywood stunt actor. Weathers was shaking his arm vigorously, yet the flame continued to eat at the gas. The motorcycle caught on fire.

Harwood aimed his pistol.

The driver swerved to avoid traffic, giving Harwood no shot.

"There!" Hinojosa shouted at the driver. She pointed at the Arco Oil hangar just inside the airport fence line.

The driver swerved to make the turn and slowed as he

followed the cloverleaf. He pulled up to the gate, which was closed. Harwood snagged his rucksack from the passenger well as he and Hinojosa jumped from the truck. The driver wasted no time in backing away, turning and heading most likely to the nearest police station.

Hinojosa pressed the intercom box and said, "Valerie Hinojosa for Emmanuel, please."

After a few seconds, a hurried voice came on the intercom.

"Valerie, the plane is about to take off!"

"We are here. Tell them to stop," she said.

The gate opened, and they ran toward the hangar. This was a United States company, but it was still sovereign Azerbaijani land. They weren't in the clear yet.

The man who must have been Emmanuel came out of the hangar driving a golf cart. Hinojosa and Emmanuel exchanged a look, something that was not lost on Harwood. He looked over his shoulder. Nothing coming, yet.

They jumped in the golf cart and Emmanuel raced them around the side of the building to the Airbus A300 that had a pushback tug tow bar connected to the front landing gear. A man was opening the door and another was driving the stairwell to the door.

Harwood and Hinojosa were up the stairs and into the cargo airplane that was outfitted with three rows of empty personnel seats. Behind those were pallets with equipment strapped atop them. He dumped his rucksack in one of the seats, studied the aircraft.

The plane pushed back, taxied, and screamed down the runway.

He looked out the small window. Blue lights were circling an accident on the highway to the airport. Weathers. Did he make it out alive? And where was Stone?

All that mattered now was that Weathers and Stone weren't on this airplane.

Harwood turned his head, never one to discount the improbable. Stone wasn't in the seats and no one appeared to be hiding among the pallets. To be sure, he walked to the rear of the aircraft, inspecting behind each one. The pallets contained pipes, cables, and engines. This was a maintenance run back to the United States.

Neither Stone nor Weathers was hiding behind the pallets.

He sat next to Hinojosa as the plane gained altitude over the Caspian Sea, the blue lights of the police vehicles replaced by the azure blue waters of the inland sea.

"Who's Emmanuel?"

"FBI field agent," she said.

"I saw the look. He's more than that."

She was staring at her lap then tilted her eyes up at Harwood.

"Emmanuel Hinojosa. He's my ex. FBI. Gets around this part of Asia."

Harwood looked away and thought about it. Big coincidence? What did it matter? They were on an airplane flying to the United States.

"I'm glad he was there for you," Harwood said.

"Not an accident. I gave him a heads-up when I got alerted that our cover was gone."

Harwood nodded.

"So you're Sammie's sister?"

"Yes. I'm on the list. Bronson gave me a heads-up."

"Bronson?" Harwood smiled. His first legitimate feeling of ease in forty-eight hours.

"Deke's a good man," Hinojosa said. "Cut him some slack."

"We shall see," Harwood said.

The cockpit door opened as the plane leveled into a smooth glide heading west.

The pilot was a tall, gray-haired man wearing a white short-sleeve shirt and black slacks. He smiled and said, "Get comfortable. Fourteen hours to Dulles. Understand you're a military couple returning from your honeymoon?"

Harwood almost bust out laughing. That was the cover her ex-husband had provided the Arco team?

"Yes, thank you. Just hiking through the Caucusus," Hinojosa said.

"Well, congratulations, and I'm glad you caught us before takeoff."

The pilot smiled again, nodded, and then opened the latrine door.

The steward stepped forward and provided them drinks and food. Steak, cheese, eggs, and dinner rolls. Harwood and Hinojosa ate it all.

In between bites, Hinojosa said, "So, do you want to know what's next?"

"I know what's next. I'm going to kill every son of a bitch who framed Sammie and find out who actually killed him."

Hinojosa stared at him, possibly frightened by the ferocity of his words.

"But first let me borrow your phone. I need to talk to some-one."

Hinojosa handed him the satellite phone that had a good signal. He made the call.

"Reaper!"

"Hey, Monisha, just checking on you."

"I'm good. I'm here with Sergeant Major now. Where you at?"

"Ask me the right way and I'll tell you."

He could feel Monisha rolling her eyes.

"Okay, where are you?"

"I'm on an airplane. Just wanted to check on you. Glad you're okay. Put the sergeant major on, please."

"Wait. I want to talk some," she said. "I miss our nightly talks."

"I miss them, too, but I'm kind of in a rush." His voice was clipped and Monisha got the picture.

"Talk." Sergeant Major Murdoch was a legend in the Ranger community and a man of few words.

"In some serious stuff. Team Valid turned on me. Headed where you sent me. Will need a secure ride to somewhere safe."

"Roger. Out."

He handed the phone back to Hinojosa.

"That your girl?" she asked.

"Yeah, Monisha's my fifteen-year-old ball of fury."

"Thought you said you'd never been married?"

He didn't recall saying that but responded, "I'm not, never have been. Found her in a bad situation a year ago and adopted her. Thought Sammie might have told you."

Hinojosa nodded and looked away. Harwood leaned back in his chair, thinking, *something's not right*, but sleep overcame him for almost the entire flight.

CHAPTER 15

Sloane Brookes was drinking a glass of wine at a trendy bar at the Wharf in southwest D.C.'s newly gentrified district. She sat across from Deke Bronson, the FBI agent in charge of the Camp David Ambush investigation.

He had suggested they meet, and him being something of a playboy, she agreed. Perhaps she could nudge him that fifty-one percent to be on her side, should anything untoward come to light. It was always good to have a hole card.

Her phone buzzed and displayed UNKNOWN CALLER.

Jessup. From whom a call was extraordinarily rare.

She had no desire to head back to her estate, get in her boat and travel to Tangier Island, so she didn't.

"Excuse me," she said to Bronson, who stood as she slid past him, her fingernail accidentally grazing his thigh. Bronson was physically fit and a sharp dresser. He had an open English spread white collar above a light blue shirt. He wore a silk sport coat that had to be either Canali or Zegna, cut perfectly to show off his

V-shaped physique. Perfectly creased dark slacks fell atop shiny-as-a-mirror burgundy Berluti Scritto slip-on loafers. She had been considering a way to get him in the sack when Jessup called.

She stepped outside and walked toward the Potomac River. Traffic zipped on the 14th Street bridge just a few hundred yards away. She was alone and feeling vulnerable. Her black Oscar de la Renta cocktail dress, which set her back five thousand dollars, rustled as she walked in her five-inch Louboutin heels. She was always leveraging her height to her advantage, but Bronson appeared almost as tall as her and not the least bit intimidated. He was a former marine, and that kind of turned her on.

But still, Jessup. He was a total buzzkill.

Just tell me, she texted to Jessup. He called, and she answered. Their communications, he assured her, were filtered through a secure server that bounced the data packets all over the world before being received on either end.

"Check Maximus Anon Twitter," he said.

She pulled up the Twitter account of the handle Maximus Anon, saw that his number of followers had fallen from one million plus to just under one hundred thousand. That wasn't the concern, though. He had just tweeted:

1. The #CampDavidAmbush is not what it seems. It's far worse. Follow my logic.

2. As you recall before I was shut down, I reported that Carly Masters had discovered something sinister within the Senate Intel Comm. It is my belief she gave this info to Army Ranger CPL Samuelson.

3. CPL Samuelson had a silver MacBook in the background of his FB live video feed. Reports are that the

FBI never found that MacBook. There are reports that @SloaneBrookes is missing a laptop. Brookes was on SIC.

4. Samuelson's best friend, Vick Harwood, aka The Reaper, is army Ranger sniper. Harwood was on mission called #TeamValid that U.S. government abandoned after Perza and Sultan families were killed.

5. The Reaper is nowhere to be found, but his name was leaked by the government to me. They want me to know and they want you to know. Why would they want this?

6. Well, just as Samuelson is the fall guy for the Camp David Ambush, the Reaper will be the fall guy for killing the Perza and Sultan families. Their deaths have already been confirmed by the Iranian and Russian governments.

7. But get this: there is no evidence that Perza and Sultan had anything to do with the Camp David Ambush, which makes us wonder, why would someone want their families killed?

8. It all goes back to Carly Masters. One unreported fact NO ONE is covering is the murder of Raafe Khoury, the "IT guy" for the Democrats. Khoury worked specifically for Sloane Brookes for a short time.

9. All magnetic compasses are all starting to point at Sloane Brookes.

Her stomach sank.

"Um, that's kind of specific and defamatory, don't you think?"

"I've tried to shut him down, but he must be running something inside Twitter, because he's still up," Jessup said.

"Remember, this is what I pay you for, though," Brookes said.

"I know. I'm trying, but this is bad," Jessup said. "I think this Reaper guy might have something to do with it, not sure."

"What makes you think that?"

"They didn't get him in Baku. He's on an airplane right now headed to Dulles. Weathers and Stone are messed up pretty bad, but they're on their way back, too. I got them an airplane."

She hung up. Bad was not what she needed right now. Everything she had carefully put together needed to stay glued together. This wasn't Crossfire Hurricane. This was nothing. There was no code name for this non-operation. It was her playing Machiavellian politics in an effort to get the upper hand. All was fair in love and war, as the saying went, and this country was at war with itself. High crimes were being overlooked. Threats directly against the president were okay in today's political environment.

She ran through what Jessup had told her and distilled it down to three points. First, the Reaper was a loose end that needed to go away. They had tried to nip that in the bud at the outset, but he had escaped. He had an adoptive daughter. Was there something they could do there? Some leverage? She thought so. Second, someone in Twitter was not cooperating with their longstanding unofficial policy to shut down conservative "conspiracy theorists." Who might that be? Could it be someone from the FBI? Could it be Bronson and might that be why he invited her tonight? Perhaps. She would play that by ear. Third, someone was feeding information from the government to Maximus Anon. Again, was it possible this was Bronson? Bronson had called to speak with her informally. Was he just hitting on her or was he investigating her? Trying to entrap her? She was accustomed to all the crazy conspiracy theories about her that were tossed around like a beach ball at a Jimmy Buffett concert. The idea that someone would seize upon any one of them—she was a lesbian, she was a man, she was an arms dealer, she was selling intelligence, she had a secret love child—and do anything beyond create more name buzz for her seemed ludicrous.

But she was concerned.

She texted Ravenswood: *Camera ready. Then meet at your place in an hour.*

He replied immediately, as he was trained to do. Fortunately for Brookes, Ravenswood was in the top-floor penthouse of the condo building next to the restaurant where she had met Bronson.

She walked back into the dimly lit establishment. It was flush with people of all walks and ages mingling, having dinner, laughing, and shouting. People were enjoying the area that used to be a fisherman's wharf. Seemed like a good upgrade.

"Everything okay?" Bronson asked, standing.

"Yes. As I prepare my campaign, I have more calls than I care to take. But this was essential. Seems we're polling well in some of the battleground states," she said. She placed her hand on his knee as they sat in chairs placed at ninety degrees. He looked at her hand then in her eyes. Based on the smoky gaze, Brookes knew what he wanted.

"I'm sure you are," he said.

"Tell me, Special Agent, don't you usually go for much younger women?" she asked him.

"I go for intelligent, beautiful women, and you get a solid checkmark in both of those boxes."

"Well said." Brookes smiled, flashing her perfect white teeth at him. She'd chosen a muted red lipstick that accentuated her smile.

"Seeing how we just met, though, and that I'm a gentleman, I'd like to get to know you a little bit, first."

"First? What's second?" she purred.

Bronson shifted in his seat, obviously aroused.

"I like to focus on one thing at a time," he said.

"So, what are we focusing on tonight?"

"Pick your poison," Bronson said. He smiled. He was a beautiful man, she thought. Shaved head. Caramel skin. Perfect smile. Piercing copper eyes. Stylish dresser.

"I prefer to focus on you," she said. "This is a pleasant surprise."

"Likewise. Where should we do all this focusing you're suggesting?"

"I'm sure you have a place in mind," she said.

"Well, I live upstairs. We could always enjoy the view along the river."

"I'm following your lead tonight," she said.

He laid a one hundred dollar bill on the table, nodded at the waitress, who had probably seen him do this move more than once. They took the elevator up to the penthouse and stepped directly into his large apartment. It smelled new. Freshly painted and lacquered. Pristine condition. The view was better than the one Ravenswood had one building over. They stepped onto the balcony and she leaned against the rail. He pressed up behind her and whispered in her ear.

"Beautiful women are my weakness."

She could feel him pressing into her back. He was definitely excited. He placed one hand on her waist and pulled her to him, as he slid his other hand around her throat.

She turned so that she was facing him, the hand now on her back and the other cupping her neck. He pulled her to him and they kissed. It was a perfect kiss. She was buzzing with excitement. He was deft and gentle, but still firm and seemed to be on the verge of forceful. Mystery combined with anticipation.

They held the kiss as he slid her dress up her legs and tucked the hem inside her thong. He ran a thumb along her wetness and she shivered. She unzipped his pants and was surprised to find he was commando. He spun her around slowly and slid her thong to the side as he entered her.

There, on the balcony, they did what Sloane Brookes liked to do—have sex with good-looking, powerful men. This was her secret and she didn't care if every camera in the world was watching.

Plus, and more importantly, she was compromising the man in charge of investigating the Camp David Ambush.

She closed her eyes and rode the wave of pleasure, felt him quicken, and they both released, breathing heavily. He leaned across her back, pulled her hair, and made one final thrust, a knight skewering an opponent.

Afterward, they were on his sofa, drinking sparkling water.

"You're welcome to spend the night," he said.

"I'd love to," she lied. "But I have business to attend to. I'm hopeful we can repeat this soon . . . and often."

"Your wish. My command," he said, pointing from her to him.

"I doubt that. You seemed pretty commanding."

He walked her to the elevator, they kissed, the doors opened, and she stepped in. Pressing the lobby button, she turned and looked at him. His eyes followed her until the doors snapped shut.

What was that look? Conquering hero? Satisfaction? This was as close to a random hookup that she had had in a long time, maybe even since her college days.

She left the lobby of Bronson's apartment building and received a text from Jessup as she was stepping into the elevator to Ravenswood's apartment.

BRONSON MADE A PHONE CALL

AS SOON AS YOU LEFT.

K. WHO?

TRACING IT. DC NUMBER.

TELL ME.

NAME BLOCKED. CAN'T GET IT.

MAXIMUS ANON?

MAYBE.

ANY ADDRESS?

LET ME WORK IT.

K

She stepped into Ravenswood's apartment.

"Did you get that?"

"Did I get it? Yes. Full facial pictures. You shouldn't have acted like you enjoyed it so much, though," he said. He showed her his SVR camera and multiple close-up pictures of her and Bronson obviously being intimate on his balcony.

"Who said I was acting?"

Ravenswood paused.

"Don't be jealous. You know I use my men for my purposes."

"Well, this is big. He's the pivot point on the Camp David thing."

Jessup called this time.

"The number he called was someone named Maxwell Winsome. He's former army intelligence and was part of the DIA for a bit. I've traced his server activity. He's definitely Maximus Anon. He was wounded in Iraq, lost both legs, and now is on disability in an apartment near Capitol Hill. He sits at home, researches and posts on Twitter. I've got the address."

She wrote down the address and handed it to Ravenswood.

"Make it look like a suicide," she said. "Meanwhile, I'm calling my physician."

Ravenswood took his elevator down to the lobby, leaving Brookes
in his apartment. He was still seething from watching the FBI agent
rail her on the balcony just fifty yards away. Using his camera he
snapped away and captured the incriminating evidence as she had
requested. He had thought they were going to have a conversation and wanted to capture them talking. He even had a direc-
tional microphone, which only picked up her moaning and his
grunting.

He had his share of women, but as a marine who was now out
of the service, he was a possessive alpha male. He had nailed
Brookes right there in his apartment. She was good. He had felt
the power, the conquest. He was fucking a former U.S. senator
and current presidential candidate. It had been a rush, but she
had been cold, calculating. When they were finished, she was
up and out of the bed. It felt more like a transaction than making love, if it was possible to call it that.

The bitch of it was that he had the goods on Brookes. He knew
what she had done and continued to do. He hadn't wanted any
part of her scheme, but had gotten sucked in like he guessed so
many other men had. The interesting thing about the way Brookes
had let Bronson take her on the balcony was that even though she
said she enjoyed herself, she also appeared to struggle and resist,
then came the choke hold. Fine acting. She could legitimately
blackmail him for rape and expected that she would if it came to
that. *Meanwhile, I'm calling my physician.*

He shook off the anger and jealousy and retrieved a burner
phone from his blazer inside pocket and pressed Dial on the only
number in the address book.

"Hola."

"*El lugar habitual, ahora.*"

"*Sí.*"

He snapped the phone shut and walked four blocks to the Metro. Took the Orange Line to East Falls Church. Keeping his ball cap pulled low over his head, he exited the station and walked four blocks into the dilapidated neighborhood of small, post-World War II, low-slung brick ramblers. He spotted the watchers, who he hoped had been alerted he was on the way. They liked his money and he liked their results.

One of the young Hispanic men held a cell phone to his ear as Ravenswood walked down the street. He felt the eyes peering at him from behind the shuttered blinds. He'd been here before, a few times, only when he needed something unsavory done.

The porch light on the next house flickered twice. That was the signal to walk two houses beyond and hook into a small gravel alley behind the second house. There was a detached brick garage that had a recently whitewashed one-car garage door. On the side of the structure was a white door that was cracked partially open.

Ravenswood approached, feeling the two men close in behind him, ninjas quietly following. He rapped lightly on the door and someone pulled it open. The two men behind him closed quickly. He stepped inside and was staring at five hardened MS-13 gang members, tattoos crawling all over their faces, necks, arms, and chests. A couple bared evil grins, while two men in the back stood stone-faced with their arms crossed. One was seated and sucking on a giant bong.

Exactly what he needed: to be in a room full of stoned stone-cold killers from one of MS-13's most hardened *clicas*.

"*Dinero,*" said the man with the giant MS-13 stamped on his forehead. He was taller than the others and seemed to be the alpha among alphas.

Ravenswood retrieved ten thousand dollars, knowing this was only the opening bid.

He felt the air moving behind him when an arm circled his neck and placed him in a vise-grip choke hold. The move was not unexpected, so he remained loose. He had intentionally brought an older burned military Beretta pistol, knowing it would be taken in the entry. There was no avoiding the meet. MS-13 wanted their money delivered in person. There was a reasonable probability you wouldn't walk out alive if you didn't bring enough cash. Ravenswood knew the game was typically about three pat downs. He had forty thousand dollars total dispersed amongst his two pants pockets, his two inner coat pockets, and his hand.

Two men approached, one smiling and showing that his lips and inner gums had been tattooed. He was missing a few teeth and had gold caps on his incisors.

He took the money and laughed.

"*Diez* mil? Brodda', wat you tinking? Las' jobe was *treinta* mil."

"*Sí*," Ravenswood said. "This is an easier job."

They expected some type of negotiation, so he gave it to them. It was all part of the process. A pair of hands from behind wrenched the pistol from his hip holster and held it to his head. The man whispered, "Muthafuka" in his ear. They were swarming him like maggots, hands and stale, nasty breath pouring over him. Spanish and broken English words tumbled over one another into a low crowd noise. Soon, they had all fifty thousand dollars and his pistol. He had left his wallet at home and taped his Metro card on the inside of his sport coat.

"*Muy bien*," the tall man said. "Come."

He walked past the man sitting on the natty sofa and still hitting the bong. The tall man walked him from the living room into one of the bedrooms that had been converted to an office. A large, shirtless man with ripped muscles sat with his arms folded in front of a gray metal desk with a shiny new MacBook. The man had full tat sleeves, but his chest was tattoo-free save two hearts with arrows on each pectoral, one that read PADRE and the other MADRE. In the corner of the room were three AR-15s and two M4s with silencers, all most likely stolen military equipment.

"Hector makes the call," the tall man said in decent English.

"Forty thousand?" Hector said, arms crossed, muscles pushing on muscles.

"Simple job," Ravenswood said.

"No such thing," Hector countered. "For thirty we took care of the IT guy. I watch the news. Follow certain . . . clients . . . on Twitter. Your girl is in trouble."

The last thing Ravenswood expected was that Hector was a social media expert, but he didn't know why he suspected he wasn't. Everyone's information was so public today it only made sense for a team of professional assassins to monitor all of the outlets, Twitter, Facebook, and Instagram.

"No trouble," Ravenswood said.

Hector smiled. "Then why are you here, my friend? For the second time in less than two weeks."

He paused, could feel himself start to sweat a bit, which was not a good thing to do in front of these ruthless killers.

"Another business transaction," Ravenswood said.

"Tell me."

Ravenswood laid out the target and what he wanted done to the man.

"Suicide is not our thing. We are more . . . brutal," Hector said.

"We need suicide," Ravenswood said, as if ordering from a menu.

"Then this forty thousand is a down payment and we get another forty when we do the job."

"That's ridiculous," Ravenswood said.

"What is ridiculous is that you think you can dump your dirty laundry here with us, have us do a flawless job, and you never follow up with a bonus or tip. So, we will do your job and then you will, within twenty-four hours, bring another forty thousand to this exact location. Or we can take you to the other room."

One of the MS-13 teams had shown him "the other room" when he was there two weeks ago. Nooses hung from a steel pipe. Black bloodstains inked the floor and walls. It was a torture and murder room, no question.

"I think that's fair," Ravenswood said.

"We will take care of this guy," Hector said. "And then you will pay us the other half. If not?" He shrugged and looked through the open door at the closed door across the hallway. "We can't promise a quick death, but we can promise death eventually."

Ravenswood felt a tingle crawl up his spine, like a spider.

"Deal," he said. "Twenty-four hours."

Hector nodded.

"We never discussed a rush job. So, it will be an even one hundred thousand."

Ravenswood nodded. He knew he wasn't getting out of there alive if he argued. That was the risk in doing business with MS-13. They were brutal, which was also the reward.

"Of course. And there may be another opportunity soon."

Hector smiled as the tall man escorted him out.

As he stepped onto the gravel alley, one of the gangbangers tossed his pistol. It landed with a scraping noise.

"Piece of shit," he said.

Ravenswood picked up his pistol and retraced his steps to the Metro. His burner phone buzzed in his pocket. It was a text from the MS-13 house.

This guy next?

It was a picture of Vick Harwood, the Reaper. How did they know? More than a simple gang, less than the mafia, MS-13 had evidently learned the value of mining intelligence. It was more than a simple question. The text was a statement. *We are inside your head. We know what you are thinking. You have every reason to fear us. We can find you.*

He stared at Harwood's face and texted in return, *Yes.*

CHAPTER 16

Harwood awoke when the plane landed at Dulles International Airport, thirty miles west of Washington, D.C., in the Virginia countryside near midnight of the same day they had taken off from Baku.

Hinojosa was awake, holding her smartphone, which was buzzing and chiming.

"Holy shit," she said.

He rubbed his eyes. "What?"

"This Twitter guy has posted this entire theory about what happened at Camp David and it's so real."

"You're on Twitter?"

"I mean, everybody has to be nowadays. It's how Smart communicates. Pole-vaults over all the media and just puts it out there."

"Makes sense. So, what's this dude's theory?"

"Basically, that former Senator Brookes from Virginia is behind it. That she needed Carly killed because she found out something about her. He mentions a missing laptop and connects it to an IT guy who was killed."

Harwood thought about the MacBook. He had not mentioned that to anyone other than Bronson and Hinojosa, both with the FBI.

"Killing someone is no simple thing," Harwood said.

"Unless you have someone else do it for you," Hinojosa countered.

"I get that, but still. Twelve family members and another ten Secret Service agents killed in that ambush. That's a terrorist attack, not a hit. And the lack of morals that would come with that. Who would kill that many people just to protect themselves?"

Hinojosa looked at him. The plane stopped outside the Arco hangar.

"You're cute, Vick. I like your innocence. You're a killing machine, but you kill in the name of righteousness. You've operated at the soldier level. I've operated at the political level. Two different animals. These people will do anything to save themselves and preserve their power. It's a drug. And they kill for it."

He nodded.

"Okay."

Harwood felt a rush, as if the escape from Iran and Baku were back on. Perhaps it was? He didn't know what to expect now that they were on U.S. soil. A U.S. government–sanctioned team of assassins was trying to kill him and Hinojosa. They wanted him dead because he knew too much about the operations in Crimea and Iran, he presumed. And they wanted Hinojosa dead because she was Samuelson's sister. He hadn't actually seen any proof that she was related to Samuelson, but he had taken her at face value given the intensity of everything else that had taken place. They had been chased hard by Stone and Weathers. As he had slept and drifted in and out of dreams, he found himself thinking about Samuelson and why he might have been framed. If what Hinojosa said was true, that Sammie and Carly were an item, then it was possible she had told him her secrets, possibly even invited him to the outing at Camp David that day. Harwood remembered that Samuelson had been excited during their last few phone calls, as if life was finally looking up for him.

But why make him the shooter? It made no sense. ISIS was proud to take credit for their terrorist attacks and they had yet to do so regarding the Camp David Ambush. He remembered the number of people who genuinely hated the current president and those who also truly admired the man. What percentage of those who hated him would actually slaughter family members of the President's cabinet? It was the work of a terrorist, for sure, but foreign or domestic?

The names that had been given to them produced no further leads. Was the intelligence community following up and fleshing out the details? He'd been on assignment practically since the beginning and without an opportunity to analyze anything about the original attack that put everything in motion.

The facts as he knew them were that Stone and Weathers dumped him in Iran, presumably leaving him behind to die and as evidence of American involvement. Their pursuit confirmed that he wasn't supposed to make it back alive to the United States. A second bothersome fact was the additional person at the Perza compound in Iran, a man who looked exactly like Basier Perza, Laleh's twin, and the Iranian terrorist that the FBI claimed was involved in the Camp David Ambush. There was very little chance he had conducted the raid at Camp David and then returned that rapidly to his family compound. What did that say about the accuracy of the reports on the shooters? Or their mission, for that matter? Lastly, he knew for certain that Samuelson had a MacBook in the Facebook Live suicide and that MacBook was missing when he arrived on the scene.

What did all of this mean? He wasn't sure but knew that he needed answers. His life was in jeopardy, and by extension, he guessed, so was Monisha's. If these people were willing to randomly kill family members at Camp David, they would come back to his home in Columbus, Georgia. While Command Sergeant Major Murdoch and his family were tough, they couldn't be on guard twenty-four hours a day. He would call Monisha and Murdoch in the morning.

He knew that clearing Samuelson was the only path to the truth, which would, as the saying went, potentially set him free. Rarely one to think about politics, Harwood considered the ramifications of the political conflict raging in the country today. Polar extremes in a struggle for the ideological identity of the nation. As a black man he had his own struggles and views but kept them mostly to himself. It was his vote and nobody's business who he supported. Everything being so public today, there was an expectation that you brand yourself as either left or right. Liberal or conservative. As a soldier, he again had his own perspective on American foreign policy. He didn't like it when a commander in chief announced timelines and troop deployments. He believed President Smart was wise not to disclose numbers of deploying troops and where they were going to fight.

All of that said, he was a patriot. He loved the United States and all that it stood for. He knew that some had globalist agendas, which meant erasing the boundaries and watering down the liberties that every serviceman and -woman fought hard for. Still, he didn't believe that framing Samuelson had anything to do with politics, per se. Samuelson had information and someone determined he needed to die. That someone could either outright kill

Samuelson or get creative and use him for a purpose beyond just eliminating a threat.

Who would want that done and why?

That was his starting point.

Turning to Hinojosa, he said, "Find an address on this Twitter guy and let's head there first."

"Already got it. He lives in southeast D.C. near the baseball stadium. Registered to Maximus Anon, LLC," she said. "The trick is going to be getting out of here."

"A company?" Harwood asked.

"We will find out."

Blue lights were flashing in the distance, racing their way. The ramp opened and Harwood slung his rucksack over his shoulder. The Arco pilots and steward seemed oblivious to their status or predicament, which was fine with Harwood.

He raced down the steps and saw the Signature Terminal, knowing it was the private jet facility he'd landed at just a few days ago.

"I've got an Uber coming in three minutes," Hinojosa said.

"Uber? You're broadcasting where we are. Your credit card is lighting up. The FBI GPS trackers are pinging. And they're alerting the cops that we are here by using some bullshit narrative."

"Hadn't thought of that. You slept, I couldn't."

They were walking toward the Signature VIP door when a black sedan pulled up in the parking lot on the opposite side of the gate. A G550 Gulfstream was taxiing up to the left of the Airbus A300. The police lights were still a few minutes away, the sirens wailing. He had no idea if the police were coming for them or if it was some random act. Harwood led Hinojosa into the private jet terminal and quickly escorted her out the front into the parking lot.

"Follow me," he said. They approached the Town Car from the

rear. He heard a snick as the driver unlocked the doors and stepped outside. He was an older black gentleman wearing a black suit and white shirt. He noticed Harwood and Hinojosa and squinted.

"Who's your principal?" Harwood asked, stepping up to the man quickly.

"Right this way, sir."

"What?" Hinojosa asked.

"You're not the only one with connections," Harwood said. "Murdoch did this. Our driver is actually an infantryman from the Old Guard at Fort Myer near the Pentagon."

They were in the Town Car and sliding through the gate, hooking a series of lefts and rights that put them on the Dulles Toll Road toward Washington, D.C. The police lights passed them coming into the airport traffic network as they were leaving it. The car seats were black leather. A smoky divider separating them from the driver lowered.

"I'm Jonesy," the driver said. "Murdoch calls, Jonesy delivers. No questions. I imagine you're somebody to him, which makes you somebody to me. Where we going?"

"Thanks, Jonesy," Harwood said. "Nationals baseball stadium will be just fine."

The driver's face crinkled with a smile.

"Roger that."

The sliding glass window rose and gave Harwood and Hinojosa some privacy to talk and plan.

"Tell me about this Twitter guy," Harwood said.

"Not much to know. Twitter allows you to have fake accounts, fake names, whatever. He goes by Maximus Anon. Some people get doxed—outed—but the good ones are able to stay one step ahead of the pursuers trying to embarrass people, silence them, etc."

"Doxed?"

"Internet slang for someone uncovering an alias and exposing them. Usually relates to government bureaucrats just being vocal on Twitter or maybe some other forum when some asshole comes along and uncovers their identity and informs the boss or supervisor. People have been fired, especially if you vocally support the current president."

"That's messed up. What happened to the First Amendment?"

Hinojosa chuckled. "Yeah, well, its application seems episodic."

"Is this guy friend or foe?" Harwood was trying to steer the conversation toward something he could more readily understand. He wasn't on social media other than to post the occasional Instagram photo of him and Monisha, mainly because she wanted it out there that she was related to "the Reaper."

"We don't know, but it's more likely that he's neutral. A lot of these guys are trying to protect the Constitution. There has been considerable erosion of privacy rights, as Operation Crossfire Hurricane showed us. So there's this loose-knit cabal of researchers with hidden identities. Some parody an elected official. Some are more serious or ominous. Some, like Maximus Anon, are brazen."

"So more than likely, he'll be neutral," Harwood said.

"More than likely, but he may be pissed that we've found his house. If he doesn't want his true identity uncovered, then we can imagine how he'll feel about us showing up on his doorstep."

"If it's his doorstep."

"There's that," Hinojosa agreed.

Forty-five minutes later it was nearly 2 A.M. and the streets of Southeast, Washington, D.C., were quiet, but not empty. The shaded separator came down and Jonesy said, "Be safe."

"Roger that. You, too."

Jonesy nodded and his right hand flicked out with a card.

"Ever need a favor in this area, give me a call. I don't know who you are or what you're doing, but Murdoch saved my life in Iraq so I'll be there when he or anyone he supports needs me."

"You're a good man, Jonesy. I'll pass that along to Sergeant Major," Harwood said.

Jonesy shook his head. "No need. He knows, but thanks."

They jumped into the pleasant morning mist, a slight wind blowing off the Anacostia River, just beyond the stadium. Tall buildings surrounded the stadium, as if they were all leaning over trying to get a view inside. Random cars motored by with purpose; no one cruised this part of Washington, D.C., ever, much less at 2 A.M.

"That way," Hinojosa said, looking at her phone.

Harwood led them across M Street, Southeast, beyond high-rise condominiums, and into a series of two- and three-story D.C.-style brownstones with flat rooftops. The streets had a planned-community feel to them. Small trees were planted every ten yards along the small yards. Every home had a version of a low white picket fence. Interstate 395 hummed with light traffic less than a mile to the north. Beyond that the Capitol rose from the teeming rooftops like a morning sun lifting above the ocean.

"Next block," Hinojosa said.

"Wait," Harwood replied. He held his hand across Hinojosa, blocking her movement. Then he pulled her down.

There were two cars parked on the street less than half a block from them. Heads were moving back and forth, as if they were chatting. The windows were slightly fogged. Enough to write something in, Harwood thought, which meant they had been shut off for a while.

"Two cars. Count about six guys, three in each, including drivers. Where's our target?"

"Right around the corner from them. I mean directly around. Two houses down."

A car came around the corner, sweeping them with its head-lights. It stopped, and two men poured out. Harwood stood and stepped in front of Hinojosa while drawing his pistol and knife in opposing hands.

The men were tattooed and scarred. They were baring teeth, looking like inked-up gargoyles, lips rolled back, teeth bared, muscles prominent. Like pit bulls without leashes, they leapt toward Harwood, two on one. Harwood sliced up with his knife and caught one man across the jaw, spewing blood everywhere. He spun and landed a back kick into the attacker on his right. The man rolled toward Hinojosa and was up and leaping at her. Harwood pistol-whipped the first man, his head as hard as concrete. Two more slaps with the pistol and he went down. He spun around to find Hinojosa and the second man squared off in a knife duel, circling like two wrestlers. Where Hinojosa had gotten the knife, he didn't know, but was glad she had one. Maybe three seconds had passed since the whole thing started. He lifted his pistol and shot the man squaring off with Hinojosa then whirled in time to put three rounds into the windshield of the car careening their way. Its tires lurched up onto the curb and sent the car airborne. It landed with a thud on the first attacker that Harwood had knocked unconscious. The car bottomed out and spun into a telephone pole, dragging the man's body beneath. If not for the pole, the car might have slammed Harwood into the brick wall behind him.

Hinojosa cleared the dead gang member of a knife and Glock. Harwood checked the driver's seat. One of his bullets had clipped the neck of the driver; the carotid artery was pumping blood out of the side like oil from a quart jug.

"This was a diversion," Harwood said. "They were rear secu-rity. These guys were sent to get the Twitter guy."

Two blocks down the four MS-13 assassins were out of their

two cars, drivers remaining at the wheels. Two were looking in their direction and two were headed around the block. Like their dead brethren, these two men were wearing jeans and no shirts. They walked quickly, then began jogging, then transitioned to a full two-block sprint. Each was carrying a gun. Harwood's shots had been "silenced," but they were still loud enough to wake the neighbors. They had maybe five minutes to escape the area before the police came, if that.

Harwood and Hinojosa bolted to the right into an alley. Hinojosa kept running, the rabbit, as Harwood pressed into a small doorway alcove before the attackers pinwheeled and followed into the narrow darkness. As the first man approached, Harwood lashed out with his knife, blade out running along his forearm. The man's momentum carried him forward, but Harwood knew that he had scored a direct hit on the carotid artery. Blood was spewing like water from a cut high-pressure hose.

Harwood's momentum carried him into a frontal collision with the second man. He sliced at the man's gun carrying hand, causing him to slow. He was confused, naked, without his weapon, so he retrieved a knife and locked on to Harwood in an odd wrestling move, like a front headlock. Both men had knives that were swinging wildly like two pendulums sparking off one another. Harwood's rucksack made his movements more cumbersome and the MS-13 gangbanger was strong.

Harwood spun and slammed the man into the alcove where he had been hiding. He jabbed up with his knife, but the angle that they were both keeping on one another prevented him from gaining any leverage. They were A-framed, powerful arms locked against each other's shoulders, heads butting. Harwood's short uppercuts with the knife hand were blocked by the gang member's powerful forearm. He needed room to operate and this small area wasn't helpful. He spun and let go all at once, risking turning his back to the man for a brief moment. The gangbanger was quick, though, a street fighter, and landed two rabbit punches in Harwood's kidneys that felt like hammer blows. He was beyond the arc of the slashing knife, but just barely. Sirens began to blare loudly in the distance. Looking into the man's eyes, Harwood saw evil. The irises looked elliptical, like a deadly serpent's.

There was movement beyond his attacker.

Hinojosa.

She held up her pistol and fired twice. The man braced, as if punched in the back. He stood there for a moment, staring at Harwood, blood beginning to trickle from his mouth. The man smiled, blood gurgling against what few teeth he had. He raised his knife hand and waved it at Harwood, stepping forward like a robot with a dying battery.

Programmed to hate and kill, the man stumbled forward. Harwood retrieved his own pistol and shot him nearly point-blank between the eyes. Wasting no time, he ran to Hinojosa who had turned toward the address they had for Maximus Anon, the Twitter researcher. They were standing in a courtyard with four sets of back decks opening to the manicured lawn that was twenty yards across. Like a square, people in sixteen townhomes could potentially see what was happening. Hinojosa's gunshot, while necessary, was loud, and lights were flicking on.

"Second from the right," Hinojosa said. She was taking deep breaths, no doubt fueled by adrenaline.

They raced up onto the wooden deck of the townhome reportedly owned by Maximus Anon, LLC. The tax records did not show an individual's name associated with the ownership. Harwood had no idea what to expect. He slowed as they approached the back door, noticing two stories up and possibly a basement. Corrugated metal half-moons filled with gravel were protecting two small windows at ground level that peeked up at them.

Through the window off the deck, the radiant beams of flashlights crossed like dueling light sabers. They were too late. The MS-13 gang members were searching the house.

The doorknob rattled. The deadbolt unlocked. Harwood and Hinojosa pressed up against the sliver of brick wall in between the window and the door. The door opened inward and away from them. The flashlight made a quick sweep of the wooden planks, its arc barely grazing Harwood's boots. Someone shouted, "Hey!" from across the courtyard. The door shut, and two voices ricocheted in Spanish. Harwood looked at Hinojosa.

"Nobody's here. Let's haul ass." She translated for him.

The front door slammed shut. Harwood waited ten painful seconds, wondering if it was a trap. The car doors slammed. The sirens grew louder. Harwood opened the door. Hinojosa followed as they raced through the kitchen into a family and dining room. The house was neat, well kept. Furniture was perfectly arranged, like a showroom.

He said, "Check upstairs, I'll take the basement."

Hinojosa flew up the stairs as Harwood opened the door that led into a darkened cellar. He flicked on the light switch, listening to Hinojosa's footsteps thunder above. He didn't like splitting up, but they had about thirty seconds to finish what they needed to do. Entering the basement, to the left was a laundry room with a large washbasin and white washer and dryer. To the right was a door and wall that looked like an add-on after construction. Harwood tried the doorknob but it was locked. He stabbed his knife into the drywall, carved a quick hole, and then punched his fist through the smaller opening to make a bigger one. His hand felt around for the inner knob, found it and twisted. He opened the door and shouldered through while awkwardly retrieving his arm.

Inside the room was a series of servers and monitors, like a hacker's wet dream. He spun through the room and took inventory.

No sign of anyone hiding anywhere. Something caught his eye. It was a small insignia decal on the side of one of the server racks. A red one-inch oval on the side of the black surface. He studied it for a second and recognized it immediately.

Semper fidelis. Always faithful.

The Marine motto.

No time left to research further, he raced up the steps in tune with Hinojosa's footfalls coming down. They met at the front door, opened and shot out like burglars chased by an alarm.

Across the street was a similar warren of townhomes. They fled through an alley as police cars screeched to a halt on the side road where the MS-13 gang cars had been parked. They sprinted at full throttle through two more neighborhoods, crossed under I-395, drifted farther east, toward Anacostia, and found a public housing project that fronted Southeast Boulevard.

They dove into the open doors, raced up the steps until they were on the roof. A couple of homeless people were laid out in sleeping bags on one side, so Harwood and Hinojosa jogged twenty yards the other way and knelt. He knew they were treed in this building, but he felt that they had moved far enough away from the scene that they could stop, plan, and move.

"Anything upstairs?" Harwood asked.

"Two perfectly made beds. Closets filled with men's suits and classy women's clothing. If we'd had more time I would have tried on a few things."

Harwood nodded, smiled. First joke in a while. A good sign.

"The basement had servers and computers in it. Almost like a hacker lived in there, but as we were running the thought occurred to me that someone could be punching into that system from the outside. Like it's a place just to house the electronics."

"Could be, but why?"

"Obviously Maximus Anon doesn't want to be discovered," Harwood said.

"Doxed. So he or she has an important job," Hinojosa said.

Below them cars sped along the Southeast Freeway. Beyond that headlights cut a path across the Anacostia River on I-395. New construction was sprouting along the north bank. Half-built condominium buildings towered over the District Yacht Club. The piers poked into the water like bony fingers, the slips half full of assorted vessels from yachts to twenty-foot speedboats.

In the distance to the south and west, the flashing blue lights from the crime scene grew in number and intensity as the police gathered. Police cars also blocked the roads leading outward from the residential area. The block was too tight, though, Harwood thought, and of course they and the MS-13 gang members had already fled. The police had four dead MS-13 bodies, provided the members didn't clear them out. But two police helicopters appeared on the scene and began working in concentric search patterns from the crime scene outward.

"Semper fidelis," Harwood said, remembering the decal on the server rack.

"Marines. Always faithful."

"Right. Maximus Anon is a marine."

"Or former marine," Hinojosa said.

"No such thing. Once a marine, always a marine," Harwood said.

"Who do you think? Know any marines?"

"Weathers," Harwood said. "He's a marine."

"Who was trying to kill us."

"Who told him to dump me?" Harwood asked. He looked at Hinojosa, searching for a tell.

"I don't know. He was communicating directly with CONUS. I suspected something based on seeing he had a burner phone, which is why I gave you the Baku bail-out option. Then I used a Jack Rabbit to find his number and eavesdrop. That's how I found out he talked to someone here in the National Capital Region who was using a voice changer. You can buy them on Amazon nowadays. But it had that low mechanical sound to it. Traced the cell number and it was a burner, also. But the directive was to dump you alive in Iran. I presume to leave evidence of American involvement in the murders. Your fingerprints were on Stone's sniper rifle and so it would have been easy to make you as the killer."

"I was the killer," Harwood said. "You directed me to kill. Who directed you?"

"Bronson gave me the instructions. Our tiff was a façade."

Harwood thought about Bronson. Good-looking black guy. Better looking than him, that was for sure. Harwood was a jagged rock to Bronson's shiny diamond. Polished and political, Bronson could be good for either Maximus Anon or the mechanical voice.

Or both.

"Bronson is a former marine," Harwood said.

"I know. I just put that together. You think he is Maximus Anon?"

"Only one way to find out," Harwood said.

Hinojosa nodded.

"But first we need to find a place to hole up, because this rooftop isn't going to hold," he said. Harwood stared at the half-built condominiums as he spoke. It was approaching 3 A.M. and the city was at the ebb of its activity. The partiers were home and fast asleep. The early risers and commuters were either hitting snooze or looking for coffee. The freeway had a rare moment of inactivity and Harwood led Hinojosa back down the stairs, passing a few stoned and sleepy drifters wandering the littered hallways. He guided her over the expressway and found a gap in the fencing. Navigating past piles of concrete blocks and rebar, he found an opening into the stairwell that would be the fire escape, most likely. He took that up as far as it went, walked onto the concrete floor that was a giant open space. Two walls were built and two of the sides were open, awaiting construction. Harwood used a flashlight to scan, saw a few fast-food bags, thought about rats, didn't see any, and decided this was as good as any place. He walked the length of the floor, saw the fire escape on the other side, checked the exfiltration route that way, and was satisfied.

But then, two police cruisers with unlit racks slowed as they slid past the construction site. He pressed them against the concrete wall, bare I-beams above. The cars continued along Southeast Freeway, going slow. Definitely looking. Two Coast Guard patrol boats slipped by along the river, searchlights swinging like a used car sale.

"Okay, the cops are everywhere. Feds, too. We stop here. I was looking at the marina, but the Coast Guard is already in the water. Maybe we hide here for an hour or two. Let things cool down. What day is it?"

Hinojosa thought for a second. "Tuesday morning." She checked her phone to be sure and nodded.

"Bronson will be in his office. You have his number?" Harwood was snapping his SR-25 together. He extended the bipods and aimed at the road then spun around and aimed at the river. He had some dead space, but he could hold there.

"I do," she said.

"Okay, we wait here, make the call, and then move right away. Even money says that someone used a smartphone to record some of what happened. Good chance we're on that recording," Harwood said.

"Oh, God." She clearly hadn't thought of that.

"We have to do everything we can to stay off the radar while still getting at Bronson. He could be the key to this. It all started with him."

"It did," Hinojosa said.

"And then we find that missing MacBook."

"The one from Samuelson's apartment," Hinojosa said.

But he had never mentioned that to Hinojosa. How the hell did she know about that and who exactly was she?

Her phone purred with an incoming call. She looked at it and tried to conceal it from Harwood.

"Bronson's calling *you*?"

CHAPTER 17

Sirens wailing from all corners of Washington, D.C., woke Sloane Brookes.

She was disoriented and confused until she remembered that she had fallen asleep in Ravenswood's guest bedroom at his Wharf penthouse as opposed to taking her helicopter back to her Virginia estate.

The floor-to-ceiling window showed the Potomac River snaking to the southeast. Reagan National Airport—where her Sikorsky S-76 luxury chopper sat idle—was just south of the river. She thought about her pilots, who were holed up in Crystal City at the ready.

Anxiety boiled in her throat, clenching, making it hard to breathe. While the sirens were just random noises, her instinct told her they were related to the mission she had directed earlier. That's right, she *had* directed a mission to kill a man. That thought scared her, now. In the early morning darkness, innocence attempted to reemerge, a white bridal gown on a prostitute, perhaps. Her power and ambition demons were resting, fueling, and preparing for the long game, the presidency. The innocent child was scared, though, without residence, having been evicted long ago. The tough façade of the brave, scheming woman rested in her makeup kit in the bathroom.

What *was* the mission?

She needed to focus. Fight-or-flight syndrome was kicking in. She reached for her clonazepam bottle but then remembered this wasn't her bed or nightstand. She had an emergency stash in her purse, which sat on the sofa across the room. She had no idea if Ravenswood had made it back or not. She knew that he dealt with seriously evil men to get their work done, but always kept a distance. She had no need or desire to know.

She checked her phone, which sat on the nightstand, the battery almost drained. How had she forgotten to plug it in and charge it? The evening began to come back to her in pieces. The late-afternoon text to meet with FBI Agent Deke Bronson. Their dinner and drinks. Sex on the balcony captured on video by Ravenswood.

Then ordering the hit on Maximus Anon, whoever that might be.

She swung her legs over the bed and padded on the granite floors to her purse, grabbed the iPhone charger, and popped a 1 mg yellow clonazepam pill, which should start smoothing her out in about fifteen minutes. She walked back to the bed, realized she had never showered after sex with Bronson and shrugged.

Whatever.

She sat on the bed and plugged her charger into the wall, causing the light on the iPhone to brighten. Because she had all messages turned off for her lock screen, she had to open the phone to see if anyone had tried to contact her.

Her green-and-white text bubble had a red icon with the number "2" in the top right-hand corner. She pressed on it. The first text was from Ravenswood. Simple: *OTW*, which meant on the way and was stupid for him to send. She didn't care if he was or not. The text placed him in a certain spot at a specific time. If the chaos going down in Southeast had anything to do with him, that was a piece of evidence he didn't need to manufacture. An unforced error, as they called it in tennis.

The second text was from Jessup, her strategic advisor, as she liked to think of him.

REALLY NEED TO TALK

The time stamp was at 1:48 A.M., just a few hours ago. He was up late, possibly all night. Almost 4 A.M. now, she decided to take a shower and change clothes. She kept a few items at Ravenswood's place, which she used as an occasional hideout when she wasn't staying in her Capitol Hill brownstone, which she used routinely when she was in the Senate. The media had grown accustomed to staking her out there and it was convenient to be able to be anonymous, or so she wished to believe.

She showered, gaining some momentum, though still concerned about the sirens. She dressed, repacked her small travel bag, and checked her phone. Another message from Jessup.

URGENT

Whatever good the clonazepam had done eroded quickly. Jessup had only texted her a few times since they had known each other and even though his phone was a burner, it was starting to freak her out. She needed to fly back to her estate, get in her boat, and meet him. It was always face-to-face with the television and fans blowing, white noise in the background.

She stepped into the living room, found Ravenswood seated on the sofa, feet propped on the coffee table as he stared out the window. He turned his head as her heels clicked on the granite.

"Morning," he said.

"Is that us?" she asked. "The sirens?"

"Most definitely. I just received a call from my contact. The cops took six men in, four of which were killed by a black man and a good-looking woman with brown hair, as they put it."

"Two alive, four dead?" she asked. "Gangs? MS-13?"

"Yes. Yes. And yes."

"The Reaper," she said. Not a question.

"Most definitely. He's back and he's alive and he's pissed off. That's not a good combination for us."

"The woman? Hinojosa?"

"Most likely. Fits her description. She was, after all, the handler for Team Valid."

"Where are Stone and Weathers?"

"Wounded relatively badly, but back on U.S. soil and equally pissed off. I'll put my two pissed-off mercenaries against a do-gooder like Harwood anytime. That Reaper bullshit is all make-believe for the media. Navy SEALs getting rich selling books. Army Rangers want to do the same thing. All marketing bullshit. That guy is no tougher than the next," Ravenswood said.

She raised an eyebrow. "Okay, slugger, then why don't you just take him out. I mean, he survived Crimea, Iran, Baku, and now apparently six of your thugs."

"Not 'my' thugs, but yes, okay, he's a survivor, but he's probably used up all of his nine lives."

"Huh, I see it a little different. He's a winner and he keeps winning. I never underestimate my enemy, and since you work for me, I'd recommend you drop that cocky ass attitude and focus on how to beat this guy."

He nodded, continued to stare at the darkness. The city was waking. The 14th Street bridge was already flowing with bright lights coming at him and red lights trailing away.

"Now that I know where he is, here in the city, I think I'll do just that. Between me, my friends who are supremely pissed off, Stone and Weathers, the FBI, and even the D.C. police, I think we've got a decent shot at wrapping him up shortly."

"Okay, then just get it done and quit talking about it. And don't fucking send me stupid texts that you don't need to send."

"Yeah, sorry about that. Was a bit unnerving and just thought you might be worried about me," Ravenswood muttered.

"I'll worry about the world before I worry about you. You're an employee. Do your job," she said.

He nodded and said, "Roger that."

She took the elevator down from his apartment to the lobby. Texted her crew to fire up the chopper, and paid cash for a cab to the private terminal at Reagan National. The helicopter flight was smooth and thirty minutes long before they settled on the helipad a hundred yards from her home. She walked inside, changed into boating clothes as the chopper repositioned to the county airfield ten miles away. Fired up the boat and sped to Tangier Island. The stars were swirling brilliantly as she entered the complete darkness of the Chesapeake Bay. There was no ambient light to mute the stark beauty of the firmament. Still, the anxiety ate at her until she palmed another clonazepam and dulled her senses. She docked the boat and walked up the pier to Jessup's home.

He met her outside again, ushered her inside, and they sat on the porch. The sounds of nature coming to life were like a symphony. Fish smacking at the surface in ritual morning feeding.

Birds waking and diving into the clear water, unfettered by the wind, which would pick up later in the morning.

They sat in the wicker chairs with oversized cushions. The music played through the speakers. The ceiling fan whirred and an ancient floor fan blew across the screened porch. Jessup placed two water bottles on the table next to the two computer terminals.

"First, the good news. I shut down Maximus Anon. His Twitter account is indefinitely suspended and I've recovered about three hundred screen captures from different users. There are probably more, but I started with those with the highest number of followers and worked backwards. You're not paying me enough, by the way."

"I'll determine that."

He nodded and continued.

"The rest isn't looking so hot. We're moving from staying ahead of this to falling behind. If we fall behind, everything unravels. Harwood was never supposed to return. He knows too much about Samuelson and whether he's figured it out or not yet, he will. And when he does, it's not good."

"I agree. So, what's the plan? Where is he?"

"Here," he said, pointing at his MacBook. The grainy video images showed Harwood and Hinojosa running from a run-down project building in Southeast, across the freeway, and into a construction site. Jessup switched to another video that was part of the I-395 traffic monitoring system, which had enough downward angle to show Harwood and Hinojosa picking their way through a fence gap and into a construction site.

"Still there?"

"As far as I know. I'm inside the IC command and control system, which gives me every camera in the area. The highways, the marina, the Coast Guard, the airport. There are cameras and sensors everywhere. If they move, we will see them. He's a combat guy, not used to being in today's modern city. He's trapped himself in the location. The urgency of this situation is I wanted to discuss with you how we deal with this. He's back up against the river and two freeways. Really has one way to go, which is due west toward the Navy Yard, which has cameras everywhere, also, in addition to being a bitch to get into." The IC, or intelligence community, maintained a continuously growing and networked community of cameras.

"Options?" But she was thinking already. She could let Ravenswood and his heathens handle the situation. They could tip off the police. They could steer Stone and Weathers in his direction. Or they could get the FBI involved.

"All of what you're thinking," he said. "I see your mind working."

"I guess part of the decision rests on what's happening with Maximus Anon," she said.

Jessup typed some commands and brought up a series of cameras focused on the brownstone row house that had no less than ten police cars parked in front. Two ambulances were on location, both open at the back. Emergency personnel were pushing gurneys with dead bodies covered by bloodstained white sheets into the back of both ambulances.

"I'm reading the SIGACTS of the D.C. police department," Jessup said. He pointed at another monitor, which showed a scrolling matrix of significant activities, including information such as location, time, activity, response, and status. "If you look here, there were four killed. Several photos were taken and there are two videos showing Harwood and Hinojosa entering the home of Maximus Anon."

"Who are the dead people?"

"The reports are it was gang violence. MS-13. Five dead," he said.

Brookes whistled and shook her head. What had Ravenswood gotten himself into? No wonder he was staring out the window like a zombie. He figured himself a dead man. He ran a group of MS-13 into the meat grinder thinking it was going to be an easy job. Find some fat computer guy and loop a belt around his neck and let him dangle from a two-by-four in the basement. That was all she'd wanted to have happen. Now this.

"Okay. Well, you know everything, so I'll talk it out with you. Ravenswood doesn't know about you, but you know about him."

"Let's keep it that way, Senator," Jessup said.

"No worries there. He'll be lucky to live another day if that truly was MS-13 on the ground. What I'm seeing is that we need the Reaper dead to cover the Samuelson side of the story. If he's gone, he can't uncover anything else or tell his side of the Team Valid story. The Sultans and Perzas are dead and that's what we needed."

"Yes. I've confirmed that they're dead and I've been able to hack into their networks and delete anything that might be . . . uncomfortable. Before, they had someone monitoring their system twenty-four-seven. With the chaos, they had a break where I was able to get into each system and do what I needed."

"Okay, so that problem is cleared up, but the Reaper is the new problem. If he even goes public about Team Valid we're screwed."

"I doubt he'll go public. Hinojosa is there and she'll convince him, rightfully, that his best options are to stay off the radar."

"Which brings up a good point. What do I do about Hinojosa? Is she collateral damage here?"

"That's your call," Jessup said.

She pulled at her lip, thinking. "You're right. Let me work it over."

"I don't need to know," Jessup said. "I already know more than I want to."

"Well, you're all in, so you're going to hear it. What I'm thinking is that we give Stone and Weathers the mission to kill the Reaper, however they determine is the best way. Then we tip Ravenswood as to the location so that MS-13 can power up and do their thing, also. I think we keep D.C. police and the FBI as hole cards for now. They'll be following these clues, also, so I doubt they'll need much from us."

Jessup nodded. "I like it. It needs to happen fast. The Reaper could call any newspaper or TV station and blow this thing up. I'm not sure he realizes what he's got, but he's going to figure it out, sooner or later. And when he does, he's doing two things: coming after us and going public."

She nodded, took a sip of ice water. "He wants justice," she said. "But so do I."

Jessup clicked some keys and said, "I've got a message ready to send to Stone."

"Content?"

"It's the lat/long of the Reaper and Hinojosa's location with a screenshot of the building they're in. I include the instructions: Leave no trace."

"Leave no trace. I like it. What about the gang? As backup."

"Your wish, my command," Jessup said. "Your pal used a burner to contact them in East Falls Church. They're in a brick rambler." He pulled up a Google Earth image and zoomed onto the house that looked like a post-WWII baby boom house. Every house on the street looked the same. Red bricks, black, decaying shingles on the rooftops, and chain-link fences with circular tracks in the backyard, most likely from pit bulls or Dobermans.

"Okay. Get them moving. They're pissed off, too. Best to get everyone going while Reaper and Hinojosa are tired and everyone else is mad."

Jessup typed in some commands and said, "Okay, done."

"It's really that easy? Send a text from Ravenswood's phone to some gangbanger?"

"Yes. I can even do it from your phone," he said. "But I never would."

She stared at him a second, catching his eyes, pulling them up to hers.

"I swear," he reiterated.

"Okay," she said.

After a few minutes, Jessup turned his monitors toward her.

"Here we go. Camera in East Falls Church shows activity at the gang house. Piling into two cars. Carrying weapons. Camera on this screen showing Stone and Weathers rolling in a Land Rover from their safe house in Alexandria."

Brookes nodded. "And the girl. In Georgia? Where are we on that?"

"I've got someone from the original team moving on her. She's staying with the parents of the Ranger command sergeant major. I imagine that we're only getting one shot, so to speak, at her. I wouldn't want the wrath of any Ranger coming back on me."

"Then do it right. Kill him, too."

Jessup stared at her. "I know what needs to be done. You see the irony in you ordering all of this to happen while trying to preserve the image of your integrity to maintain your presidential viability, right?"

"I see clear purpose. How is this any different than fighting to maintain national security? The resistance is too important. I'm their leader. I have an obligation. And while I don't necessarily identify with them, they support me, see me as the path to reclaiming their progressive agenda. Whatever we need to do to stop this madman, Smart, well, a few bodies are worth the price."

Jessup swallowed. "Including a kid?"

Brookes nodded.

"I've never seen it put so starkly, but it's your plan."

"You've got that right," she said.

CHAPTER 18

Hinojosa answered the phone. Harwood listened, catching only one side of the conversation.

"Yes, Special Agent . . . roger . . . he's with me . . . I'll tell him . . . I'm not sure about that . . . I'll ask him . . . okay, I'll call. . . ."

She hung up and looked at Harwood.

"He wanted me to tell you that he wants to meet with you to discuss something," she said. "It's about Samuelson."

"Your brother," he said, looking her in the eyes.

"Yes, my brother."

"Not Sammie?"

"You're questioning me? He's my brother, okay? He's dead. I'm dealing with it the best I can. Did you ever think it might help me cope to use our last name? What everyone else calls him?"

Harwood nodded. Not convinced, but it was a somewhat persuasive argument. Unable to grieve her brother's death, perhaps she called him by an emotionally detached moniker—their last name—that allowed her to compartmentalize. Sure. He'd done it in combat. There was no reason to believe it wasn't the same for her. But still. There was something ringing hollow.

"So when do we meet?"

"He said he would send somebody and to hang tight."

"Hang tight?"

"He said that you would know what that means."

Harwood thought about it for a second. Bronson had been a marine in Fallujah. He'd served in Force Recon and knew all the tricks for inserting and exfiltrating an area of operations. They were in a tough position. Bronson knew exactly where they were. If he didn't before, he did now because he most likely geolocated her phone. He studied the half-constructed building. Open to the south with the river, which was an easily intercepted escape route. He turned and studied the freeways to the north. Simple to block, unless of course you had an FBI escort with lights flashing. That wasn't Bronson's style. He looked up.

Open sky, save a few I-beams the crew had put in place.

"Okay, I think I understand." He reached into his rucksack and retrieved two twelve-foot lengths of rope and two snap links. He showed Hinojosa how to tie off the Swiss rappelling seat and properly insert the snap hook.

"Not sure what this does."

"I'm not sure it's what he's talking about, but we'll need to be ready if the time comes."

"In the meantime?"

"We've got good high ground here," Harwood said. "But the workers will show up in about two hours, sunrise, and that's if we don't get pinged before then. Cameras are everywhere. We're vulnerable."

"He said he would take care of it. Two hours. Can we hold for two hours?"

"You're the one with all the inside information. You tell me." He looked at his SR-25 splayed out on the concrete.

"I'm no strategic genius, but I'd say when the sun comes up, we're toast."

"If this is where Bronson says he's getting us, we need to give him that opportunity."

"Okay."

Harwood kept a furrowed brow aimed at Hinojosa.

"Jesus. You still don't believe me."

"It doesn't matter what I believe. Only the truth."

Hinojosa removed her backpack and set it next to her as she laid with her back against the wall, hugging the pack like a pillow as if she were spooning with it. Her eyes closed as Harwood continued to scan for anything coming their way.

After thirty minutes, mist and fog clouded the Potomac River to the east. He held his night-vision goggle to his right eye, his tie-down keeping it secure around his neck. The moonlight was weak, fading into the west. Low clouds blocked the starlight. Still, he could see well enough and Harwood had seen this before. The truism that it was darkest before the dawn coupled with the natural ebb of the human circadian rhythm made this the most dangerous time for warriors. Sleep was the enemy's prostitute, seducing even the most alert and awake sentries. Worse, what was to come was even more precarious, the transition from full black with night-vision equipment to the temporary and changing hues of sunrise. The eyes had to adjust from full dilation as more light became available for the irises to process. Things that were not seen during darkness became visible; likewise, items that had been noticed would be different and starker. Harwood scanned his sector to the north. The concrete block piles were still covered in darkness, but he saw that there were more than just the one they had passed. Construction cranes loomed over top of the building.

His fields of fire were decent, but close in. There was dead space at the base of the building and if Stone and Weathers were coming after him, they had plenty of good sniper hides from which to shoot. He walked to the far side of the building, looking south. The lights of Anacostia winked at him. Directly across the river was a park and beyond that was Ward 8, the poorest section of Washington, D.C. Every other house was probably abandoned or a full-up drug and gun laundering operation. But he determined his biggest threat to be from the front, the way they had entered. The water was at least a barrier to keep pursuers from easily closing on them.

Defend to the north; be prepared to escape to the south.

The morning dew brought a chill into the open concrete bay. He walked back to the north side of the building, about a fifty-yard trek, and found Hinojosa, asleep, tired, exhausted.

"Cameras everywhere," he said to himself this time, thinking his way through the problem set. "Two hours not good enough."

Hinojosa grunted; okay, maybe half asleep. The traffic on the interstate and freeway was picking up, hissing and rumbling as it echoed into the concrete cavern. After thinking another minute, he reached into her small backpack and retrieved her phone, pressed her thumb against the button and dialed Monisha's phone from memory.

On the third ring a sleepy voice said, "Yeah?"

"Monisha—"

"Reaper?" She awakened quickly.

"Yes. Don't have much time."

"Been trying to reach you. Your voice mail is full and it doesn't ring."

"It broke," he said, which was one way to describe deliberately destroying it.

"Sammie left me something, Reaper. Sent me a flash drive," she said.

"Don't open it," Harwood said.

"Too late," she replied.

"Give it to Sergeant Major," Harwood directed.

Monisha was silent. There was a noise in the background. Some mumbling and then in a hurried voice she said, "It's all about that Pakistani guy. Sounds like the basketball player, Steph Curry. They saying you killed the wrong people. That you were doing someone else's bidding."

"What?" Harwood asked.

The muffled voices grew louder. Then there was a thump, which could have been the phone dropping on the floor. Breaking glass rattled through the speaker. A loud explosion erupted and everything went silent.

"Monisha!" he shouted into the phone.

His voice woke Hinojosa.

"What's going on?"

"Something happened to Monisha!" His mind raced as the world spun beneath him. An inescapable feeling of helplessness enveloped him. He never quit. He never let the odds, no matter how stacked against him, deter him. But now, perhaps for the first time ever, he felt a fresh vulnerability. Sure, he'd been scared in combat before. Anyone who said they weren't was lying. But when it was just him, it was okay. He was usually square with his values and his God and if he bit it, well then, so be it. It *had* been just him. Now, the larger responsibility for Monisha, a young girl who had been abandoned much as he had been when he was a child, weighed heavily on him.

That fatal feeling of failure slid around him like a python, suffocating him.

"Reaper, we've got to go!" Hinojosa shouted.

Two cars screeched to a halt outside of the fence.

Harwood focused.

"How the hell?"

He had been right. The most likely axis of attack had come from the north. In the morning darkness, tattooed MS-13 gang members poured out of the cars carrying shotguns, five from each vehicle. Even the drivers were joining the fray. One group of five raced to the northwest corner while another went to the northeast corner.

Harwood made a command decision.

He laid down beneath his SR-25 and aimed through his Leupold scope at the lead gang member at the nearest entrance to them. With the darkness and mist obscuring his sight picture, he was going for body shots. No margin for error. He needed to slow the advance and then stop it.

One pull, first man down. Another pull, second man down. The muffled shots still ratcheted loudly in the concrete cavern. The two followers split left and right. Harwood tracked to the left and winged the third man. The fourth had hidden behind the big pile of concrete blocks they had passed earlier. He slewed to the right and fired twice, hitting two men who had failed to gain cover.

Five down, five to go. It was a numbers problem. He had to kill as many as possible outside the building.

"What the hell?" Hinojosa said. She pulled her pistol out and backed against the wall, eyes darting nervously to the left and right as if they were in a last-stand fight. Perhaps they were.

"Watch this stairwell," Harwood said. He pointed at the northwest stairwell they had entered earlier.

He repositioned to get a better angle on the northeast attackers. They were moving more methodically this time. One was covering, while the other would move. Bounding overwatch, a tactic taught in the military. He lined up beside an open window and peered through the gap. One man was motioning for the other to move forward.

Harwood slowly raised his rifle. The man moved. Harwood fired. The man fell. He switched to the lead gang member, fired again, hitting the man's weapon. That wasn't his target, but he would take it. But it was the only shot he could get before the attacker sprinted to the base of the building. Dead space. One coming from each direction. He needed to rely on Hinojosa, whatever her real identity and purpose might be.

Her pistol boomed, echoing along the open bay. Harwood made the mistake of wheeling in her direction to confirm her status. She was standing over the man who had come racing up the stairwell.

A noise to his rear caused him to wheel around in time to receive a roundhouse kick to the head from a fully tatted gang member. Harwood spun, held on to the rifle, but quickly dropped it as he rolled away and came up with his knife. The man had bare feet and looked like a tribal warrior from a different century. Swirling tattoos and bared teeth. Demonic eyes. Hands flashing with two knives. He lunged at Harwood, who deflected the thrust with his own knife, the blades sparking in the darkness.

Harwood slashed with his knife, but the man leaned back in an acrobatic and athletic move that didn't bode well for Harwood. He corrected quickly and took up a knife fighter's stance. They circled, slashing and grunting. They were moving too quick for Hinojosa to get a shot. He concentrated on the task at hand. Expected no rescue. He was a fighter and he would win.

The man lunged. Harwood was quick to step left and rake his knife upward against the gangbanger's tatted arm. The knife bit, causing the man to drop one of his two knives. He recoiled in pain, while keeping his eyes on Harwood, who pursued success and spun, switched the knife to his left hand, and used the force of his whirling body to slam the blade into the man's abdomen.

His attacker doubled over. Harwood leaned in and lifted the blade up to the sternum, cutting everything two inches deep inside his abdominal cavity. Blood poured over his hands as the gangbanger head butted him, causing him to step back. The man retrieved the knife, even though his guts were literally beginning to unfold from his torso. His movements weren't as quick as before, but he was coming at Harwood, who was regaining focus.

The knife was slashing down at him when he heard the pistol bellow. The back chunk of the man's skull shattered, blood spraying onto Harwood. He grabbed his knife from the man as he fell to the concrete.

"Nice shot," he said to Hinojosa, who hefted his rucksack and passed it to his blood-soaked hands.

They ran to the southeast exit before any first responders could descend upon them. Harwood scouted the marina, the river, and then the far side using his night-vision goggle again. The sun was threatening, but begin morning nautical twilight was just arriving, the first hint of gray on the horizon. He had done some quick mental calculations on countersniper operations. The rooftop where they had first stopped was a decent nest. The park was less than a half mile across the river. The first row of homes along the road were good spots as well.

As they approached the southeast stairwell that would lead them out the back way toward the marina, an anomaly registered in Harwood's night-vision goggle. It was the slightest aberration, but it was there. He couldn't place it, thought about it a moment, lost it, and then said, "Down!"

He grabbed Hinojosa as he dropped the night-vision goggle, let it swing by its lanyard around his neck and he saw the muzzle flash from the weapon. It was on top of a row house five houses in from the bridge over the Anacostia River, just above the park. The bullet smacked into Hinojosa's backpack with such force that she spun around, sort of a pirouette. Two more shots sprayed concrete dust into their faces, but they were safe behind a block wall that would soon be a fire escape for the building. Harwood tucked Hinojosa behind him. Her breaths were raspy.

"You okay?" Harwood asked.

Hinojosa nodded. "Backpack took a direct hit. That would have been me," she said. "Thanks."

"If you really are Samuelson's sister, I'm assuming he'd want you to stay alive."

"I am, and he would," she replied. Her voice was clipped, pissed off.

He retrieved a device from his rucksack as he collapsed the bipods. He snapped a small tripod into place with telescoping levers connected to the rail system on the barrel and the buttstock. He plugged a micro-USB cable into the remote aiming device and nudged the rifle barrel around the corner of the stairwell so that the muzzle and scope had clear line of sight across the river. He powered up the remote camera in the palm of his hand and manipulated the controls on the touch screen until the weapon was aimed at the building where he had seen the two men on top. With each adjustment on the screen, the weapon moved microscopically. Harwood focused the scope on the rooftop. The thermal imaging was clear and defined. Two men in dark clothes were lying side by side and looking in his direction. They were talking, heads turned toward one another. The remote also had a trigger pull that simulated Harwood's typical pressure from his trigger finger. He focused the scope, which blurred for a second before becoming high-definition clear on the remote pad.

"Snipers. Has to be Stone and Weathers. Saw two lumps laying on the roof," he said.

Harwood had the crosshairs on the dark-haired Weathers, who was serving as sniper. He was surprised the former Marine Force Recon sniper had missed. It must have been closer than he realized. Stone was motioning in their general direction, looking through binoculars. They were acting as if they knew their position was burned, which was fine with Harwood.

He put his finger on the remote-control trigger button on the plasma screen.

A helicopter sang in the distance, the blades chopping through the black sky.

Bronson.

It was flying low along the Anacostia River, sweeping circular contrails of moisture in its wake. The helicopter would cross the path of Stone and Weathers. Harwood fired twice and he saw them roll away. He had only used the remote device a few times and it wasn't as accurate as him holding the weapon to his cheek. Stone and Weathers had to know they were burned though, and like suppressive fire on a landing zone, his shots might have bought them time to do what Bronson had in mind. He quickly collapsed his gear, stuffed it into his rucksack, retrieved his infrared strobe, turned it on and tossed it into the middle of the open concrete floor.

As he turned, he heard, "Vick."

Hinojosa was standing in front of an MS-13 gang thug, who was holding a knife to her throat. He was shirtless with blue jeans and bare feet. He had a large block-lettered DIAZ across his forehead. Whether that was his name or an homage to Miguel Diaz, the East Coast leader of MS-13, Harwood didn't know. Her entire body was blocking everything but his left eye and a fraction of his face. Hinojosa's pistol was tucked beneath the Swiss Seat. No good options. Harwood's pistol was slung low on his hip, like a Western gunfighter's. His rucksack weighed on his back. The helicopter was on the way, growing louder. They knew it was for them. The attacker had no idea.

"*Venganza*," the man said.

Revenge.

As the man spoke, the helicopter flared over the open bay. Diaz craned his neck toward the loud machine whirring overhead. Hinojosa pulled at the man's arm and ducked.

Harwood drew the pistol and fired twice, clipping Diaz's forehead, enough to make him stumble back, allow Hinojosa to spin free, and for Harwood to grab Hinojosa and race toward the SPIE rope the crew chief had dropped. There were two snap hooks about five feet apart. The special patrol insertion and extraction technique was a Marine invention. Bronson was a marine turned FBI special agent. Harwood had guessed right. He snapped Hinojosa into the first one and said, "Hold the rope!" All the while, Harwood was feeling an uneasy presence to his rear. Was Diaz dead or alive?

He pulled the second snap hook to him and clicked himself into the SPIE rope, which he then tugged. The helicopter began lifting away slowly at first, pulling Harwood's feet off the concrete and beginning to raise him above from the construction site.

Diaz leapt and grabbed Harwood from behind, causing the rope to sway and slam into a side wall of concrete block. The attacker clawed his way up Harwood's rucksack and reached around his outer tactical vest. Harwood released his hands and was suspended by the snap hook secured into the SPIE's rope. Diaz's thrashing caused him to lie flat until he used one hand to grasp the rope again, while reaching for his pistol with the other hand. As he spun wildly, Harwood caught a glimpse of Hinojosa looking down from five feet above, helpless.

Diaz ripped open the Velcro tab on Harwood's knife case and retrieved the blade. He flipped it open about the same time that

Harwood had his pistol in his hand. The helicopter lifted above the future condo building, nosed over and sped south along the Potomac River. It was flying so fast that the rope, which was suspending Hinojosa, Harwood, and now Diaz, was nearly at a forty-five-degree angle beneath the helicopter.

Harwood and Diaz were locked in an isometric stalemate. Harwood was holding the knife hand of Diaz and the pistol with his other hand, while Diaz was clutching to Harwood's tactical vest and pressing down toward Harwood's neck. Diaz kicked his leg up onto Harwood, who was nearly horizontal and parallel with the Potomac River gliding by beneath, causing Harwood to loosen his grip on Diaz's wrist. Diaz's knife hand was free and arcing toward Harwood, who blocked the move with his forearm.

The knife missed him by a fraction, glanced off his shoulder, and bit into the SPIE rope. They free-fell from forty feet above the river into the water. Eye to eye with the crazed killer, Harwood saw the look of abject fear on Diaz's face and figured one of two things: He was afraid of heights or he couldn't swim. Harwood used the opening to head butt Diaz, who was now clinging onto him with both hands, and snatch the loose knife that was tumbling from Diaz's hand. As they impacted the water, Harwood's rucksack absorbed much of the fall. Diaz did a back flop into the dark water. While morning was just over the horizon, darkness enveloped them. Harwood tumbled through the water, feeling the weight of his rucksack as water gathered inside. He stabbed the knife into the water where Diaz had landed, thought he hit something solid a couple of times, and then did the combat water survival sidestroke.

Surfacing, he saw nothing but river to the east and a wooded area to the west. He stroked until he hit a muddy bottom. Keeping his gaze on the water where Diaz might emerge, he felt his way up the bank and rolled onto a flat piece of ground, an animal trail.

He lifted the night-vision goggle to his eye. About fifty meters out, Diaz was thrashing the water.

Couldn't swim. Maybe stabbed.

He looked skyward. No helicopter. The sound of the engines had dissipated. They weren't coming back, at least, not yet. Hinojosa had no way to communicate to the pilots and while the crew may have suspected a struggle, there was very little that they could have done other than putting them on the ground.

Harwood turned and used the goggle to pick a path through the forest. After walking for thirty minutes, he was still in deep woods and climbing out of the river valley. The sun was beginning to nose over the horizon and he saw a small clearing with large rocks jutting up from the ground.

Better still, after walking another hundred meters, the rocks were more prominent, some with overhangs. He chose a small, protected area and emptied his rucksack, allowing his items to dry. He cleaned and assembled his SR-25 and Sig Sauer pistol. He made sure the Blackhawk spec ops knife was clean, sharpened, and in its sheath.

After repacking all of his gear, he improved his position with camouflage and chopped away some fields of fire toward the river. The sun had risen and he was combat ready for Diaz or whatever might come his way.

He waited, hearing the faint noise of highways and suburban life. Kids shouting at each other. School buses braking with a screech and a hiss. Mothers shouting out not to forget something. After an hour of remaining perfectly still in his sniper hide, he carefully removed his handheld global positioning system from his rucksack's outer pocket and pressed the power button.

He knew it was a risky move. Stone and Weathers had probably regrouped and were trying to determine his location. Whoever had unleashed the MS-13 zombies on him was assuredly looking for him, also. Whether he could trust the FBI remained to be seen. Regardless, knowing his location was crucial.

The map appeared on the display and showed he was near Quantico Creek, which was partially on the Marine Corps Base Quantico. The western portion of the base included the FBI Training Academy. It was a discreet location, one that Bronson would have thought of using either to secure him and Hinojosa or to dispose of them. He didn't believe Bronson had turned, but at the moment, everyone was suspect to him.

He powered off the GPS, knowing he may well have given away his location, but he didn't plan on staying in one spot too long. He had to get to the source of who was framing Samuelson and why.

Twigs snapped above him. Then the sound of two whispering voices was just around the corner from his hide site. Younger voices. Not anyone looking for him, he didn't believe. The couple turned the corner and began kissing. Two teenagers going for a quickie before school.

"Hurry up," the boy said, removing his letterman's jacket. They dropped their backpacks and began undressing. The boy removed his jeans as a text came into the girl's phone.

"It's Sandy, I told her to give me a ten-minute heads-up before she got to the house."

"Only need five," the boy said, smiling.

"Don't I know," she said, rolling her eyes. She put her phone on her backpack as she removed her skinny jeans and black Disturbed T-shirt.

Harwood waited until they were engaged in sex before he bolted from his camouflaged hide site, raced past them, snatched the girl's phone, and scrambled down the trail.

The girl, who had been leaning forward over a rock formation, screamed, "Hey!"

The boy, who was focused on what most teenage males would have been concentrating on, took a second too long to figure out what was happening.

Harwood was in the bush before either of them could possibly identify him, which would be easy enough once he made his call. He dashed another two hundred meters, found a cave, maybe even a tunnel, and hid for about a half an hour. Reemerging from the cave, he checked for a signal, knowing that he had a limited time to use the phone. He was banking on the teenage girl not wanting to report that she and her boyfriend were having a quickie in the woods before school.

The signal was good, and he dialed Bronson's number from memory, having earlier seen it appear on Hinojosa's phone.

"Bronson," he answered.

"It's Harwood."

After a pause, Bronson said, "Reaper, good to hear from you. Was concerned you were fish bait in the Potomac. Is Valerie with you?"

"Valerie is supposed to be with you. Didn't the helicopter arrive?"

Bronson said, "Not yet."

It didn't make sense. Enough time had elapsed where Hinojosa should have been safely delivered back to the FBI Training Academy, where he presumed Bronson was taking them.

"What happened?"

"I lost comms with the helicopter and it hasn't come to this side of Quantico yet. I'm concerned."

They had squared off before, when Harwood had been on the run, accused of murdering army generals and politicians. Bronson had been on his trail and they had ultimately established an armistice. Neither was one hundred percent comfortable with the other, but there was a bond there that neither could quite

identify, also. Perhaps even a brotherhood. Maybe it was that both had served in combat, or maybe it was because they were both black. Harwood wasn't sure. It probably had something to do with both.

"Before we talk about anything, I need you to get a team in Columbus, Georgia, down to check on Monisha."

"Already done. She's fine. It seems the same bad guys that tried to break and enter your house before you left tracked Monisha from school, followed Murdoch's parents home, staked her out, and then got the go order."

Harwood exhaled, long and steady, releasing compartmentalized anxiety. He felt a weight lift from his shoulders.

"Murdoch's dad was a paratrooper and drill instructor. His house was outfitted with layered security cameras and sensors. He saw the two-man team coming, got Monisha to a safe spot, and then dispatched the two intruders."

"Dispatched? Either still alive?" Harwood asked.

"One is, but he's in a coma. Hoping he comes around. Meanwhile, we're exploiting their phones. One of the numbers leads to the same burner that called MS-13 last night and this morning."

"We're getting somewhere," Harwood said. "Where is she now?"

"Safe with the Murdochs."

"Okay, Hinojosa?"

"Not on the phone."

"Fair enough. Why are you making Samuelson for this thing, Bronson? You know he had nothing to do with it."

"I know now," Bronson said. "So, Reaper, where are you? Quantico Creek? We need to talk face-to-face."

He knew the FBI, among others, was tracking him but didn't care. He would be gone before they could react. He didn't want to wait for a meet that might never happen, though, so he pressed

on. "Explain how you know Sammie had nothing to do with this," Harwood replied.

"Again, not on the phone. I'll come get you. This thing is coming to a head in the next twenty-four hours. I've got your location. Move up four hundred meters to the west and you'll be on Possum Point Road. Throw something on the road as a marker, go hide, and I'll find you."

Harwood clicked off, walked until he found the road, and broke a small tree limb in two pieces. He laid them across each other on the desolate, uneven pavement framed by scrub brush on the creek side and thick forest on the north side.

X marks the spot. Not original, but sufficient. He moved north about one hundred meters and then west, found a good sniper hide, and aimed his SR-25 at the X. Then he scouted to the west. Within thirty minutes a tan military Humvee was moving slowly along the road. Bronson's shaved head was visible through the windshield. The Humvee stopped at the X and Bronson stepped out. Bronson held his arms wide and lifted his sunglasses. After a few minutes, Harwood picked a path to the road and kept his SR-25 trained on Bronson. He was wearing a black windbreaker with gold FBI letters on the back and left breast, black cargo pants, and tan combat boots. Harwood remembered that he was usually a dapper dresser and guessed that Bronson was in tactical mode given the situation.

"Reaper, good to see you, too. Lower the weapon," Bronson said.

"Just a second," he said.

He inspected the rear of the Humvee and then the two seats, which were empty. He tossed the girl's phone in Quantico Creek and slid into the rear left seat.

"Okay, let's roll," Harwood said. They drove forty-five minutes not to a wooded area on the FBI Training Academy grounds, as he expected, but to Aquia Harbour Marina. Bronson parked the Humvee and opened Harwood's door.

"Bring your stuff," he said.

Harwood had first met Bronson when he was on a boat in the salt marshes of Savannah, Georgia. Perhaps he was being nostalgic. Dozens of sleek white speedboats of varying sizes were moored to the wooden piers, lines secured around metal cleats. They walked to the end of one of the piers and stepped into a Formula 310 with twin MerCruiser engines. Harwood scanned and there was nowhere to go belowdecks other than a small equipment hold. A Y-frame sunken boat trailer modification was secured to the starboard and port corners of the aft. A Sea-Doo jet ski was lashed to the metal trailer floating in the water.

"Figured you for something a little more roomy . . . and private," Harwood said.

Bronson smiled. "That one is up by my place at the Wharf. Just use this for hitting the beaches on the bay and buzzing around in that jet ski." He chinned toward the rear of the vessel.

Harwood should have guessed the playboy would want to be able to take women onto the boat to impress them. He dropped his ruck while Bronson stood at the console.

"Undo the lines and pull in those fenders," Bronson said.

Harwood did as Bronson asked. No time to get in an ego match with a man whose ego was larger than the boat engines. Bronson backed the boat out of the slip and motored into Aquia Creek toward the Potomac River. The banks on either side surrounded them with tall hardwood trees and steep ravines that fed into the widening creek.

As he steered the vessel, he sped up when they left the no wake zone.

"Moving target is always harder to hit. Right, Reaper?" Bronson shouted above the buzz of the motor.

"You know it," he said, but wasn't sure if Bronson heard or cared to hear.

They cleared the mouth of the creek and were soon in the middle of the Potomac River. Bronson sped across the full breadth of the river, maybe two miles, approached the Maryland side, and slowed as they entered a small creek that narrowed quickly. It turned hard left where Bronson shut the engine.

"Also, when you don't have privacy on board, well, you find your own," Bronson said.

Harwood had little time for Bronson's theatrics, but played along.

"I get it. This is where you bird-dog some chicks. What are *we* doing here?"

"Talk. Tell you stuff. And see if you can't tell me stuff."

"All this time we've known each other, Bronson, and I still don't know what team you play for," Harwood said.

"I'm one of the good guys," Bronson said.

"So you say. Are you on Team Bronson? Team USA? Team Brookes? I've learned that 'good' is mostly in the eye of the beholder."

"Fair enough. Not on Brookes's team, though I did tap that just for sport. Pretty cool to say I bent a senator and potential president over my balcony."

"I'm sure you were the one who was played, based on what I've heard," Harwood said.

"Huh. Hadn't thought of that," Bronson said.

"Just brace yourself for the pictures. If she's under investigation, those will come out at an opportune time. I have no real information, but I've been dealing with these people for a few days now. It's all about the power and they will stop at nothing to gain it."

"You're probably right, but I'm not part of all that. Might have still been worth it, even if."

Harwood shook his head. "You're a good agent, as far as I can tell. Nothing worth throwing away your career."

Bronson was sitting opposite him in the white cushioned seats. "Maybe so," he said, looking away at the trees above them.

"Tell me about Sammie. Hinojosa. That's what I want to hear. Not about some piece of ass," Harwood said.

Fish smacked at the surface. A copperhead snake was coiled tightly on some gray rocks about ten yards away. The cove came to a tight V where the creek was nothing but a trill some fifty yards away. Steep banks dove in from all directions. There was no long-distance shot and if someone had been following Bronson in Virginia, they would have to swim or jump in a boat to find them.

"Okay. We interrogated Malik Sultan, the one we captured at Dulles," Bronson said. "He had nothing to do with the ambush at Camp David. Was here on a business deal, but his counterparts never showed up."

"Lured here just to be seen and be captured?" Harwood asked.

"Bingo."

"Okay," Harwood said. "But Sultan and Perza were legit bad guys, correct?"

The morality of killing the right person was important to him.

"Yes, they were funneling funds from the U.S. to help build nuclear weapons in violation of the new president's foreign policy."

"Okay, go on. I'm solid."

"The expended brass you found in the next room over? Fingerprints belonged to Stone, from Team Valid. Someone had planted Sultan's fingerprints in the database to appear if we queried Stone's. Max made the wrong call initially, but he cross-checked against the international database in West Virginia and they were different. We had Sultan's prints from IEDs in Crimea. And the more I dug, the more it was clear that Team Valid is not a presidential order. It came from Kilmartin, the director of the FBI. Completely rogue and off the books."

"Let me guess. Stone and Weathers did the ambush to kill Carly Masters. They framed Samuelson and implicated the Sultans and Perzas. Someone needed the Sultan and Perza families killed and this gave that person the catalyst for establishing Team Valid," Harwood said.

Bronson chuckled. "I guess we're done here. You got it figured out."

"I've been living it, Deke."

Deke. Building the trust.

"Well, Vick, we have more to learn, but it appears there is a group of people from the previous administration that opposes the current administration. Imagine that. And some of that group have been conducting a shadow series of negotiations and diplomacy to keep alive canceled treaties such as the Iran nuclear deal. And it's one thing to express support, but an entirely different thing to keep financing going in violation of U.S. law."

"A deal got canceled. No biggie. How is that worth killing for?"

"If these people's identities are revealed in any kind of credible forum other than Maximus Anon's Twitter page, then they have a serious problem. It appears top-secret comparted and Q-level classified secrets were being sold to Iran as well. Stuff from the Senate Intel Committee. We're talking jail time. Sedition. Treason. Big stuff."

"I buy that. Anon seems pretty accurate," Harwood said, eyeing Bronson. Remembering the Marine logo on the side of the server rack, he added. "Semper Fi and all."

Bronson smiled.

"We've been trying to find that person, just so you know. For the record, Maximus hasn't been wrong, yet."

Harwood listened. There wasn't a denial in his statement. Was Bronson Maximus Anon?

"How did Sammie get in the middle of this? He was off the grid," Harwood said.

"Partially off the grid. He was seeing Carly Masters, who had a soft spot for Army Rangers. They met during his rehab in Walter Reed. Her brother had been wounded in Syria and was one bunk over. Their relationship grew to the point that Samuelson got as close to D.C. as he could stomach."

"He wasn't a city boy," Harwood said.

"That's right," Bronson continued. "Valerie told me. They had lost touch. She said she saw him in the hospital after we got him back from the Chechen thing, but he was too proud. Didn't want anyone's help. Couldn't understand why he was having PTSD or memory issues. He was really struggling. She tried to intervene, but duty called for her, too."

"I'm still noncommittal on her," Harwood said.

"About what? Whether she's with us or them?"

"Yeah, something like that."

"She's with us. We . . . had a thing," Bronson said.

"Please, that's half the women in the D.C. metro area," Harwood said.

Bronson smiled. "Maybe not half."

"Still, you get my point. Doesn't mean anything."

"Well, I've never seen proof that she's Samuelson's sister, but that doesn't mean she's working for the other side."

"Then why the charade? Why put herself on the Team Valid kill list?"

"Maybe something to do with Carly Masters? They were friends," Bronson said.

"Lots of maybes. Ever going to get to telling me why she isn't here?"

"Yeah, some asshole hacked our secure communications system and gave my Black Hawk a signal to waive off. The helicopter that picked you up was off the radar."

"So I'm fortunate an MS-13 gangbanger jumped on me like a freaking zombie. Otherwise I might be wherever Hinojosa is?"

"Maybe."

"My money says either way, good guy or bad guy, she's with Brookes in that compound."

"Maybe."

"Okay, so fill in the blanks for me," Harwood said.

"Sammie still had his security clearance and he'd just started a job with a defense contracting company. Masters caught Khoury, the senate IT guy, one night downloading top-secret information. She didn't confront him. She just remotely monitored his activity. She gave Sammie the names of the people who were involved. Evidently, there were some people skimming off the financial transactions of the Iran deal and selling information, as I said. When that got canceled, two things happened."

"They got exposed and they quit receiving their stipends," Harwood said.

"Again. We're done here," Bronson said. "But seriously, Carly Masters telling Samuelson was technically not a smart thing to do for two reasons. First, it is considered leaking, particularly in today's environment. And second, it obviously got her killed."

"These same people I'm guessing killed Khoury the IT guy that Masters found?" Harwood asked, recalling his brief conversation with Monisha.

"Yes. Khoury, who mysteriously committed suicide with a bullet to the forehead, was the broker of this information. Corent did the forensics and Khoury's head was moving when he was shot. Not conclusive, but still suspicious. He was the cutout who was gathering the technical details of our nuclear capabilities and enabling the financial transactions to take place. It is a complicated network of banks that are violating U.S. law to continue the flow of money to Iran that the previous administration promised and agreed upon. Smart undid that and shut down the flow. As you said, once the deal was off it trapped some people that were skimming from the billions. One of those people appears to be Senator Sloane Brookes."

"You're saying Maximus Anon is right then. Brookes had Stone and Weathers ambush the families at Camp David to kill Carly Masters and establish the need for Team Valid? Then they planted the names of Sultan and Perza so Team Valid would kill them? Perza and Sultan weren't anywhere near Camp David."

Bronson pointed at him. "That's what it looks like."

Harwood whistled a low, soft tune. "I've been thinking it, but it's hard to believe. And they're trying to make Sammie for the Camp David ambush?"

Bronson held up his phone, punched an icon on the screen, and a news video began to play. It highlighted that another terrorist had been identified along with Samuelson. Vick Harwood, the Reaper.

"Me?"

"You."

"Why?"

"They want you out of the way. Shooting you dead in your sleep is always an option, but my guess is that some folks have this outsized impression that you're a big badass or something and can actually fight back."

Harwood smiled. "Well, that's a possibility."

Bronson returned the smile. "I'm actually starting to like you."

"Don't," Harwood said, deadpan. "Just tell me how our country got so fucked up while we were overseas protecting everyone back here. Hard to believe."

"Not so hard," Bronson said. "Look at Crossfire Hurricane and all the Spygate stuff. It's insane, but it's real. Nothing is outrageous anymore. People are openly threatening President Smart and the Secret Service doesn't do squat. These people we're talking about actually got so comfortable that they were planning the overthrow of the government. My people. The FBI. All the pinheads in HQ." Bronson pointed at his chest. "That's unacceptable. And this bullshit is just a step down, you know, aiding and abetting our enemies."

"Brookes is capable of all this? Just to cover her ass?"

"Well, she plans to run for president, also. So, there's that. But no, it was basically just power and money."

"Well, she's toast now," Harwood said.

"Not so fast, gunslinger. There's a trail, most of it has evaporated, and just because Maximus Anon says it's so, doesn't make it provable in court."

"You're kidding."

"Actually, I'm not. And this is why I saved your ass."

"My ass was just fine," Harwood said.

"About ten dead MS-13 gang members out there. Local cops will be thanking you. But Stone and Weathers are still on the mission."

"Well, I've got three objectives. Clear Samuelson's name. Make the people that killed him pay. Keep Hinojosa alive, because that's what Sammie would want, if she's his sister."

"And this is where I have to step in as an FBI officer of the law," Bronson said. "You can't work on this case. He's your friend."

"It's a free country," Harwood said. "I can do as I please."

Bronson nodded. "That it is. For example, if I were to tell you that a playboy named Chip Ravenswood who lives at the Wharf in Washington, D.C., was working for Sloane Brookes and he may hold the key to everything, there would be nothing I could do to stop you from paying a visit to his condo or her compound."

"And you can't pay him a visit because this entire operation is being run by your boss, the director of the FBI, who hopes to be attorney general one day in a President Brookes administration."

"Bingo," Bronson said, pointing a finger like a gun at Harwood. "And we've got about twenty-four hours to sew this up."

Bronson held his phone up that showed the latest tweet from three minutes ago.

Maximus Anon: A LOT of activity in SE DC. MS-13 acting as hitmen for dems looking for yours truly, but not to worry. I'm safe. They want me bc I know the truth. Sloane Brookes had Raafe Khoury killed to conceal her involvement in Iran $& intel laundering. #CampDavidAmbush her doing too. @FBI Director Kilmartin is wrapping things up fast. Is he involved? #Brookesgate

Harwood knew that if Maximus Anon was right, Team Valid would be coming after him within the next few hours. Somehow, they were tracking his location even after he and Hinojosa had inspected every bit of gear and discarded two tracking devices.

"If this is Brookes, how is she tracking us?"

"Like I said. You're off the case. But remember the rules of engagement. Every soldier has the right to self-defense."

Bronson's phone buzzed with a call.

"This might be for you. Georgia area code."

Harwood took the phone and answered.

"Reaper, you're one hard person to get in touch with," Monisha said.

"Are you okay?"

"Yeah, thanks for checking up on me," she said with a bite of sarcasm. "Minnie and Pops are taking real good care of me, though."

"I've been talking to Bronson about you. He said you're fine."

"He's the one who's fine. Seen pictures of him," Monisha said.

"Focus, Monisha, what's up?"

"Like I was telling you before, you know, those guys tried to kill me and I single-handedly took them down," she said, pausing.

"That's the story everyone is telling," Harwood said.

"Yeah, right, Reaper. Listen, I'm uploading this document and texting to this number. I researched it and I wish I was there to help you, but Sergeant Major says I can't go."

"Okay, do that. Speaking of which, put Sergeant Major on. I'm glad you're okay."

"Yeah, the love is just oozing out of you," Monisha said.

There was a slight rustling as the phone changed hands and Murdoch said, "Ranger, don't waste my time."

"Roger that, Sergeant Major. Trying to figure something out."

"I've looked at what Monisha has. Her notes are good. Take a look at those. You got about three different problem sets you have to deal with. And I'm telling you this is big stuff. If you solve this, we'll send you to the Middle East to solve world peace."

"No thanks, Sergeant Major. Been there, done that. I've got that T-shirt."

"Roger that." They both hung up about the time Monisha's text came through with a Word document attachment. Harwood opened the document as Bronson leaned over his shoulder.

"Damn, Reaper, you stink," Bronson said.

"Rather this than your aftershave. Okay, here it is." Harwood and Bronson read the text on his outsized smartphone:

Carly gave Sammie flash drive. Didn't trust cloud. BLUF: Brookes was dealing with Perza and Sultan fams to get money to mullahs in Iran to continue nuke deal after nuke deal canceled. Masters found emails that have now disappeared. Only copy on the flash drive-don't worry CSM has it ;). Stone and Weathers are bad guys. They will kill you. (Pls don't get killed). Sammie said that whatever Hinojosa tells you, she may be Sammie's sister, but they didn't get along at all. She ain't that cute, btw.

Harwood looked up at Bronson, who had obviously read ahead.

"Hinojosa's cute," Bronson said.

"True, but where is she? What's her deal?"

"Anyone's guess. The helicopter's transponder is off."

"You don't seem that worried," Harwood said.

"I'm concerned. Someone told my helicopter to stand down. That's not cool. Someone else knew where you were and pulled you out using the exact same method I intended. That's a level of penetration I've not seen before," Bronson said.

Harwood nodded. "Maybe so." But what he was really thinking was that while Bronson was looking him in the eyes, he was communicating something else. They were tucked away in a cove talking about a conspiracy to aid an enemy of the state, Iran, and conduct espionage by selling nuclear secrets to the number one state sponsor of terrorism around the world. To what end? The divisions in the country ran deep, but people weren't insane enough about politics to want to have damage done to the country, were they?

"If Iran developed a nuclear device more rapidly, then President Smart canceling the Iran deal would look pretty stupid," Harwood said.

Bronson pointed his finger at him like a gun, the thumb collapsed like a cocked hammer as he said, "We have a winner."

"All that bullshit aside, these people killed Sammie and his girlfriend," Harwood said. "All because the girlfriend tripped over something and tried to do the right thing."

Bronson nodded, as if urging him to continue.

"They're meeting tonight at the senator's compound. Everybody who is responsible," Harwood continued.

Bronson nodded.

"They'll have security, including this Ravenswood guy. Team Valid, most likely, will be defending the compound," Harwood said.

Another nod.

"Justice will never be done to any of these people because bureaucrats just survive like cockroaches," Harwood said. "And you can't do anything because you're government."

Bronson spoke finally.

"And you're off the case."

As Bronson was stepping from the boat to the jet ski, he detached the jet ski from the small trailer to which it had been secured. He led the nose of the jet ski to the side of the boat, lifted the trailer, which stood about three feet high above the motors, and locked it into place. He stepped onto the jet ski and pushed the ignition button.

As the engine coughed, Harwood said, "Are you Maximus Anon?"

Bronson held his gaze, shook his head with no sign of evasion. If Bronson wasn't Anon, then who could it be?

"Kilmartin? The FBI director?"

"Think about it, Ranger. You'll figure it out. What's that Snow White saying? Who is the fairest of them all?"

"Don't do fairy tales. Too much real life," Harwood said.

"Kilmartin doesn't make sense, though, because he's covering for Brookes," Harwood replied. "All I can think is that Iran is nothing but a terror state. You know that from Iraq."

"That's why Smart canceled it. Anti-Israeli elements here in the United States have actually been assisting Iran all along. The plan has been to enable the Islamic forces surrounding Israel. Brookes is a major anti-Semite. Kilmartin is just a politico who was playing the odds and thought Brookes was going to be president. What we've got is a bunch of people who thought she was going to win, so they lied, cheated, and stole while jockeying for position, and now they're all holding their jockstraps in their hand watching from the sidelines like a kid with a snot bubble coming out of his nose."

"So why not just arrest them tonight?"

"Nothing against the law about having friends over to your house," Bronson said. The jet ski engine whined.

Harwood paused, processed what he thought Bronson was telling him, and asked, "What's your perfect world here?"

"The senator has committed crimes. It's unlikely that she will pay any price. She's got something on Kilmartin, so he's covering for her. They've already killed your best friend, his girlfriend, and tried to kill your daughter. They're not going to stop."

"You're telling me stuff I already know, but I think I understand you. You want evidence that you can use in court to take down Kilmartin. That enhances your position in the FBI and accelerates you even further to becoming the first black FBI director."

Bronson smiled.

"Who made you so smart?"

"Thirty-three kills, plus a few extra. That doesn't just happen."

"Go on," Bronson said.

"You want to break this case wide open. You've got inside information. You're using me as a tool, but I'm good with it, because as you said, they're coming after me and my people. Nobody does that."

"They're not an easy target, Reaper. They've got a media genius on TV every night. The president's briefer is slanting stuff every morning, throwing a slider or curveball ever so slightly. Former CIA director. Former U.S. senator. And there's a wild card. Someone is giving them perfect information. Plus, some pretty heavy muscle with Ravenswood, Stone, Weathers, and some muscle around Fort Benning, near your house. But the unknown person may be the key to it all."

"No ideas?"

"Not yet. World-class hacker, though."

"Can you call off Stone and Weathers?"

"They are working for Brookes. Team Valid is her concept. I have no influence there."

"Blunt force trauma, then," Harwood said.

"Sometimes that's the only way," Bronson said.

Harwood watched him speed off into the Potomac River, rooster tail spitting water twenty feet into the air.

CHAPTER 19

Sloane Brookes stood on her deck and stared at her boathouse, thinking, *Should I just get in that fancy boat and go far away?*

The idea had been a good one. Once Smart canceled the Iran nuclear deal, funnel some discreet information to Iran to help them build a bomb that would embarrass Smart. Classic Machiavellian politics. Over a two-year period, Khoury had probably cashiered thousands of Q-level access secrets through the Sultans to the Perzas. Iran's scientific community was robust, but kick-starting them with basic plans on how to build a nuclear device in the image of the U.S. arsenal seemed wise. Brookes assumed that the U.S. military would be able to defend against its own nukes better than something that the Iranians had randomly developed.

The race between giving enough information and money to Iran so that they could accelerate their program versus chasing down Carly Masters had been filled with tension. Masters was about to get out of control, according to Jessup, as she worked with Samuelson to figure out what everything meant. Jessup had been monitoring their phones, computers, and clouds. The Camp David thing seemed like the perfect plan. Invite one of the Sultans to America, put him at Dulles about the time everything was going down, and then have Jessup work some digital magic to implicate the Sultan and Perza families as well as Samuelson. Lots of moving parts, but most had gone according to plan. They still had a chance to pull it off, but they had to meet tonight. No electronics. Spoken word only.

But still, should she just get the hell out of Dodge, she wondered?

It was all working out just fine until this Reaper came along and began sniffing around. He was supposed to die in Iran, which would have been the perfect ending. Instead, she felt as if things were just beginning.

Her phone dinged with a text from Jessup.

I BELIEVE MAXIMUS ANON IS DEKE BRON-
SON, FBI SPECIAL AGENT
YOU KNOW WHAT TO DO THEN IF YOU'RE
CONVINCED
WORKING IT
?
WILL TELL YOU TONIGHT
K

She went through the motion of flinging her phone through the window, but never released it. Snipers were supposed to kill people. She was planning to have Kilmartin's ass tonight when he arrived. One of his agents had been leaking through Twitter as an anonymous source, laying out the entire conspiracy. The only upside was that it was so insanely crazy that only Fox News was covering it and the rest of the media was blowing it off as another lame conspiracy. Which of course it was so far fetched that it was easy for the journalists of the mainstream media to spin as tinfoil-hat kind of stuff.

She had Ravenswood, Stone, and Weathers. Surely, they could kill two men who should already be dead. She looked at the high compound walls and thought more about her security. There was a safe room in her basement with a tunnel that led to the boat-house. All of her windows were blast- and bulletproof. There were three elevated areas within a mile where someone could have line of sight into the compound, but they were tough shots, if any shot at all. Like threading a needle. One was from the rock formation where she had met with Henry and the president's briefer the previous morning. There were two other similar hillocks where a sniper could set up. Naturally, she had instructed Stone and Weathers to lie in wait at two of the three, assuming Harwood would occupy one of them.

She dug through her pocket and retrieved two clonazepam pills she kept for emergencies. The stress was building and she needed a kick of the psycho-sedative. She crunched them dry in her mouth, tasting their sweetness, but swallowing with antici-pation nonetheless. How many people had she killed? Well, zero exactly. But of course, she'd had killed the twenty-two in the Camp David Ambush. Four at the Sultan compound. Another seven at the Perza compound. Then of course there was Samuelson, but that was more Weathers and Stone's idea, according to Ravenswood. Then there were the MS-13 gangbangers, which she didn't really give a shit about, but still, she was oddly interested in the total number. Jessup had told her there were at least nine MS-13 mem-bers killed. She was already at forty-four dead at her direction. She wondered if battlefield generals felt this way—anxious but detached. Morbidly curious, even. These were part enemy, part in-nocent, part friendly. Was combat any different? She had always read about friendly fire and how they were an unwelcome but necessary cost of waging war.

And war it was. Brookes's drive for power wasn't so much connected to ideology or lust for money. She didn't care so much about the one percent difference between her and some opposing party member in Congress. And she had more money than she could spend in several lifetimes. Rather, her drive derived from a Kennedyesque belief that because she was Virginia royalty, she owed it to her heritage to assume the throne of power. Her contributors had eagerly donated to her, like subjects laying alms at her feet. The dinners, speeches, television shows, adoring believers, and unlimited access to everything were the perks of the powerful and she was at the pinnacle of her party.

She believed in the party, for sure, but only as a vessel to transport her to her rightful place in history. Everyone dies; only legacies mattered. Her impact on history remained to be seen, and so far was diluted into a bunch of votes that made a difference on the margins. Not that making a difference was important to her, either. She needed that lasting impact. The one big thing. Obama had his healthcare deal, which turned out to be a nightmare, but still that was his legacy. Bush was remembered for the Iraq war and killing Saddam Hussein. That was a good news, bad news legacy that she wouldn't mind having. At least it mattered in the grand scheme of geopolitics. Smart had his North Korea deal and tax cuts, both of which could change at any moment.

Her big idea was to keep the Iran nuclear deal alive, give them a bomb, show how incompetent Smart was, defeat Smart, and then formalize the agreement again, which would require the elimination of the bomb she helped create. With all the diplomats out there having secret meetings with Iranian mullahs, she figured her using Jessup's expertise at funneling the money, along with the skimming operation, was child's play. Khoury the IT guy was supposed to be collecting the intelligence reports, feeding them to Jessup so that he could then provide them to Iran.

Saving the world from the burgeoning Iranian nuclear threat would be her legacy.

But she had to defeat Smart first before he got any more traction.

Ravenswood walked up from the basement into the backyard.

"Good to go," he said. He was wearing dark brown cargo pants and an outer tactical vest with full ammunition pouches over a black stretch shirt that hugged his body. He flipped his shades down over his eyes and adjusted the M4 carbine that hung from a three-point sling looped into a snap hook on his vest.

"She still alive?"

Ravenswood nodded, obviously feeling the rush of wearing his equipment and torturing a captive.

"That was a good intercept you provided me," Ravenswood said. "Curious where you're getting your info."

"Like I said, everything's compartmentalized. You of all people should know that. Need-to-know basis," she said.

"I jump through my ass to get on your helicopter and rig a SPIE system while someone hacked into the FBI air operations and gave a stand down to their helicopter. As always, I'm half impressed and half pissed off."

"That's my definition of winning," Brookes said.

"Ugh, did you really have to say that?"

"It's about time we started winning, Chip. So let's finish this up. She give you anything useful?"

"Said MS-13 banger jumped on the rope and they cut away into the Potomac somewhere near Quantico. The Reaper is pissed about Samuelson and she is, of course, upset about her brother."

"Stone and Weathers?"

"They're tracking him by following Bronson."

"Maximus Anon."

"Bronson?"

"Yes. He's Maximus Anon. Been leaking like a garden hose through Twitter."

"Mostly an echo chamber. No one is taking him seriously."

"He's not naming you in a conspiracy, Chip."

"Might as well be. Your fortunes are my fortunes. I want the power trip as much as you do," he said.

She nodded then changed the topic. "I'd like to see her. Is she blindfolded?"

"Yes. She has no idea where she is."

Ravenswood led them into her expansive basement. The estate was built upon a foundation that had once been a plantation home. Accordingly, it had the necessary shackles and chains to bind slaves.

Valerie Hinojosa was hanging almost Christlike in the dungeon. Her hands were hanging limply from black iron wrist cuffs. Her ankles were bound in a similar, but wider, cuff. Her head was drooped with her chin nearly on her chest. Ravenswood had stripped her down to her bra and panties. Red welts had formed along her side where he had whipped her. A black kerchief was tight across her eyes and Bose noise-canceling headphones covered her ears.

"Did you . . . do anything?" Brookes asked in a whisper.

Ravenswood smirked. "I'd like to, but not in the mood to leave behind any DNA."

"You think she's sufficient bait for this Reaper guy?"

"Could be. We'll see."

"We need to do better than see. He's the only thing keeping her alive. Once we've got her, Bronson, and the Reaper, we'll be in the clear. Jessup can handle the rest."

Ravenswood shot her a sharp glance.

"Who's Jessup?"

"My hole card. Let's get out of here. Gives me the creeps."

They ascended the steps and instead of heading onto the deck, took the entryway to the kitchen, the path the slaves used to take. Sitting at the dining room table, Brookes said, "Have a seat."

Above them was a crystal chandelier and layered trey ceiling with ornate dentil molding reminiscent of the castle-like façade of the compound.

"Let's go over the plan," she said. "I want no mistakes."

Ravenswood nodded and began talking.

CHAPTER 20

Harwood nudged Bronson's boat into the sand seventy miles north of the Brookes compound. He had decided to head south, toward Reedville and the compound, as opposed to north toward the Wharf and Ravenswood, as Bronson had suggested. Harwood's guess was that if Brookes was having a face-to-face meeting at her remote estate, Ravenswood would be there and most likely running security with Team Valid: Stone and Weathers.

He secured his rucksack, which he had inspected and repacked, and tied off the bowline to a weathered tree trunk. The Potomac River was murky with silt as it gathered near the Chesapeake Bay.

The map showed a cell tower nearby. Knowing that he didn't have much time, if any, to evade the ghosts in the wires that were looking for him, he used the Bronson-provided burner cell phone to call Monisha's number by memory.

"Who's this?"

Monisha. Always showing the love.

"It's me," he said.

"Reaper!"

"Keep it down, Monisha. I don't have much time and I don't want anyone to know where I am."

After a pause, she said, "Okay."

"There's something very important on that flash drive I need you to find for me," Harwood said.

"Reaper, I gave it to Sergeant Major like you told me. Besides, I've looked at everything on that. There's nothing more than what I sent you," Monisha said.

"If I know you, you downloaded it onto your hard drive," he said.

The line went silent.

"So that's a yes. Before you delete that information, which you will do, tell me if you see anywhere in the text where Sammie says, 'Send it'?"

During the silence, he could visualize her reading. She was a bright child and he had high hopes for her. With every day she seemed to grow and mature. He was making it up as he went, never before having been a guardian or parent. But he knew the power of love or, conversely, the pain of its absence.

"Yeah, right here. Doesn't really make sense. He just finishes what he's saying with 'send it,' then adds his name beneath it."

"Move the cursor over 'send it.'"

After a second, "Oh my God. It's a hyperlink. Usually they're blue or something."

"Click on it," he directed. "Hurry."

She was silent for a long time, presumably as she read.

"This is some wild shit," Monisha said.

He didn't correct her profanity. No time to waste.

"Is it financial transactions?"

"More than that. It shows bank transfers to Perza in Iran and

Sultan in Crimea, but also has something called HUMINT, SIGINT, and ELINT." Each time she spelled the acronyms for human intelligence, signals intelligence, and electronic intelligence.

"Okay, and who is doing the transactions? I need to confirm that what I'm about to do is the right thing."

Another moment of silence before she said, "There's only names on the receiving end. There's a company account it looks like. Something called Acme, Incorporated. Like the roadrunner." She cackled a bit, but got serious again. "Looks like billions with a *B* going to Perza and Sultan and every time there's a transaction a little bit goes to Acme."

"A little bit every time adds up to a lot when you're talking billions," Harwood said.

"O.M.G.," Monisha said. She had a flair for the dramatic, but still, Harwood perked up.

"Yes?"

"There's a basic step-by-step guide for how to build a nuclear bomb in here."

"Like a diagram?" Harwood asked.

"Yes. A picture with instructions."

"So they have a plan and they have the money," Harwood said.

She didn't respond.

"You there?" he said.

"Yeah. This is a lot of money, Reaper. People where I come from kill for a hundred dollars. There's a lot of killing going on over this money."

"I know. And because of that, you need to delete all of that information, Monisha. Seriously. They have someone who can track that information and find you."

"There's one more thing here. I didn't tell you about it before, but it's a photocopy of a letter," Monisha said.

"Read it to me quickly," Harwood said.

"'Dear Melinda, I'm sorry that our marriage didn't quite work out as planned. I don't know what the best thing to do here is, but I can't imagine life without Sammie and Valerie. The Solomon approach would be for each of us to raise one, but they are brother and sister, and that would be cruel to the children. As long as you don't move and allow me unlimited visitation, I will agree for you to have custody with me as the joint custodian. I will forever love you, William.'"

"But Sammie said he lived with his dad?" Harwood said.

"Maybe he just left. Felt sorry for him. At least he had one," Monisha quipped.

"What am I? Chopped liver?"

"Heck, I don't know if you're coming back tomorrow, Reaper," she said.

That was more like it. He smiled.

"But the point is that it confirms Valerie Hinojosa is his sister," Harwood said.

"Says Valerie. Nothing about Hinojosa," Monisha said. She was good at focusing on the simple facts before her.

"Good point. See if you can find a Valerie Samuelson or Hinojosa that is connected to Sammie. Meanwhile, I've got some business to take care of."

She chuckled. "You make it sound like you're in a business suit getting ready to go into an office building when you're probably in the woods somewhere looking down your rifle scope."

Not far off, he thought.

"Okay, now delete that stuff, Monisha."

There was clicking over the airwaves, then Monisha said, "I trust you, Reaper. I just double deleted it. Into the trash bin and then emptied the trash bin."

"Okay, good. I know what I need to know, I think. Enough to go on. I'll see you soon, Monisha."

"K, Reaper." She paused. "I miss you," she said. Harwood wasn't expecting that. They dealt with those kinds of emotions with shallow jokes or gallows humor, cutting at one another. The crasser the joke, the deeper the love. He did miss her, though, and there was no harm in letting his adoptive daughter know that she was worthy of affection.

"I miss you, too, Monisha. Think good thoughts," he said. Hanging up the phone, he moved to a perch that overlooked the boat from about fifty yards away. It was a flat area with twenty- to thirty-foot-tall trees and some boulders, one of which was like a small table. He removed his rucksack and retrieved the paper map that Bronson had given him. Studying the terrain around Brookes's compound, Harwood identified three obvious sniper locations that Stone and Weathers would most likely be lying in wait. The issue was that there were two of them and three locations. He numbered them one through three as he used to do in combat, with number one being the best hide site and three being the least desirable.

Countersniper operations necessarily involved stalking, but he was actually countering the countersniper operation. He anticipated that Stone and Weathers would be in hide sites within one hundred meters of the top two sniper locations. The map showed some decent depressions and ridges they could hide behind to eventually ambush him.

Those locations would be his targets. He numbered the potential ambush locations around each of the sniper hides. He assumed they would have all of the latest kit, including night-vision goggles, and briefly debated whether it was better to strike now when they would least be expecting him, but decided the cover of darkness was always an advantage to the attacker.

He had no particular feeling toward Hinojosa. She was professional and did her job well. But what really counted to Harwood was what was on that flash drive. While Hinojosa was most likely Samuelson's sister, the real motivation here was stopping the espionage that was enabling Iran to build a nuclear weapon.

He waited until darkness, passing the time by eating combat rations and drinking two bottles of water Bronson had left for him in the boat. He stripped and cleaned his SR-25 and Sig Sauer pistol. He used a whetstone to sharpen his knife as he sat cross-legged leaning against the rocks. Under the last remnants of daylight, he reassembled and packed his rucksack. His magazines were full.

He studied his map, memorized everything he needed, and then picked his way to the boat, which was sitting idle at the base of the vertical bluff he had last parked it. He boarded, programmed the GPS, cranked the engine, and navigated the Potomac River, finding a rhythm and a sense of anonymity in the middle of the widening waterway. At least a mile on either side, the land rose more abruptly on the west side than on the east. He watched the wheel adjust slightly every time the GPS hit a waypoint that he had programmed. By his calculation, he had nearly two and a half hours at thirty knots to travel nearly eighty miles from his position opposite Aquia Harbour to the jetties on the Northern Neck of Virginia. The area was famous for its fishing industry, especially the menhaden, which produced all of the omega proteins that Harwood gulped on a daily basis.

The sun was hanging in the west, sinking slowly, painting a picture with orange and purple hues mixed with green forests and the muted brown river. Bronson's boat purred with efficiency, propelling Harwood toward Brookes's compound. He had clear vision and purpose. Enemies of the state were aiding and abetting foreign threats. More personally, they had killed his former spotter, as well as twenty-two innocent souls in the Camp David

Ambush. How many had been killed, total? The body count was high when factoring in the Perza, Sultan, and even MS-13 goons.

Harwood was square with his God, though. Deep down, he believed Hinojosa was on the side of good and was most likely held captive by Ravenswood. He would find out soon enough. As the sun dipped below the bluffs to the west, the moon nosed above the horizon in the east. Harwood took this as a sign that everything would soon be in balance, the way nature intended it to be. He was working hard to be a good father figure to Monisha and be a good Army Ranger. That was what counted in his life.

And doing those things well meant eliminating threats to his family and avenging the obvious murder of Samuelson. He didn't care who pulled the trigger—Stone or Weathers—he knew it wasn't Samuelson.

Nobody fucked with an Army Ranger without paying the price. The creed to leave no soldier behind applied beyond the battlefield, as well.

The boat slowed and turned in between two jetties. He passed a couple of shrimp boats with their nets hanging over the side like misshapen wings. The fishermen were returning to the docks as darkness enveloped them. Part of his strategy had been to hit the jetties at darkness, but he hadn't accounted for the extra sets of eyes, figuring most of the fishermen would have already docked and processed their harvest.

He motored past them and was swallowed into the darkness of a cove. The GPS, operating like autopilot on an aircraft, turned the wheel sharply into another cove, following tidal streams deep inland. He'd traveled about a mile from the jetties through several tunnellike coves that led deeper into the Virginia countryside when the boat slowed. He recognized the water tower that marked the point he was looking for.

He took control of the wheel, floated the boat into the muddy

bank, shut the engine, grabbed his ruck, and leapt onto the bank. He secured the bowline around a tree trunk, hefted his ruck onto his shoulders, snapped a modified helmet onto his head, and flipped down his night-vision sight.

He patted his Sig Sauer P320 X-Five Full-Size with side rail mounted infrared laser and flashlight. With the flip of a thumb he could toggle between infrared aiming that was aligned and bore scoped to his pistol barrel and white light that would be visible to the naked eye. He screwed the SRD9 suppressor onto the bore of the pistol and felt it click into place. After ascending the bluff, he oriented himself and began the roughly two-and-a-half-mile walk to the first sniper hide ambush location.

Countering the countersniper.

He kept his SR-25 disassembled and secure in his rucksack. If done correctly, his operation involved knife fighting, then using his silenced pistol. He had searched for sniper hides that might have line of sight on the ambush locations, but those sites were all low ground, not easily targetable from any distance. And a miss might tip off the entire security detail that he was on location. Surprise was his friend, at the moment.

When he got to within one hundred meters of the first sniper hide he knelt next to a field of tall grass along the edge of the forest. Water tumbled along a small, rocky stream no more than three feet wide between the woods and the field. There was a deer stand about thirty meters to his front, which meant there were probably others. The grass and proximity to water would make this prime hunting grounds. The rise to the elevated sniper hide was prominent across the field. If he were to ambush the sniper hide, it would be from one of the deer stands.

He stepped back into the darkness of the woods and took cover behind a tree. Listening intently, he heard the usual rhythmic

sounds of night in the country. The gurgling stream, the rustle of squirrels in the trees, and the occasional rut of a deer.

But the scrape of metal against wood was an unnatural sound among nature's symphony. The noise came from his two o'clock, across the fifty-meter-wide field. It occurred to him that the sliding sound might have been a long gun scraping in his direction along a wooden support. He carefully moved to the opposite side of the tree he was using as cover and snuck a quick glance across the field. A figure was moving in the deer stand, which was about twenty feet up a tall hardwood tree of some type. Harwood lowered onto all fours and then onto his stomach, low crawled to the base of the tree holding the deer stand nearest him. He carefully opened his rucksack, using the sound of the stream as audible concealment as well. Assembling his SR-25 to include his Knight's Armament suppressor and ATN THoR HD thermal scope, he quietly slid a magazine into the well, depressing the release as he seated it to avoid the loud click.

Leaving his rucksack at the base of the tree, he ascended the angled two-by-fours that served as steps to the deer stand, each time running his hand along the step above, checking for traps, IEDs, or trip wires. He quietly placed his rifle on the weathered floor of the stand. The entire process took him fifteen minutes to get fully into a shooter's position. He laid a T-shirt in the corner where he expected the brass to kick in anticipation of deadening the noise and preventing it from rattling around the stand. When he powered up the THoR scope, he slowly charged the weapon, sliding one round into the chamber.

So far, so good. He moved the weapon onto the small ledge and sighted in the general direction of the scraping noise. The optical display within the retina gave him distance, wind speed and direction, altitude, and a variety of other essential shooting information.

With the scope on white hot, he immediately saw a body moving in the deer stand. His shot was either at the head or an oblique shoulder or chest shot. He needed a first shot, first kill so whoever it might be didn't make a radio call. The scope calculated everything he needed to do as Harwood placed the crosshairs on the man's head. His thumb flicked the safety off as his trigger finger pulled directly back.

It occurred to Harwood that it might not be Stone or Weathers in the stand, that it could be a random deer hunter. He considered that it wasn't deer season and deer weren't generally on the move at night. Rather, dusk and dawn were their preferred times and he was an hour past dusk now.

The man in the opposing deer stand was sighting a long weapon of some type directly at his number one sniper hide selection. All of the circumstantial evidence pointed at this being Stone or Weathers. Harwood's guess was that it was Stone. Weathers was the better shot of the two and more of an alpha. While Stone was a boisterous hothead, he was reasonably lost when it came to the strategic picture. Weathers was the consummate quiet professional. As the alpha, Weathers would want Stone on the first line of defense because he was expendable. And while he didn't know Ravenswood, he still considered that Weathers would be calling the operational shots of defense of the compound for this meeting.

The trigger gave way. The suppressed shot resonated loudly across the field, mostly the machinelike action of the bolt chambering another round, which pinged loudly. The brass kicked and landed soundlessly toward the end of the T-shirt. The man's head kicked back. His weapon fell into the deer stand with a thud.

Harwood scanned the tree line, finding what looked like four other deer stands, all empty. He saw movement to the southeast, toward the compound, of a vapory figure galloping away. Because of the optics, it was difficult to tell if it was a person or an animal, but it was definitely animate based on the heat signature. After ten minutes of no activity, he collected his T-shirt and brass, lowered himself from the stand, and shouldered his ruck.

He carefully chose a concealed path around the open field to get to the deer stand on the far side. Dropping his ruck at the base of the tree, he climbed and found Stone's dead eyes open and staring at him. He checked for a pulse and got nothing in return. Climbing over Stone, he found the entry wound center mass of the skull above his left ear. He'd been going for the temple, but this was equally effective.

Harwood turned and sighted along the same general azimuth that Stone had been looking. Harwood could clearly see the hillock that was his number one sniper hide prediction. It appeared that fields of fire had been cleared. The shot was wide open at about one hundred meters. Even Stone would have been able to make this shot, he mused.

He scanned to the southeast, looking for whatever he had seen. No joy. He turned and inspected Stone, finding a personal mobile radio and cell phone. He probably had regular intervals he was supposed to report. Harwood looked at the smartphone and saw that it was 8:40 P.M. The scratching noise had probably been Stone reporting back to Weathers or Ravenswood and he'd gotten careless.

Harwood gathered Stone's SR-25 rifle, Glock pistol, and K-Bar knife, and found his wallet and some receipts in his cargo pockets. He was careless in the Crimea and Iran fights and he was careless here. It had gotten him killed. Harwood felt no remorse.

He retraced the route to his rucksack and secured the smaller items while disassembling Stone's rifle and tossing the parts in different directions.

Quickly, he shouldered his ruck and began moving toward the

southeast of Brookes's compound when a small light appeared from his outer tactical vest indicating a text had come into his burner phone. He found a hollow surrounded by trees, took a knee, and covered the phone as he looked at the text.

It was from Monisha. Three words and a picture.

CHECK THIS OUT

He stared at the picture, nodded his head, and made a decision.

CHAPTER 21

Sloane Brookes paced in the room filled with the current FBI director Seamus Kilmartin, the president's briefer Miles Everett, broken nose and all, former CIA director Josh Henry, media anchor Rocky Campagne, and Chip Ravenswood.

"Everybody is in this thing," Brookes said. She stopped walking, stared at the giant fireplace, thought she heard a noise, looked out the window, and continued. "As Ben Franklin said, 'We must indeed all hang together, because most assuredly we shall all hang separately.'"

"I haven't done anything illegal," Everett said.

"Shut up," Sloane snapped. "You've been feeding bullshit to the president. It's called lying. Treason. Sedition. Suck on your pistol now if you don't have the stones to power through this."

The two clonazepam had smoothed her out and helped her summon the courage to focus on the issues at hand, which were that the Reaper and Hinojosa were still alive. Hinojosa was the bait and the Reaper would come to them. It was that simple. She wanted the entire cabal present when it went down so that they could all be sworn to secrecy on the entire plan going forward and of course they would all be culpable in the deaths of the Reaper and Hinojosa.

"Sloane," Kilmartin said, "I think everyone just needs to focus here."

"I'm focused. This thing is within reach." Turning to former CIA director Henry, she said, "Josh, where is Iran on screwing the nuke to a missile?"

"Close. Both the funding and the technology have helped. It will be within the next twenty-four hours. They'll start cold by testing on Israel. Their current missiles can range there now and with the miniaturized nuclear plans we've delivered, they believe they can score a first-time hit."

"Okay, good. So dipshit Smart cancels the Iran nuclear deal. Iran says okay fuck you and builds a nuke. Then nukes Israel. I like it. Smart will look like the dumbass he is and, Rocky, you can run me twenty-four-seven picking Smart and his administration apart." She pointed at Campagne with a long manicured finger.

Campagne nodded.

"I didn't sign up for this," Everett said. "I've got a family. A pension I need to worry about."

"Too late for that, dipshit. How did Dillinger ever pick you to be the president's briefer?"

"Easy, Sloane," Henry said. "We all have a role here. Everett's job was to dampen everything you've been saying about Iran. You're on Rocky's show hammering away that Iran is a threat and he should have never canceled the deal. Everett is inside telling the president you're just a stupid bitch and don't know what you're talking about."

"Has the convenience of being true," Everett said.

Brookes walked up to him and slapped him across the face. "You little cocksucker."

Everett smiled. "Been wanting to say that. Plus, it's like method acting. If I believe it, I'm more convincing."

Brookes nodded.

"What's the word from Iran on launch? Can they go sooner than twenty-four hours?"

"I'll ask," Henry said. He stood and walked into the dining room, putting his phone to his ear.

"And for anyone wondering here. This isn't sedition. Iran's not an enemy we are at war with and they're attacking Israel, not the United States."

"Well, I still wouldn't go bragging to the *Washington Post*," Kilmartin said.

"No need. I've got Rocky."

Ravenswood looked at his phone, pressed a detent button on his neck, and said, "Go." He walked away from the group into the hallway.

"Better be some good news," Brookes said.

"Sloane, I think it's best if we each leave shortly. We don't need to be here for whatever is about to happen," Kilmartin said.

"Okay. You don't, but I wanted to finish the conversation. I'm all about planning for success. When the nuke hits Tel Aviv, Rocky, I'm your first guest. And I want max airtime on this. Everett, whatever Dillinger gives you, dilute it even more. The reports coming in will be confusing at first and everyone will be focused on Israel more than Iran. Our role in this is covered after tonight."

"Yeah, with about forty bodies," Everett said.

She leveled a hard stare at the briefer and then continued. "Seamus, I want you to start an investigation into the Smart administration's decision-making in canceling the Iran deal. What were Smart's dealings with Israel? Did any of his businesses profit before or after he canceled that thing?"

Kilmartin nodded. "We can do that."

"See that, shithead, that's how you operate," she said to Everett, who pushed his glasses up his nose using his middle finger.

Henry walked back in and said, "My contacts tell me they can go in twelve hours."

"Twelve is good."

Ravenswood walked back in and said, "Stone has missed two reporting windows. Weathers is on the move. Everyone needs to stay inside for their own safety."

Brookes nodded and said, "Okay. We stay, for now."

"Roger. I'm heading downstairs to check on our guest."

CHAPTER 22

Harwood carefully circled down to the Chesapeake Bay, found the fortress that Brookes called home, and took a knee.

The water lapped harmlessly at the sandy shore. Facing the bluff he had just descended, he knelt and studied his surroundings. To his right was an estuary that emptied into the bay, which was to his rear, vast and seemingly endless. To his left was a pier and boathouse. He backed into a crevice in the bluff and removed his phone, punched up the image that Monisha had forwarded, studied it, and shut the phone down.

Carefully, he walked south toward the boathouse and pier. The house seemed built into the bluff and extended a considerable amount of distance onto the pier. It was made of the same rustic wood as the pier, had a steep roof with black shingles, and a small weather vane on the top. Harwood reached the boathouse, aware there were most likely cameras and sensors everywhere.

Monisha had sent him a map that showed an underground anomaly that appeared to be a tunnel connecting the house to the bay and, more specifically, to the boathouse. He studied the structure, built with wide wood planks that dove vertically into the beach from the base of the pier and ran horizontally above the pier. Reaching the vertical slats, he pressed against the wood and determined they were not budging. He walked chest deep into the water and found an opening for the boats on the bay side. Submerging himself until the only thing above water was his night-vision goggle, he slipped into the boathouse listening to the echoing sounds of dripping water.

He walked in slow motion bouncing off the bottom of the bay, treading water with his arms as he held the SR-25. He presumed that Weathers had scouted the entire area and was familiar with all of the points of entry and egress. If there was a tunnel, though, Harwood was banking on the notion that Brookes may want to have an escape route for herself.

He used his hands to pull himself around the side of a large white-hulled boat. Reaching the swim platform and engines, he flipped up his NVG and sighted down the sniper rifle through his thermal sight. He instantly saw what he thought he was looking for. The naked eye would most likely not have been able to see it, but the thermal optics showed an oval that was warmer than the rest of the terrain. He moved to the oval, keeping his weapon at the ready. Emerging from the water, he walked up the sandy bank, rolled across the pier, and approached the oval. He felt around the sand and grass on the side of the bluff, found a small rope handle and tugged.

The door gave way and he inspected the immediate environment before stepping into the tunnel. Once in, he closed the door behind him and didn't move for five minutes. There was no time to waste, but if he were dead, then time wouldn't matter. He used the thermal scope to study the tunnel, but it provided little feedback other than differing hues of gray and black that descended into darkness. More useful was his night-vision goggle with infrared flashlight switched on in the lock position. He also flipped the AN/PAQ-4C aiming light that gave him some infrared light penetration deeper into the tunnel. It was a pinpoint beam but could reflect possible danger back at him.

Keeping his pace count, he walked nearly a hundred meters before reaching a wall. There was a door with a levered handle, not a regular doorknob. He inspected the entire doorframe for wires or sensors, almost like doing a jumpmaster door check. Finding a drop bar lock on the outside of the door surprised him. Someone had at one time locked people *inside* the rooms beyond. He lifted the heavy two-by-four from the U-shaped brackets, which appeared to be heavy-duty metal and as big as his hand. The wood bar fit snugly in the two brackets. No one would get out, ever, unless there was some way to lift the bar from the inside. He considered the possibility and felt around the door, finding a small protrusion, something like the latch on a car hood. He visualized someone on the other side being able to push down on a mechanism and lift the two-by-four out of the brackets.

Interesting.

He kept the two-by-four on the path next to him and took five minutes to disassemble his weapon and store it in his rucksack. He checked his pistol and knife, knowing that he would be better off with these weapons in the tight confines of the Brookes mansion. He found a small alcove and hid his rucksack in the tunnel near the door to the basement. He was going in light on this mission, despite his credo to never allow more than five feet between him and his gear. After a new thought occurred to him, he used a white light flashlight to manipulate his weapons and make some modifications that could be useful to him. Finally, he removed his helmet and placed it atop his ruck. He wanted no sensory deprivation going into the room. In fact, he wanted to be able to feel a slight breeze across his scalp. Every moment counted in close-quarters combat.

He pressed down on the door latch and it gave. He slowly pulled the door open, light sneaking into the small crack of tunnel darkness. He transitioned from his goggle to the naked eye, let his retinas adjust, and focused on the room.

The far wall was old brick, some of the mortar having receded over the years, leaving the impression that this was an older, unrestored basement of some type. A dim fluorescent bulb hung from the ceiling casting a pale glow in what appeared to be a dungeon. The floor was brick, as well. Harwood eased the door open a bit more, its hinges squeaking in high-pitched musical octaves.

A moan came from somewhere to his left.

Pistol at the ready, he spun into the room, clearing left, center, and then right. Back to the left was an open doorway. Leaving the door open, he walked slowly into the room and passed through the door into a similar room he had just left.

Shackled to the wall was Hinojosa. Her head hung limp. She was stripped to her underwear. Had been beaten, possibly worse. Definitely not working for the other side. Probably Samuelson's sister.

He cleared to the far side of the room, found a series of steps that assuredly led to the main living quarters. Harwood saw other black shackles along the wall and realized that this was a slave holding area for a plantation owner. There were a brick chimney and some old firewood logs at the far end of the room.

Hearing noises upstairs, Harwood searched for the keys to the shackles. Like an old-time jail, the key was hanging on the far wall, an impossible reach for someone secured to the opposite wall. He immediately secured the key and started with the one shackle around both ankles, then the left arm and lastly the right. He kept her blindfolded and gagged, though he removed the noise-canceling earphones. She struggled against him, probably unsure of whether he was friend or foe. He didn't have time to waste, though, if the information Monisha had sent him was correct.

A nuclear Iran with a missile that could range Israel.

He slung Hinojosa over his shoulder, her weakened body struggling against Harwood's powerful frame. He sat her next to the door to the tunnel and turned at a noise behind him. Pistol at the ready, he came up firing when a man in tactical gear turned the corner into the room. He remembered the picture that Bronson had shown him.

Ravenswood.

"Fucking Reaper," Ravenswood said. He raised a pistol, but Harwood's first bullet caught his shooting hand, causing him to drop his pistol onto the brick floor. Ravenswood was relentless, though, coming up with a knife and flinging it as fast as Harwood could pull the trigger of the pistol. The muffled shots were still loud in the cavernous basement. Ravenswood spun and was possibly hit but kept coming at him. The knife had grazed Harwood's left arm, drawing blood. Ravenswood tackled Harwood with a quick leap. The bear hug prevented Harwood from getting his weapon angled correctly, negating his advantage.

He reached up and managed to extract his knife from his outer tactical vest, sliding his hand between the pressure of the bear hug. Harwood flicked open the knife as Ravenswood reared back in preparation for a head butt. He used that moment to slide the knife beneath Ravenswood's body armor. The sharpened blade punctured his abdomen and slid up until he reached the vest. Ravenswood's head came forward and glanced off Harwood's forehead. Not a crushing blow, but not a total miss, either.

Ravenswood's forward momentum carried him behind Harwood, who raked the knife laterally beneath the lip of the body armor. Blood was spilling over Harwood's hands as he retrieved the knife and plunged it into Ravenswood's neck. The knife made a wet sucking sound as he removed it from Ravenswood's neck. He pushed the body to the brick floor and wiped his blade on the man's pants.

Hinojosa had removed her gag and blindfold. She stared at Harwood with an expression of confusion and fright. She had grabbed Ravenswood's Glock and was aiming it at Harwood.

"I'm here to help you," Harwood said.

Hinojosa tossed her hair out of her eyes.

"Reaper, this isn't what you think it is," Hinojosa said.

A new voice to the scene made Harwood's stomach sink.

"Reaper. So good to see you," Weathers said, stepping from the tunnel into the brick dungeon. He was holding a large pistol. "You know, Semper Fi and all that bullshit. Talked to Maximus Anon lately?"

Then Weathers shot Harwood in the head.

"What's all that commotion?" Campagne asked.

A helicopter buzzing the house reverberated overhead, drowning out their voices for a moment. When the helicopter cleared the airspace, Brookes said, "Could have just been something from Pax River. They're always flying different helicopters up and down the bay, testing new stuff."

Naval Air Station Patuxent River was less than fifty miles north of Brookes's compound and had a potpourri of aircraft with which the military was constantly experimenting.

"Where's Ravenswood?" former CIA director Henry asked.

"He went to check on Weathers. He's our only guy."

"That helicopter is flying inside your compound, Senator," Everett said. "You mentioned another way out of here."

"I don't recall saying that," she said.

"What about your boat?" Kilmartin asked. "We can get to your boathouse and then get to the boat and then disperse somewhere in Maryland or wherever."

"I've got a plan," she said.

She had a plan for herself, for sure. Her calculation had been wrong, though. It wasn't just Harwood and Hinojosa who knew what she had been doing. Everyone in this room could be squeezed by the FBI or CIA or Secret Service and ultimately spoil her chances.

She walked across the room and listened to the commotion in the basement. It sounded like Ravenswood had finally earned his keep. Now she needed to put in place the rest of her plan. A helicopter searchlight swept back and forth across the expansive front lawn inside the compound walls. The rotor blades chopped overhead like a beating drum on the roof.

"Okay, things are getting dicey," Brookes said. "Helicopters from Pax River don't normally shine spotlights in my yard."

"We can use the tunnel, Sloane," Henry said. "I just got an update from Weathers."

Brookes looked at the former CIA director with a stony gaze.

"Very well. We can go into the basement and get out that way."

Brookes's nerves began to get the best of her. Henry had suggested this as the nuclear option, but she never liked it. Sure, they could always find another reporter to provide them constant coverage. And she wouldn't worry about the beta male briefer, Everett. Kilmartin was a different issue, but still, he was expendable if there was no one alive who knew any of her crimes.

She led them into the basement, a bit anxious at being the first one into the shackle room. The first thing she noticed was that Hinojosa was no longer captive against the wall. That could be either really good news or just the opposite. She continued walking to the small entryway that led to the tunnel. Peeking beyond the opening, she noticed the room was empty, though there was a dark, wet stain on the bricks.

"Sometimes the oil leaks in here," Brookes said. The group had gathered inside the small brick room and were facing the door to the tunnel. "But this is the way to my boat. We can get into the boathouse and slip out this way," she said.

"That's not oil. That's blood!" Everett shrieked.

Weathers stepped from the tunnel through the doorway and leveled the pistol Harwood had been carrying at Everett's face, frozen open in a silent scream. Weathers pulled the trigger, the bullet caught Everett directly beneath his broken nose, and entered his brain.

Campagne turned and ran toward the opening when Weathers fired a second muffled shot into the back of Campagne's head.

"Hang on a minute!" Kilmartin said, reaching for his weapon concealed in a shoulder holster beneath his suit jacket.

Weathers glanced at Brookes, who nodded, and then he shot Kilmartin in the forehead. He quickly turned his pistol on Henry, but Henry had his pistol up and was locked in a shooter's stance, knees flexed, Beretta aimed at Weathers.

"I could have already shot you, Marine. Now it's just the three of us and that was the plan unless Stone made it and it doesn't look like he did."

Weathers glanced at Brookes, who shook her head. "Don't do it," she said, which was a reverse signal, because Weathers pulled the trigger while he was still looking at Brookes. The bullet caught Henry in the neck, causing him to spin and fire at the same time. His Beretta sounded like a cannon in the small space. Weathers took a step toward Henry and fired a bullet into his head.

"Oh my God," Brookes said, trembling.

"It's done," Weathers said. "It's what you wanted, ultimately."

Still reeling from the shock, she was having a hard time processing everything that had just happened. These were friends. Well, as close to friends as she would find in the Washington, D.C., area.

"Call the pilot and tell him he can quit buzzing the house," Brookes said.

Weathers nodded.

"You okay?"

She trembled and stepped toward him. "Let's get out of here. Finish this."

"Good idea."

"Where are the Reaper and Hinojosa? Already dead?"

"Something like that," Weathers said. "Insurance policy until we're clear. I'll get you to the boat and then come back and clean this up as much as possible. There's blankets out there to keep you warm."

"I want to go to Tangier," she said. She was thinking of Jessup, perhaps her only true friend.

"Not yet. Let this cool off," Weathers said.

Brookes had met Weathers on the campaign trail. She needed an advance man who could double as security. He was smart, reliable, and strategic. She didn't realize he was a stone-cold killer until he had hatched the plan one night after sex. Lying in bed, he'd said, "What if Iran got a nuke? That'd make Smart look dumb, right?"

And from that conversation, she had kept him closer and closer to her side. When Carly Masters had found Khoury stealing the intel and working the finances, they knew they had to do something. A solo hit on Masters seemed like the best option, but then she'd involved Samuelson, a former Army Ranger sniper.

Weathers, having been a Force Recon Marine sniper, had the idea to catch Masters from a distance when she was in public. Then

Brookes had mentioned, as long as we're killing people, the Perzas and Sultans need to be dispatched as well.

Dispatch was her euphemism. She still hadn't pulled the trigger and didn't know if she could. In fact, she was pretty sure she couldn't. But Weathers again had come up with the concept of Team Zero, he and Stone and Team Valid, which included Harwood, because there was some suspicion that Harwood knew something.

Before she knew it, the bloodthirsty marine had walked her into over forty deaths of some variety. Murder or self-defense, it didn't matter. The term, "For want of a nail . . ." came to her as she followed Weathers onto the pier and into the boat.

"Where are they?"

"They're in a good place, Sloane, now relax, please."

Shivering, she pulled a blanket around herself as she sat in the seat of the boat she used to regularly shuttle to Tangier. She was thinking of Jessup as she huddled onto the padded bench seat. What had he said to her? He was working to shut down Maximus Anon, but never seemed to be able to keep the Twitter phenom down for the count. Who else had such perfect knowledge other than Jessup?

"Oh my God," she whispered to herself.

"Give me fifteen minutes," Weathers said. "Then we'll get out of here."

Brookes nodded, looking at her shoes.

"Look at me, Sloane," Weathers demanded. She looked up. His countenance had all the fury of a lightning storm. "Stay here until I get back."

"Okay," she said.

He jogged back into the tunnel.

CHAPTER 23

Harwood had felt the beanbag strike his head, knew what was happening as Weathers pulled the trigger on the nonlethal weapon. He didn't know how long he'd been unconscious, but he was awake enough to have heard Weathers shout at Hinojosa and then slap her.

"Your stupid, fucking brother jacked this all up. It was a simple kill on one person!" Weathers said.

"Stop it," Hinojosa pleaded.

"Tell me, Valerie, did you fuck Harwood?"

"No, Griffin, I *never* had sex with Harwood. I've been loyal to you even though I know you banged that senator in there."

"Among others."

The best he could tell was that Hinojosa was on the other side of the tunnel a few feet from him with Weathers standing in between them. He opened his eyes and saw a hazy image of Weathers standing over Hinojosa aiming a pistol at her head.

"You and Harwood. Murder-suicide. Means you go first."

Then the voices could be heard from the room just meters away.

"That's not oil. That's blood!" someone shouted.

Weathers didn't hesitate. He moved through the tunnel door into the same small room through which he had entered the home less than an hour ago. Several gunshots followed before he was escorting Sloane Brookes toward the boathouse.

As he faded in and out of consciousness, Harwood was aware Weathers would be coming back quickly to do exactly as he had said: murder-suicide.

Harwood had used Stone's pistol not because he anticipated any of what had transpired, but because he didn't want any of his ballistic fingerprints in the Brookes compound. But that was a moot issue now.

During the moments of unconsciousness and recognition of the possibility of death, Harwood thought about lying in the sniper hide sites with Samuelson. They'd grown close as professionals and then as friends. Monisha looked up to him as a big brother. Redemption of Sammie's name was as important as anything he was doing. While he was unclear why Hinojosa had initially drawn down on him a few minutes ago, he suspected Weathers had beaten her into submission during what sounded like a tormented relationship. Never leaving a soldier behind included not leaving their reputation to be wrongly smeared. Samuelson was a good soldier, a good man. He had served his country and earned a decent life. Brookes and Weathers, at a minimum, had stolen that life from him. If Harwood needed any fuel to regain his consciousness, his righteous anger at what had happened to his fellow Ranger was plenty.

As Weathers had walked toward the boathouse, Harwood slid toward the rucksack he had stowed by the door. Now, the sound of boots slapping on the wooden pier ricocheted into the tunnel. He found Hinojosa as he slid across the path.

"Valerie," he whispered. Reaching out, he felt her head, wet with blood. Weathers had pistol-whipped her. Probably not the first time. He pressed his fingers against her neck and got a pulse.

"Come on, Valerie, we've got to move."

He crawled to his knees and grabbed her by the armpits, lifting and dragging her into the brick room. He laid her among the dead bodies. He recognized the news anchor and maybe one other, but the other two were unknown to him. It didn't matter, they were dead. Harwood stumbled to his feet, climbed out of the room and back into the tunnel, found his helmet and rucksack and dragged them back inside. By now, Hinojosa was on her hands and knees vomiting as she knelt among the dead.

The footsteps rang louder.

Bullets pinged off the door as Harwood closed it and did his best to secure the handle, but Weathers was already bulldozing through. He fired at Hinojosa, but Harwood surprised him with a hand-to-hand combat eye gouge followed by a throat punch, and a kick to the rib cage. Weathers stumbled as Harwood closed on him, chopping at the pistol with a series of fist slaps before grabbing his arm and slamming his knee into the forearm. The pistol dropped onto the back of one of the people Weathers had shot.

Weathers's surprise had worn off and he was gathering himself to fight back. Harwood felt the first of two punches reinjure an already shaky concussed brain. Still, he thought about Samuelson and fought back. He had nothing to lose, because if he quit then all would be lost. Backed into a literal corner, Harwood spun and delivered a high kick to Weathers's chin, snapping his head upward, opening Weathers up for two more throat punches and an elbow across the chin.

Weathers went for the close fight and attempted to bear-hug Harwood, who stepped aside and tripped Weathers. His opponent fell onto an older man, but he came up this time fumbling with a pistol, a Beretta to be more precise. Harwood gave Weathers no time to think about using it as he delivered a series of high kicks to Weathers's hands, causing the pistol to flip up into the air like a football.

Harwood attempted to catch it, but Weathers used that opportunity to rush Harwood and tackle him, landing a series of UFC moves that resulted in Weathers being in the position of advantage on top. Harwood arched his back, using his hands to block Weathers's relentless onslaught.

Harwood spun with force and threw Weathers off him up against the brick wall. As they backed toward the tunnel door, Harwood lured Weathers into the doorway where he grabbed the two-by-four from its perch on the side of the right U-bracket. Swinging it like a baseball bat, he connected with Weathers's head, which was evidently shockproof because the marine kept coming at Harwood, who tumbled back into his rucksack.

Instinctively, he reached for the knife in his outer tactical vest, but Weathers said, "Looking for this, bitch?" He flipped open Harwood's spec ops knife and drove it toward him. Harwood used a basic double-V blocking maneuver, where both hands caught the downward arc of Weathers's wrist. They remained frozen in isometric meltdown as Weathers tried to drive the knife into Harwood and Harwood attempted to prevent a fatal strike.

Harwood kneed Weathers in the groin, perhaps the only vulnerable area on the marine. Weathers gasped and released just long enough for Harwood to gain control of the knife and plunge it into Weathers's heart. The resistance was strong at first, but Harwood was leaning his weight into the supine frame of Weathers. He felt the knife slide to the hilt between two ribs, puncture the heart, and he knew it was only a matter of time. He twisted the knife, feeling its razor-sharp blade crunch against two ribs, giving him minimal lateral movement. When Weathers finally coughed blood and his eyes went blank with a vacant stare, Harwood said, "That was for Sammie."

He retrieved his knife and rucksack, leaned in the basement and shouted at Hinojosa. "Come on! Let's go!"

Hinojosa was up. She had a pistol.

"Just for protection," she said. "I'm on your side. I didn't know. I was just scared."

As they walked quickly through the tunnel, she paused when she saw Weathers's dead body.

"About right," she muttered, and kept walking.

When they got to the boathouse, Sloane Brookes and her boat were gone. Harwood carried his ruck up to the high ground, which was her backyard. He quickly assembled his SR-25, attached the thermal scope, extended the bipods, and climbed the steps to the back deck that afforded the best view of the Potomac.

Less than a half mile away was Brookes's boat heading due east toward Tangier Island. Had the shot been perpendicular to his line of sight, it would have been measurably more difficult.

As it was, he lined up the sight just above her head. The display in the retina gave him all the right measurements and calculations and he made the physical adjustment. Her head nearly filled the scope. Long hair was flowing with the wind as the boat slipped across the glassy Chesapeake Bay.

He placed his finger on the trigger. Exhaled. Began his squeeze.

"Cease fire, Reaper," Bronson's voice bellowed from behind. The agent was running toward him.

Brookes was the person who had Sammie killed. She needed to die.

Or at least be in prison.

"Reaper! Stand down!"

He released the pressure on the trigger. The boat slid quietly into the night toward the lights of Tangier.

"Tell me you'll get her," Harwood said.

"We'll get her." Bronson turned away and lifted his phone to his ear.

Harwood nodded, lifted his rifle, and backed away.

"Get me out of here, Deke," Harwood said.

CHAPTER 24

President Smart watched the action unfold from an iPad as he sat in the Oval Office. He held his official Twitter phone in his right hand. A call came in on his phone, but he didn't answer it. It was the signal and he smiled.

"Do we have the grid coordinate for the Iranian nuke that Brookes was having built?"

"Yes, sir." The general began to read the actual numbers.

"I don't need that. Just give me a stealth fighter or bomber to destroy it right now. Execute," Smart said.

"Execute? Iran is sovereign territory, sir."

"So's my ass but you see people kissing it every day," Smart said. "Do I need a new general to drop a bomb?"

"No, sir. Just confirming."

"Confirmed. Next fifteen minutes. I want it done."

"Roger that, sir."

The general stood and departed.

"And, General?"

The four-star stopped and turned around.

"Yes, sir?"

"When you're done, I want to talk to this Reaper guy."

"Roger that, sir."

When his office was empty, he banged out a quick draft tweet.

Maximus Anon: A LOT of activity at former Senator Sloane's house tonight. Getting reports that I'll try to confirm as soon as possible. Appears she was involved in some very shady dealings. Instead of Slippery Sloane, maybe her new nickname should be NOT SO SLIM SHADY! Explosive stuff!

He pressed Send, but of course it didn't go to his own Twitter account. A man named Jessup received the tweet and bounced it around sufficiently to disguise its origin. In a moment, Smart saw the tweet appear on Maximus Anon's account as it instantly began receiving thousands of comments, likes, and retweets.

He stood and walked from the Oval Office carrying his iPad, watching the real-time streaming video satellite shot of Sloane Brookes pulling up to Jessup's dock on Tangier Island.

When she shut the engine, the boat exploded and fire engulfed the sun-bleached planks of Jessup's pier and house in seconds.

No survivors.

President Smart smiled and tucked his iPad under his arm as he watched Maximus Anon's tweet boil around the world.

Passing a young staffer working the midnight shift, he pointed at her and said, "And that's how it's done."

EPILOGUE

Harwood looked down at Monisha, whose eyes were staring at Samuelson's casket. She reached up and grabbed his hand, an uncommon gesture for her. He was wearing his blue army uniform, like many in the large crowd of Rangers, family, and friends.

Hinojosa sat in the corner right chair next to her parents. The Ranger Regiment colonel knelt on one knee, handing a flag to each of them, saying, "On behalf of a grateful nation . . ."

When the colonel was done, seven sergeants from the Third Ranger Battalion stood erect, like statues, tan berets folded over their right ears, jump boots black and glossy, crisp blue uniforms creased and perfect, white gloves holding M1 rifles glistening with wood oil.

One sergeant commanded, "Ready, aim, fire."

The shots rang out as if they were one. Seven rifles fired with military precision. Port arms, charging handle jacked, rifle back at the shoulder, another volley. And another.

Three volleys, seven rifles, twenty-one-gun salute.

Tears cut fresh paths over Harwood's cheeks. He stood next to Monisha, who held his left hand tightly. She jolted at each volley, showing uncharacteristic vulnerability. By now, she was weeping openly, convulsing even, unable to hold back the flood of emotions. Perhaps the tough exterior had been penetrated, but to what end? He wondered if she could grow from the trauma of losing a close friend like Samuelson, or if she would further tighten the shutters, sealing herself off from the pain.

He saluted when the bugle belted out taps, the final note of the service. The Rangers marched away. The crowd dissipated. Hinojosa approached Harwood and Monisha, clutching to her chest the flag that had been draped over Sammie's casket. Her makeup was destroyed from crying.

Monisha squeezed Harwood's hand so tight he felt a bite of pain, not only his own, but hers as well.

Hinojosa stepped into him and laid her head on his shoulder. She wept quietly, the flag pressing into his chest. Monisha folded into them and put her arm around Hinojosa's back as she released Harwood's hand and hugged him as well.

With her head just above the folded flag, Monisha whispered, "Be okay. Yeah, this will be okay. We'll *make* it okay."

He felt her squeeze tightly and quit wondering about her emotional maturity. They stood there for several minutes, embracing, reinforcing, and holding each other up, most likely. Each had suffered a singular, unique loss: Hinojosa a brother, Harwood a Ranger buddy, and Monisha an adult friend who had been a rare role model in her life.

As the sun set, they walked from Arlington National Cemetery and found a restaurant nearby. As they found a table, Harwood sat next to Monisha, who was seated across from Hinojosa.

Harwood ordered three beers and Monisha said, "Damn, Reaper. Going all rogue on homegirl. Letting me drink beer?"

"I need two," Harwood said.

Monisha smiled, the best she could do.

Hinojosa sighed and then smirked. "You can have a sip of mine," she said.

"I don't know, Hinojosa. You look like someone out of a zombie movie. Your makeup is trashed."

"Ha! You don't look any better!" Hinojosa shot back.

Harwood leaned back and thought, *Yeah, we'll make it okay.*

The beers came and they toasted.

"To Sammie."